SEA CHANGE

A Nina Bannister Mystery

by

T'Gracie Reese and Joe Reese

For information, email **Cozy Cat Press**, cozycatpress@aol.com or visit our website at: www.cozycatpress.com

COZY CAT
PRESS

ISBN: 978-1-939816-08-5
Printed in the United States of America

Cover design by Laura Redmond
http://lauradawnsky.info

1 2 3 4 5 6 7 8 9 10

We would like to dedicate this book to the memory of all great teachers, and especially Joe's mother, Marie Reese. The jails in Texas are filled with hardened criminals who, if asked, might say, "I didn't like school much except fourth grade. There was nobody who could read *Tom Sawyer* like Mrs. Reese."

Full fathom five thy father lies;
Of his bones are coral made:
Those are pearls that were his eyes;
Nothing of him that doth fade,
But doth suffer a sea change
Into something rich and strange.
Sea nymphs hourly ring his knell:
Hark! now I hear them, ding-dong bell.

The Tempest, William Shakespeare

CHAPTER ONE: BAY ST. LUCY

"In Vineyard's Haven, on Martha's Vineyard, mostly I love the soft collision here of harbor and shore, the subtle haunting briny quality that all small towns have when they are situated on the sea."

William Styron

"Women and cats will do as they please, and men and dogs should relax and get used to the idea."

Robert Heinlein

"So, how do you teach *Beowulf?*"

The sea spilled calmly out of a sun which, blood red while rising, had now mildewed into a kind of chalk white, and was making its way upward as slowly as the tide was creeping outward.

"For which class?" asked Nina Bannister. "The eight o'clocks?"

"No, no, they're incorrigible. There's nothing to do with them but make sure they can't get at the piñata."

"There's a piñata?"

"Yes. Room 220 doubles as the Spanish classroom fourth period, when I'm off. Señora Fitzwilliams insists on having a piñata hanging from the ceiling."

"Why, for heavens sake?"

"I don't know. It causes all kinds of mayhem."

"I can imagine. More coffee?"

"Just a bit, please."

Macy Peterson held a half-filled cup across the table while Nina poured, careful to miss neither the exact center of the dark brown circle beneath her, nor anything transpiring on the morning beach.

There was, she decided, nothing to miss.

Late September in Bay St. Lucy. Most of the tourists gone, the bed and breakfast owners resigned to the fact, the sea not caring about it in the least.

Nor the gulls, which spun screeching, dived occasionally, made pests of themselves by attacking garbage cans beside the beach houses—cans which Nina had resolved long ago could not possibly have resembled in any way the whitefish and sea trout which the gulls were supposed to be making the most of.

"Stupid birds," she found herself whispering over the slight splash of the coffee.

"Pardon?"

"Nothing. Just me coming to grips with dotage."

"Is that what you're in? I'd rather refer to you as a 'senior.' Isn't that better?"

"Yes. I don't mind being a senior. I'm just a bit concerned about graduate school."

It took a while for that to penetrate and, when it did, Macy struggled to keep the most recent slurp of coffee in her mouth.

"That's funny," she was finally able to say.

She had always laughed at the right time, even when she was a sophomore in Nina's world literature class.

When had that been? When had Macy been fifteen years old?

Ten years ago.

Pffffft. The time going by.

Pfffft.

"That's very funny, Nina. Graduate school."

"Yes. Well, I've applications pending at two places. I suppose we all have. I do so want to get my first choice."

"That's funny, too."

"I was just thinking. Ten years since you took world literature from me."

"Seems like yesterday, Nina. Except I keep wanting to call you Ms. Bannister."

"I do, too. That's what worries me."

"So how did you teach *Beowulf?*"

"Well. Don't just emphasize the monsters, Grendel and his mother The girls won't really care about them and the boys will have seen the video games."

"There are video games?"

"I'm sure there are, but if they're not in the stores they're certainly on the computer. There is nothing more perfectly commensurate with Anglo Saxon oral literature than You Tube."

"That's probably true. But you will come tomorrow and work with them? Ten o'clock?"

"All right. Ten o'clock. Just a few remarks."

"I wish you'd come and teach them more. Once a week, maybe."

"No. Forty years is time enough for me."

"You don't miss teaching, now that you're retired?"

"It is stunning how little I miss it. Even the good students, even those few years when I had a good principal. No. I miss none of it. Every good memory is counterbalanced by visions of chewing gum in the drinking fountains."

They smiled quietly for a time at each other, the smiles mixing like cream in steam rising from the porcelain coffee pot. *Amazing,* Nina found herself thinking. There she herself was, sitting across from her as though from a mirror, a young teacher with everything in front of her. Not at all similar physically of course. Macy was tall and slender, perhaps five eight, with long straight blonde hair—the exact opposite of Nina herself—who had always preferred the description of "elfin" to other things that are said about people five foot three. Her mouse brown hair, cut short, framed her face with her up-turned nose that might look a little elf-like.

But that did not matter.

What mattered was a look in Macy's eye, which told the world and all her students that learning would take place, that Shakespeare was important, that poetry condensed truth and that there was such a thing as truth and it was preferable to its opposite, that being not falsehood—which was truth in another container—but simply noise without any meaning at all.

Macy was, in short, an idealist.

"You have to go, Macy."

"I know."

Nina rose, knowing by the bells at St. John Cathedral in the middle of town that it was seven o'clock.

And knowing, of course, Macy's schedule as well as she had always known her own.

Seven thirty, teachers' meeting.

Seven forty five, in class, papers sorted, everything ready.

Seven fifty five, first bell.

They had entered the house, crossed the living room, and made their way out to the front staircase when Macy turned and threw up her hands:

"I forgot! I forgot!"

"What?"

"It was the first thing I was going to tell you, and I completely forgot it!"

"What is it, Macy?"

It was cool this morning, cooler than it had a right to be in late September. Macy's wire-rimmed glasses had fogged over with the same kind of mist that was hovering over the dunes beneath and behind the house.

She tugged, almost nervously, as the turquoise scarf that settled so securely into her white windbreaker.

"Broussard! Broussard is coming tonight!"

"Tom Broussard?"

"Nina, there is only one!"

"No, there are a lot. We're in Gulf Coast Mississippi here. There are as many Broussards as there are yellow perch. Not as many as there are Fontenots of course, or Guidrys, and not as many as there would be farther west, over in Louisiana—but still enough."

"He's agreed to come! He's going to talk to us!"

"When?"

"Tonight!"

"You've got to be kidding."

"No. Edie Towler called me at six this morning. Six o'clock in the morning! She's so excited."

"Well…"

"A real writer! The man has published, I don't know, how many books?"

"A lot."

"A dozen, anyway. And he's coming to our little writers' group. Nina, I've got so many things I want to ask him."

"You're sure you want to ask him these things?"

"Of course! Why wouldn't I? Why wouldn't we all?"

"It's just…"

"We're all really dedicated to writing well, and some of us will get published. I know it. Some of us will."

"I'm sure that's true."

"But to have the chance to learn from a writer the caliber of Tom Broussard…it's once in a lifetime."

"I guess that's right."

"So you'll come, right?"

"I'm not always good in writers' groups, Macy."

"But you know Tom! Some people say you even persuaded him to come!"

"I talked to him about it; I'm not sure if I was the one who ultimately persuaded him. And, yes, if it comes to that, I guess I do know Tom Broussard as well as anybody can know him."

"You taught him didn't you?"

"He was in my class. Whether I taught him anything...."

"Didn't he dedicate one of his books to you?"

"I think it was one of the books that didn't sell."

"Oh you! But do be there, won't you?"

"I'll try."

"Library, seven o'clock."

"Ok. I'll come."

"Great. Well...I'm late now. Gotta go."

Nina watched her descend the stairs, catch her pumps on the rickety, next-to-bottom step that still had to be fixed, scrape across white shell-gravel, climb onto her bicycle, and pedal away.

"Have fun with *Beowulf* and the piñata, Macy!"

"It will be his last adventure! The dragon is dead, and now he must attack the piñata!"

"Adieu, brave young teacher."

"Adieu..."

"Don't say old teacher!"

"I won't! See you tonight!"

Nina waved as bike tires crunched oyster shells and the cycle lurched into the sand and asphalt lane that connected the real world of Bay St. Lucy with the row of ocean front shacks where she now lived.

Then she went back inside

She walked into the kitchen, opened one of the small drawers beneath the sink, and took out cat food.

Furl, hearing this from his accustomed position on the deck, padded his way to the glass door and rubbed against it.

She poured a handful of dry particles into his bowl, and, feeling now as if she herself had begun to pad rather than walk, crossed the room and slid open the door, somnolently addressing her tan and white animal with a useless command.

Useless, since Furl was going to do exactly what he wanted to do, anyway.

"Furl!" she said.

He entered, soundlessly, on cat's feet as did the fog in Sandburg's *Chicago*—or was that a different poem? Heavens. Her mind, her mind—at any rate, Furl crossed the kitchen, ate two or three bites of whatever it was she was feeding him now, then returned to where she was still standing, having just closed the door.

All right. That was all the food he wanted.

Now he wanted out again.

"Unfurl!" she said in the same imperious, uselessly authoritative, voice.

She slid open the door and he exited.

While she thought of Tom Broussard.

"What a great writer!" Macy had said.

Yes. Well.

"This is going to be such a wonderful experience for all of us."

Nina looked at the kitchen clock above the stove.

Seven twenty.

She had promised Margot Gavin to be at the shop by eight.

Plenty of time. Enough to stand sit on the deck for five more minutes and stare out at the ocean.

"A wonderful experience," she found herself whispering as she pulled the chair closer to the rail. "A wonderful experience indeed. More like a disaster."

But no need to worry about that now.

No need to do anything now but watch the waves.

The swell seemed more powerful than she'd remembered it being. It washed within inches of the poles beneath her deck, and it growled the dark constant murmur that always came near to hypnotizing her. Foam tracings scudded on top of it, glistening in the morning light and dissipating on the dark sand as the waves receded. "Listen!" it ordered her. "You hear the grating roar of pebbles, which the waves draw back, and fling, at their return, up the high strand. Begin, and cease, and then again begin, with tremulous cadence slow, and bring the eternal note of sadness in."

Sadness? Not really, despite what that gloomy pessimist Matthew Arnold might have thought.

This was not Dover Beach.

This was the Gulf Coast.

There was, of course, always the dull and intermittent ache that had begun with Frank's death and that would never disappear completely, like the pain that amputees were said to feel for missing limbs; but that had nothing to do with the sea or its comings and goings. No, that elemental movement had always comforted her, always made her dream of distant places and bizarre adventures. She was Odysseus and not a retired high school English teacher; she was sailing forth at first light, out there, far, far, to the drear and vast edges of the world. Past the distant, ever burning lights of the oil platforms, past the cape islands that served as barriers protecting her little Ithaca of Bay St. Lucy—and all the way to the cave of the winds or the lairs of Cyclops.

None of these visions bothered her. There was instead a thrill to them. There was...

...and then she saw the porpoises.

They had come to visit again, close to shore, glistening black bodies arcing and plunging, soundlessly, there and gone, up and under, telling her that all was well at seven bells.

There! There they were again, twin shadows chasing each other southward toward Biloxi and Falls Bay, like marks of punctuation, dashes, extending an endless sentence forever across an otherwise blank and shifting Gulf of Mexico.

They were there for her every morning at the same time.

Always swimming in the same direction.

She had thoughts of naming them. Something literary of course, as were all of the other things she had named: cats, dogs, roses, mopeds, raincoats....

...but no, they were beyond naming, those two. They lived in a no-name realm, and if they experienced some immense pleasure by being together in the tide and the strong morning currents, why that pleasure was something that had no name either.

They were simply they, and that was an end to it.

And now they were gone, the glistening backs replaced by sun sparkle on the turquoise waves.

No, she thought, there was no sadness to the ocean, not a bit of melancholy in all the seas of the world.

Good morning to you, Frank, she found a voice within her saying, as though some elemental part of him was spread out there before her, his smile beaming from the red and rising sun just as it had always done from the chair across from her.

There was no answer, of course.

Or perhaps there was.

And smiling inwardly at the possibility, Nina Bannister rose, made her way inside, and got ready for the day ahead.

Her blue Vespa sputtered its way through the middle of Bay St. Lucy while she thought alternately about the scrabble of palm fronds and storefronts, bakeries and balconies, hotels and hand-painted signs saying "Apartment for Rent, Ocean Frontage, Winter Rates now Applicable"—and Tom Broussard.

She remembered him as an impossible student, all the worse for his brilliance, all the more frustrating to deal with because of an inbred certainty of his own mental superiority.

Which did, of course, exist.

But all the same—

Then the shouting matches in class, the trips together to the principal, the even louder shouting matches in the hall, the forced study sessions—all of these things had given way to a feeling of immense relief when he did finally graduate and was once and for all out of her life.

Except he wasn't.

The impossible young man had, frustratingly, learned something from her.

And wanted to keep in touch.

Occasionally one of her good students wanted to keep in touch, and did, to her great pleasure. A Christmas card now and again, or even a surprise visit to her classroom.

But Tom Broussard came to her mainly in rumors and back page newspaper articles labeled "Police Blotter."

A time in the military.

Then out of the military. Not quite a dishonorable discharge but not exactly an honorable one either. A separation labeled, in bureaucratese, something meaning essentially "Let's just call it quits and never see each other again."

Then some years on the off-shore rigs, as young coastal boys such as Tom always were bound by custom and heritage to do.

A stint in jail.

Rumors of dark drug connections.

How had she always been kept abreast of these things?

Had he written her?

Or had he just made sure the right newspapers arrived?

It was too hard to remember now; suffice to say, there had been some bond welded fast by those unendurable encounters, so that he now wanted her always in mind of what he had been, as opposed to just how bad he could really be.

And then he was in New York.

Despite herself she thought of *Death of a Salesman* and Uncle Ben.

"And when I came out of the jungle I was twenty one. And, by God, I WAS RICH!"

And he was.

Perhaps a bit older than twenty one...

...but a best selling author.

And now he was living here again, back in Bay St. Lucy.

May God protect us, she thought, weaving the small motorcycle—which, she noticed, was precisely the same shade of blue as Macy Peterson's scarf had been, and the sky should have been if the sun and elements were doing their job and not lazing about behind this oyster non-color thing that covered them every now and then in advance of storms—

—into the three-vehicle parking lot that fronted *Elementals: From the Sea and the Earth*—

—Margot Gavin's shop, beneath her bed and breakfast.

Taking off her helmet and hanging it by the chin strap to the handlebars as she propped down the kickstand, she looked up and noted Margot Gavin, puttering about in the vases section, and waving to her.

"You're just in time, Nina. I was about to actually do some work. Now you've saved me. We can go back in the garden, and I can smoke another cigarette."

Margot took two long strides toward the garden which, because she was almost six feet tall, meant that she had already halved the distance. Nina followed, still marveling at the kind of clothes Margot could wear, and wear successfully. At the present she had on a baggy sweater which, with its vertical red strips and horizontal white gashes and stars, looked less like a garment and more like a vast tent that some sultan had disassembled and was carrying over the shoulder.

"Look at the clay pots there by the door. Nice, aren't they?"

Nina looked, nodded, agreed, said so, and inquired about the potter.

"Sarah Fielding."

"I don't think I know her."

"New. Moved down last month from Vermont. I met her two weeks ago at some social or charity sale or bake sale or something. When I found out what she did, I asked her to throw some pots for me. And she has."

"They're very nice."

Of course everything in Margot's vine-enshrouded shop—all of the landscapes, seascapes, portraits, pots, knick knacks, local art, exotic art—was very nice. *That was not surprising*, Nina mused, given the woman's background; but how the most hideous possibilities could result in the most magical realities—the monstrosity of a sweater was only the latest such miracle—never ceased to amaze her.

They walked to the center of the fifteen-foot square, palm-fronded fountain-splashing garden, and sat themselves, each feeling quite civilized, in black, wrought iron chairs, the table rocking slightly on paving stones still glistening from the early morning dew.

It was all perfectly delightful and would have been Eden itself had not the scents pouring in from nearby bakeries, sea air, candy shops, and lush undergrowth, been invaded by the odor of Margot's cigarette.

"Have you had coffee this morning, Nina?"

"Two cups."

"Then you're only beginning. Sit for a few minutes; I'll make us a fresh pot."

"You really feel no need to be inside your store?"

"None at all. Actually, I shouldn't have opened the store at all this morning."

"Why not?"

"A perfectly ghastly night. I'm trying to get it out of my mind."

"What happened?"

Margot threw back her head, scrunched her face aground the cigarette, which she seemed on the point of inhaling, and blew out a cloud of gray, swirling smoke toward the colorless sky the way a fire truck belches a stream of water at a blaze.

The smoke, Nina could not help noticing, was the exact color of Margot's steel gray, short cut hair.

"I took one of my new boarders out for dinner."

Nina was silent for a time.

Finally she said, quietly:

"I warned you about that. You know you find your boarders extremely boring."

Margot nodded, her face as deeply and exquisitely wrinkled as a Kandinsky painting or a Stravinsky symphony, or, for that matter, any work of art whose creator's name ended in "insky."

Margot's face was, in short—and Nina had noted this from the moment she first saw the woman over a year ago—a work of modern art itself. As equally impossible to comprehend as to forget, and probably not even conceivable to a century that had not experienced two devastating wars.

"Why did I not listen to you?"

"I don't know. You're so intelligent otherwise. Do you want to talk about it?"

"No. Yes. I don't know. It's all so wretched."

"This wasn't a man that you took out, was it?"

"Oh heavens no. I'm not that stupid. No, it was a woman who moved in yesterday. She'll be staying two weeks. Her name is 'Wilson.' A widow from Wisconsin or Vermont or Arizona. One of those places, you know."

"States. Yes, I know. There are lots of them. Now, why don't you get us some coffee? It will make you feel better."

"No, it won't. Some gin though…"

"Too early."

"Why do people always say that? It has such a dampening effect on the day, when one hears it."

"Coffee."

"All right."

Margot rose, disappeared into the shop, and fidgeted around in the small kitchen area by the back wall, which had somehow been magically hidden away between a display of cookbooks and a table covered with children's games.

When she returned, she carried on one upward turned palm, as though the entire apparatus was weightless, a shining chrome platter—cups, sugar bowl filled with sweetener packets, creamer, and spoons all laid out upon it.

"This will do us both good," said Nina, savoring the steam scent rising as her cup filled.

"I doubt that."

"All right. It will do me good. You may be a little beyond help right now. So where did you take her?"

"Out to eat."

"Where?"

"A restaurant."

"One surprise after another. And what was so bad about it?"

Margot thought for a while, stubbed out her cigarette, took a sip of coffee—and then seemed to become aware of something on her skin. She began frantically, with one overly large palm, trying to brush from her sweater sleeves a substance which seemed to be burning her, but which Nina could not see.

"What is it?" cried Nina, alarmed.

"Get it…get it off me! Get it off me!"

"Margot, what is it?"

"It's all over me! It's on my skin! Nina, it's all over me! Get it off! Get it off!"

"Margot what is it?"

"It's boredom! There's boredom all over me! Get it off! Get it off!"

Nina sat back, wondering whether it was a good thing or a very bad thing that, somehow, gradually and against all odds, that this woman had become—should she say it?

Yes, no denying it.

Her best friend.

She waited.

Finally, the paroxysm or spasm over, Margot sank back into her chair, which tottered metallically as she did so.

"That bad, huh?" asked Nina.

Margot whispered, seemingly to herself.

"I'll never get it off. Never. It's all over me. Like the blood on Lady Macbeth's hands."

She leaned forward, stared intently at Nina, and hissed:

"I'm covered in boredom; and I'll never get it off me"

"Yes you will."

"No. She's poisoned me."

"It couldn't have been that bad."

"It was worse. She had to tell me about her late husband and what he had done for a living—"

"Which was?"

"I didn't listen."

"See, that may be a reason, Margot, why conversations tend to bore you."

"Do you think so?"

"I'm just throwing it out as a suggestion."

"Perhaps you have a point. At any rate, though, the person has children, who had to be talked about. And pets at home that someone is caring for—"

"Back in Arizona or Vermont?"

"Rhode Island, perhaps. Is there a Rhode Island?"

"I don't know, Margot. I taught English, not geography."

"Oh. I thought you might know."

"No. But anyway, Margot. You did a nice thing. The woman—what's her name?"

"Wilson. She's staying two weeks, as I said. Then she's going to New Orleans. She kept telling me, 'I've never been to New Orleans! I've never been to New Orleans!' As though I cared."

"But you did care, Margot. Good for you! This poor Mrs. Wilson is completely on her own, and you took her out and listened to her. She's never been to New

Orleans. All right. She needed to tell somebody that, and you were there for her. Now you won't have to hear it again, nor will you ever have to try to socialize with any more of your boarders for a while, or at least until you're feeling sociable."

"Thank God. Good, then. This has been quite therapeutic. Thank you, Nina."

"Not at all.

She paused to listen to the cathedral bells chime the hour, then play the first notes of a hymn whose melody she knew, but could not place. Music sifted down through the garden just as the aroma from Margot's herb garden rose up from the leaves and out over the town. *Bay St. Lucy*, she thought: *don't ever change.*

"There is this one thing, Margot, that I'm going to have to beg of you."

"What, Nina?"

"Promise me that you'll realize you are no longer the Managing Director of the Chicago Art Institute. You came here because that job was killing you, and you were developing ulcers."

"But ulcers can be dealt with. Boredom on the other hand…."

"Margot, boredom is what we grow here. It's our principle product. It isn't just the woman you were nice enough to take to dinner last night; it's all of us. We may pride ourselves on being a little artists' community, but that's all we are. We're *little* artists, emphasis on *little*. Renoir does not live here. We're not even the South of France. Margot, Bay St. Lucy is not Chicago."

"All right," Margot answered. "You're right. I'm sorry to complain. The ulcers are much better. And Nina, I do appreciate Bay St. Lucy. I'm very happy here, for all my complaining. If I were insane enough to go out socially with people in Chicago, I'd find them just as wretchedly boring. It's only that I had so much to do in connection with the museum that I never thought about such things. Here…"

"Here you're bored."

"Well, perhaps. But that leads me to another thing. Something I've been meaning to ask you for some time."

"No, I won't be your lover."

"I know. Although it would be a delicious little scrap of gossip, wouldn't it?"

"People would rank it just below the hundred pound tuna caught off the concrete jetty the other day."

"You think? No, I think it would positively thrill everyone. Still, that isn't what I want to talk with you about."

"All right, then we'll put potential lesbianism on the back burner at least for now. What then?"

"Do you have any money?"

"What, you mean on me? I think I have three dollars."

"No. I mean actual money. Money in the bank. Money in savings. Money to invest."

"I think I have three dollars."

"Be serious."

"Ok, it's actually closer to two ninety four, but there's usually some change lying around…"

"Be serious."

"OK. No."

"Not any."

"A little. Not much. Teacher retirement. You know."

"All right. No matter. The thing is, I have money."

"You do?"

"Yes. The Managing Director of The Chicago Art Institute makes an obscene amount of money. I had so much of it I was beginning to feel myself becoming a Republican. That's why I came here."

"No Republicans here."

"I should hope not. But I wondered if you would be interested in going into a project with me."

"What kind of project?"

"An investment."

"What investment?"

"I've been thinking about it for some time. Nina, do you know the Robinson mansion?"

"Of course I know the Robinson mansion. Everybody does."

"It's in disrepair."

"Yes."

"I'd like to buy it. I think we could...well, fix it up?"

"The Robinson mansion?"

"Yes. It's a wonderful location."

"Fix it up for what?"

"A hotel. Or, if you will, a truly sumptuous bed and breakfast. It looks out on the beach; it's got those wonderful Doric columns, the magnificent balconies...and we could run it together. It would be great fun."

"You would actually like to run a larger hotel? Deal with the guests, make meals, clean rooms, hear their complaints, all that sort of thing?"

"No, silly, that would be your job."

"Oh, wonderful."

"I would simply invest the money."

"Margot, it's a wonderful idea, except..."

"Except what?"

"I just...I keep forgetting what a short time you've been here."

"It's a little over a year now; so how long does one have to live in a city before one is allowed to buy property?"

"It's not that; it's just a question of *what* property."

"I don't follow you."

"You don't know about the Robinson mansion?"

"What is there to know?"

"No one has told you?"

"What are you talking about?"

"Margot, you can't buy the Robinson mansion."

"And why not?"

Incredulous that there would be an actual inhabitant of Bay St. Lucy who did not know, and who could actually ask 'and why not?'...Nina sat and stared until she realized that she was being rude.

Then, gaining as much composure as she could, she said:

"You can't buy the Robinson mansion, Margot, because it's haunted."

This pronouncement produced the effect of shock and awe that Nina expected, but the expression of complete disbelief on Margot Gavin's face seemed to have been caused by something more than the realization that supernatural forces might render impossible a business deal that she, only a few seconds before, had thought feasible.

And in fact, such was the case.

For Margot, her mouth open and her eyes wide and glazed, was looking not at Nina at all but through the small window in the door that led into the shop.

"Margot, are you all right?"

"No."

"What's the matter? Is it the Robinson place?"

"What?"

"The Robinson place."

"What about it?"

"It's haunted."

"I don't care. That's the least of our problems."

"What are you talking about?"

"Allana Delafosse has just arrived."

Nina turned, peered through the same window Margot was gazing at, and confirmed the fact.

Allana Delafosse was in fact making her way regally through the pottery section, the spectacle of her appearance extinguishing the possible existence of supernatural beings in the Robinson mansion just as completely as the sun's brilliance extinguishes minor constellations.

Margot's garden had become, in the last months, a kind of gathering place for the town's culturally elite.

Nina would never have described herself in just that way.

But Allana certainly would have.

And it was true—and becoming known throughout the village:

If you wanted to know everything, you came and sat for a while at Margot's place.

"Ok," said Nina, turning back, "so it's Allana Delafosse. Maybe she wants to buy something. Offer her coffee."

"Are you mad?"

"Why would I be mad?"

"Nina, Allana Delafosse doesn't drink coffee; she drinks tea. And I always seem to offer her the wrong kind. I try to have the best teas in the world here. But when I offer most of them to her, it's as though I've kicked her dog."

"Well, Allana Delafosse is the *de facto* leader of the city, at least as far as culture is concerned.

"But that doesn't give her the right to…"

At that moment, the door exploded open and Allana herself, dressed entirely in red, save for black leather gloves, a shining and equally black four-inch wide belt, and a white, twenty six-foot radius hat tilted slightly and perfectly askew, as though precisely in tune with the gravitational laws prescribed by the zodiac at just this time of the morning, just this spot in the universe— entered, and pronounced:

"My dear ladies!"

This in and of itself—this three word utterance—was an event worth celebrating and remembering, as was every gesture and sound connected with Madame Delafosse. It was not the "my dear" so much that needed celebrating and adoration; it was the word "ladies," which had never been said quite the same way on earth, and never would be again. Precisely what she said could not have been written, nor would any professional writer have tried. "Laaaaaydeeez," was perhaps the closest orthographic fit, but those inky marks on white pulp paper would have failed completely to recreate even part of the total effect of the thing itself or the "Ding an sich" that was Allana. It would not have the tilt of her head, the radioactive smile flashing out from her dark-coffee Creole skin like a thermide bomb detonated in the mouth of a cave.

"My dear laaaaaydeez—how aaahhhhhhrrrr yew this maaaawwwrrrrning?"

Margot, who, despite years in the great city of Chicago, and a decade or so before that in the great city of Los Angeles, and some years before that in various radical communes around The University of California at Berkley—had never encountered a creature more bizarre than she herself, was momentarily stunned, outgunned, and out-outrageoused. So it was left to Nina to reply to the verbal Daryl F. Zanuck cinemascopic presentation that was "Laaayyydeeeeeze, how aaaahhhhhrrrr yew?" by saying simply:

"We're good! How are you?"

How humiliating.

"I'm wunnnnnnderful! It's such a deviiiiiiiine maaaaaawwwwwrning, is it not? I do hope I'm not disturbing you?"

Margot had refitted herself by now, and found composure enough to rise and gesture to one of the chairs:

"We're fine, Allana. Please sit down. I was just going to get some tea."

"Oh you were?" said Allana, pulling out the chair, evaluating it, cleaning it, disdaining it, hearing its brick-scraping apology, forgiving it, and accepting the petition of the entire garden to join her realm and worship her, all with one brief sweeping magnificent gesture…

…upon the end of which she was somehow there, seated across from Nina at the table, the now-reigning queen of what had once been Margot's little shop.

She and Nina exchanged a few pleasantries, after which Margot reappeared in the doorway:

"I have several teas to offer. We can have Darjeeling or Assam if we're in an Indian mood; I have Chinese White Tea, Sencha from Japan, or Ti Kwan Yin from Taiwan."

Allana's gaze focused, narrowed, and hardened. She spoke slowly, the words drenched no longer with sweetness but with a great deal of disappointment, mixed only to a slight degree with rancor.

"Why, Assam, of course."

Margot nodded.

How, Nina found herself asking Margot mentally, *could you have asked?*

Embarrassing both of us like that!

Darjeeling indeed!

"Assam," Margot said, "it is."

Darjeeling.

The very thought.

"Dearest Nina. I must admit I am happy to have found you here. There is...well, an ISSUE that has arisen."

Strange, Nina thought, *how Allana Delafosse had the ability to speak in capital letters.*

The tea appeared, and was properly sipped.

Allana Delafosse broached the ISSUE.

"It concerns this evening, Nina. I assume you've heard."

"Oh. You mean..."

"The writer."

"Tom Broussard?"

"Yes. Mr. Broussard."

"Well. I heard he was coming to talk to the writers' group."

"Indeed. And it's just that there do exist, at least in my mind, questions of—how shall I say it?— APPROPRIATENESS. I'm sure Mr. Broussard has written some very fine things. I must admit to not having read his work myself."

Cleave Her in Indigo; Disembowelment at Dawn; Genitalia for the Generals...

...how surprising, Nina found herself thinking, *that these works were not on the shelves of Allana Delafosse's personal reading room.*

"Well. I know that Tom has been quite successful. He's sold a lot of books in the last years."

"I see."

"I know the group has been after him for some time to come and talk with them."

"Yes."

"I did speak to him myself, and, I guess, kind of persuaded him to come. Edie Towler—she's head of the group—had asked him several times. He may have been a bit curt with her. But I talked with Tom, and I think I can assure everybody involved, that he'll be a really useful guest lecturer. Now, as for what he's going to say…well, I really don't know."

"I had heard that he was your student."

"Years ago."

"I see."

"We didn't have the closest relationship."

"And yet I am informed that he dedicated one of his books to you."

"Yes."

"Which book?"

"I think it was…no…no, I guess it was *Whore Witch—Which Whore?*"

One second two seconds—

"Can I get us some more tea?" asked Margot.

Allana turned her head, frowned a smile, and said icily:

"I really must be going."

Then, to Nina:

"Dearest Nina. Several parents have contacted me. Their children trust me. They trust me. And the young people themselves are very excited about this event. Mr. Broussard, the Best Selling Author, is a celebrity to them. They want very much to hear what he has to say."

"Of course."

"If I can have your assurance that what he says will be, well, edifying…then, I shall be happy to attend tonight myself, and bring with me several of our young writers."

"Allana, I haven't talked to Tom for some time. But I'm sure he'll be fine. He wouldn't say anything inappropriate. Especially with young people there."

The smile returned.

"Wunnnnnnnndaful! Then I'm sure it will be a delicious evening! Oh! We are all so looking forward to it. Adieu, then!"

And after little more ceremony than attends the departure of any member of the Royal Family, Allana Delafosse rose, dusted from her the remnants of common folk, and was gone.

There was silence for a time, just enough for regality to dissolve into the air, and coffee to be replenished.

Somehow tea no longer seemed appropriate.

Finally Margot spoke:

"Nina, I think I can finally bond with you. There was always some—well—some distance between us before. But now I realize what it was. And now it's gone."

"What are you talking about, Margot?"

"During the entire year I've known you, I wasn't sure you were a human being."

"Why not?"

"Because I never saw you do anything truly stupid. Now, I feel much better."

Nina sighed.

"Right. Well, we'll see what happens. You don't want to come tonight, do you?"

"Are you insane?"

"Ok, so no. Well, do you want to talk about the Robinson mansion and why it's haunted?"

"No. I want to close the shop, walk on the beach for a few hours, and then take a long grand nap. I have a big day ahead tomorrow"

"Doing what?"

"Listening to the descriptions of the disaster that's going to happen tonight, at the Writers' Group. Now come on. Let's tidy up."

And they did.

CHAPTER TWO: WRITERS ON WRITING

"When audiences come to see us authors lecture, it is largely in the hope that we'll be funnier to look at than to read."

Sinclair Lewis

"There are three rules about writing a novel. Unfortunately, no one knows what they are."

Somerset Maugham

The Bay St. Lucy Public Library was located in a despicable little building on the corner of Calvin Coolidge St. and Archie Manning Drive. It resembled the elementary school (located only two blocks away), but was smaller, older, more depressing, and noisier. It's only positive attribute was a refusal to replace shelves of books with rows of computers, said refusal stemming sadly not from a surplus of principle but from a shortfall in finances.

The library did not replace its books with computers because it could not afford to.

It could also not afford large and luxuriously appointed meeting rooms, which was why Room 4, approximately thirty by forty feet with a circular table in the middle and straight chairs backed up against the walls, was overly full when Nina arrived at six fifty five p.m.

"Incredible," she whispered to herself as she made her way through groups of people still standing, all of whom were talking—pleasantly if they were visitors, earnestly if they were writers.

She found an empty chair in a far corner and sat down to survey the scene.

There, seated around the table, were the town's amateur writers.

Richard Benson, a shy and amiable man, insurance agent, office on the square, poet.   He wrote not precisely   lyric   poetry,   but   private   musings. Occasionally, one or two of them appeared in *The Bay St. Lucy Gazette*. They dealt often with weather, more specifically, the changing seasons. The melancholy feeling preceding autumn, the gaiety of spring—

—all of which was fine, Nina had often observed, except that it left him for large portions of the year— middle of July, middle of January, late November, etc.—with nothing to write about.

And there beside him sat Florence Cummings, who wrote short novels—two of them already self-published—about the charm of small towns in southern Lucyiana. The first of the books had been entitled *Lucyiana Musings* and the second *Memories of Lucyiana*. There was a great deal in each book about gardening, and there were recipes.

Two other members of the group wrote similar material, but Florence was the only one who'd actually taken the step of publishing her work.   The others— Deborah LeBlanc and Marcie Collins—declared at each meeting that they were "not ready for the big time yet" and were still compiling materials, most of which were gathered on weekend trips and summer vacations.

Nina knew these things from scattered gossip in shops and breakfast nooks rather than actual attendance at the Writers' Group meetings, which she attended only rarely, and then as a specially invited guest, by dint of her having taught literature to most of the citizens of the town at one time or another.

There, across the table from her, was Dorothy Andridge, who had at one time written short descriptions of wanderings through southern Mississippi towns, but who had undergone a literary vision some time in the last six months and had begun writing paranormal romances. Her books dealt with younger people who were vampires or ghosts.

Sitting beside her was a kind of colleague, perhaps the cause of her inspiration. Frank Whittington, large and jovial, manager of the town's only department store, was rumored to be gay and have a lover in New Orleans. That was all right; that was his business. But it did allow him to work without scandal in collaboration with Dorothy, and give her tips, since he had written two novels that were themselves related to the Paranormal Romance genre. Neither had been published, but he was "shopping" both, and considering self-publishing a complete line of "e" books suitable to Kindle transfers. Frank, eschewing the current rage of vampire romances as somewhat trite, had created a series of heroines who were young, deeply in love, and werewolves.

There were more of the usual suspects. A short story writer here, a poet there, a budding teenage Shakespeare creating odes about lost loves, an older gray-haired woman populating her small town with potential murderers in a slowly developing—but so far well reviewed by various good friends and close relatives—"cozy" mystery.

And there, in the corner precisely opposite, her retinue of students clustered about her, was Allana Delafosse.

She caught Nina's eye and nodded, smiling threateningly, then let her glance fall back to its original object...

...that being Tom Broussard.

Tom, Tom…

He had come all right, and there he was, sitting beside the group's leader, Edie Towler, his denim shirt sweat through, his hair tangled and oily, and his great stomach…for Tom was a good six foot three and, never exactly skinny, much more filled out than she remembered him from high school days—his stomach pressing against the side of the table.

Yes, there he was.

He stared downward at his hands, which were folded in his lap.

He stared at them as though he hated them.

The room was filled with murmurings.

More and more people found seats, and murmured sitting down instead of standing up.

Nina glanced up at the digital clock above the room's doorway.

Six fifty nine…

…..no, oops, seven o'clock.

"Well, then. Good evening everybody!"

Edie, the District Attorney of Bay St. Lucy, looked much as she always looked, Nina mused. Tall in her two inch pumps, professional—the suit she wore to board meetings, city council meetings, library club meetings, etc.—always looked the same, perfectly pressed, varying only in the change of one muted color for another, depending on the seasons.

Edie had never married, and there had been, at least to Nina's knowledge, no man or lover of any kind to watch the slow changing of her once sandy hair to salt and pepper gray.

A pity.

But some lives were lived like that.

"We are so happy to have this wonderful crowd! It is a very special evening for the Writers' Group of Bay

St. Lucy. I'm certain all of you are aware of the status of Tom Broussard, our guest speaker/workshop leader for the evening."

She looked down at Tom as though he were a roast turkey while applause spread around the room. Two—now four—of the writers stood, clapping as hard as they possible could. More people stood. Many were standing already. Two teenage writers, while not actually standing, did put their cell phones on the table, so that they could clap.

This went on for perhaps half a minute.

Then:

"Tom, who we all know grew up here in Bay St. Lucy, has written...."

She went on to talk about the number of novels Tom Broussard had written, and the weeks they had remained on *The New York Times* Bestseller List.

She did not, specifically, mention their titles.

Orders, Nina wondered, *from Allana Delafosse?*

All of this took two to three minutes and led to:

"So with all that said, I can safely repeat, we are indeed honored, Tom, that you've chosen to be with us tonight."

Tom looked at her.

He nodded.

She smiled, and continued.

"Our members have so many questions."

Then she looked out across the table.

"I know—John, I know you've told me about several of your questions, and they all sound so interesting!"

John Edwards, current high school English teacher, recent college graduate, beamed:

"Yes, well, Mr. Broussard, I'm just going to ask a little later about the relation you feel between description and dialogue. I mean, does one grow organically from the other, and if so, which from which? Is there a kind of...I don't know exactly the word I want here—palliative symbiosis between the two?"

Everyone at the table nodded.

All of them, Nina realized, were like the little plastic birds, who, proper weights on tails and beaks, go up and down into small containers of water.

"I just want," said Muriel Whitfield, smiling, white-haired, red-faced, author of the weekly gossip column "What Blew Throo St. Loo?"...I just want to know where you get your ideas?"

"Yes," said someone sitting beside her, someone Nina didn't know, "yes, do they come from your own experiences, or do you just make them up?"

Nina thought for a moment.

Cleave her in Indigo. Disembowelment at Dawn.

Did these books come from Tom's own experience or not?

She was not certain which answer she would have preferred.

A hand up in the back of the room:

"I want to know if he knows the ending before he starts writing!"

General laughter.

Finally, a silent room again.

Then Edie:

"Tom I guess we're also wondering about your use of workshopping. Do you workshop your chapters before finalizing them? How do you get feedback as this, this, "process," this, symbiotic moment evolves? And, of course, would you be able to join us as we try to work together, encouraging each other, helping each other—to reach the point you've achieved. Obviously we feel writing to be a group process, and we find the,

the "sharing" process—and isn't "process" such an appropriate word?"

Beaks up around the table, beaks down around the table...

"We find the "sharing" so aesthetically therapeutic, that we'd love for you to be involved in it with us."

Silence.

More applause now.

Then:

"....and so, without further ado, I introduce to you, Bay St. Lucy's best-selling author, Tom Broussard!"

He rose and leaned forward on his knuckles like one of the great apes.

His thick brown leather belt extended down from beyond its last belt loop like six inches of dog tongue panting, except no saliva fell from it.

He looked at the crowd, which for one instant, became completely, even digitally, silent.

Then he said:

"Go home and write."

Then he walked out of the room, exiting through a door immediately behind him.

Damn, Nina found herself cursing inwardly.

Silence for one second.

Two seconds.

Then there was chaos.

The most frequently heard cry was, "Well, I never!" which, strangely, Nina had very seldom—perhaps even never—heard before in actual life.

It was more a thing that dowagers said in novels and British movies.

Whatever a "dowager" was.

But it was being said here, and with great frequency.

There were other things said, too.

There was a bit of spotty laughter, as some members thought of forgiving the man, whom they viewed as simply unpredictable and eccentric.

This was, of course, not the attitude of Allana Delafosse

"Nina, dear…"

"I'm sorry, Allana."

"It's all right. This is, of course, not your fault. I only wish that you would give to Mr. Broussard, whenever you should see him, this note. It contains my sentiments concerning his—behavior—this evening. Especially in regards to the effect that behavior might have on the young LAAAAADEEEEEZ of Bay St. Lucy."

She gave Nina a letter.

In an elegant ecru envelope.

And with that she was gone, vanished somehow into the smoke of her own bright-blue bitterness.

Now Nina simply had to deal with Edie Towler.

"Did you know that he was going to do that?"

"No," said Nina.

"What was he thinking?"

"I don't know."

"I thought you were his friend."

"I'm not sure I would put it that way."

"Do you realize what he has done? We have *prepared* for him. We were all SO LOOKING FORWARD to this!"

"I know."

"You must also know that he owes all of us…he owes the whole town for that matter—an apology."

"Yes, he does."

"Are you going to see him, Nina?"

"Edie, it's not as though he and I are close friends."

"Well—if you can talk to him, please do so."

"I guess I can go to see him."

"Please do. And tell him that our invitations are over. We're sorry to have inconvenienced him. And that we will never. NEVER. See him here again."

And with that she too was gone, disappeared into yellow and purple tulip smoke exactly the way Allana had vanished into reptile blue smoke.

"People come and go," she found herself whispering down at the table, "so quickly here."

She apologized for half an hour or so, then left the building, and drove her Vespa home, astonished that Tom Broussard was still making her life miserable.

She was just taking her helmet off when she became aware of a letter protruding from the mailbox just beside her door at the top of the stairs.

"This cannot be good news," she whispered to herself

She did not know why she felt that way.

It's just that there are good news days and bad news day, and this was one of the latter.

She climbed the stairs, wishing they would collapse.

Four steps away from the mailbox.

Two steps away from the mailbox.

And, just beside her hand now, there it was.

The mailbox itself.

It was one of the kind of letters she hated the most: small, slender, official, white, and deadly.

She sighed and took it gently between thumb and forefinger.

"What in heaven's name is this?"

She unlocked the door, turned on the light, walked to the deck window, slid it open, ordered:

"Unfurl!"

She watched as her cat sauntered out; then she took a seat at the kitchen table.

She looked at the letter. It was hand addressed to her. The upper right hand corner bore the words.

ASHCROFT, BENNETT, AND SEALY: ATTORNEYS AT LAW

She slipped an index finger into the corner of the envelope, and, gently, ripped it open.

Then she opened the sheet of paper and saw two sentences, hand written:

NINA,

PLEASE COME BY THE OFFICE TOMORROW MORNING AS EARLY AS POSSIBLE.
ARTHUR ROBINSON IS DEAD.

SINCERELY,
JACKSON BENNETT

Then she took from her windbreaker pocket the letter that Allana Delafosse had given her, tore it up, and sprinkled the remnants in the wastebasket.

"Oh damn," she whispered to the blank table top before her. "And I thought tonight was bad."

Then she went to bed.

CHAPTER THREE: EXORCISM

"Honest and peace loving people shun the courts and are prepared to suffer loss rather than fall into a lawyer's clutches."

Peter de Noronka

Downtown Bay St. Lucy was as nondescript as she had remembered it. A few white limestone buildings, none over two stories high. Traffic lights at the junction of First and Main, the small and seldom used city park, a few coffee shops which seemed to change signs and owners every few years.

So hard to believe she'd come down here frequently, always looking forward to it.

Not that she dreaded it now; but there was simply no need, no reason.

She stood in front of the old building, which had not changed at all. There was the sign, hanging where it had always been, swinging slightly in the ocean breeze.

ASHCROFT, BENNETT AND SEALY

They had offered to keep Frank's name on it, and she could almost imagine the BANNISTER tacked on at the end.

It was only right of them to offer to keep the name up there, of course, since Frank had founded the firm.

And it was more than simple charity that made them offer: the name Bannister was known around town, and, if the citizenry was well aware of the demise of the company's founder, it still might keep memories of Frank's integrity, his resourcefulness, his dependability.

Keeping the name, in short, would be good for business.

But she had declined.

As Frank would have.

She stood before the door, reached for the handle, and thought of Marley's ghost appearing before Scrooge.

"Marley was dead all right."

But Frank's ghost did not appear, and she pushed open the door and walked up the same narrow stairway she had climbed all those years, when, home from teaching, she had bicycled downtown, swung by whatever coffee shop had stood on the corner, and taken two cups up to a struggling young attorney whose prospects seemed, at times, bleak indeed.

The attorney she now visited had struggled, too, in his early years.

Jackson Bennett. Who had learned in those first days that All-American football stardom did not necessarily translate into legal clients, and who might well have starved himself, a completely inexperienced African American attorney, had not Frank persuaded his two partners to take the young man in.

The door opened at the top of the stairs.

The figure towering above her—six foot three of him plus four stair steps still to be climbed—broadcast a smile much as a lighthouse emits a beam.

"Nina!"

"Hello, Jackson."

She continued to climb until his arms encircled her and lifted her up the final two steps.

"Nina, it's so good to see you."

"You too, Jackson. You too."

And it was good to see him. She'd always liked him, always enjoyed the mutual dinners together, Jackson and LaToya, then their child Alyssha scampering around, Fridays at one home, Sundays at the other.

The two men talking cases, she and LaToya talking whatever else in the world remained.

A bit of slight sadness at each parting as she and Frank realized there would not be children for them.

But no matter…there had been so many good things to make up for that one lack.

"It seems like a year since we've seen each other," he said, ushering her into the office.

It had hardly changed. The same leather sofa beside the receptionist's desk.

A different receptionist of course.

"Maya, this is Nina Bannister."

"How do you do."

A slender and attractive woman, secretarial and bespectacled.

How long had Frank been in this office before he could afford a receptionist? Two years?

More?

"Maya, Nina's husband was Frank Bannister. We all owe him our jobs. Our careers, for that matter."

"Oh my."

There was nothing for her to say to that, of course, and Nina was relieved when, pleasantries over, she was seated in Jackson's office, and the business at hand could be dealt with.

"So," she found herself saying, "he's finally gone."

Jackson's face, like a blue-black moon, darkened, and his voice rumbled over the desk as solemnly as the news it transported.

"Yesterday morning. Eight forty five A.M."

"In New Orleans?"

"Yes. That's where he'd been for some time. In private care."

"There were physical problems? And some mental?"

"So I understand. I've dealt, you understand, only with the man's attorneys for the past years."

Nina nodded. There was silence in the room for a time.

It seemed appropriate; a life halted in middle age, a life wasted in institutions. She sighed.

Finally Jackson Bennett continued:

"This is, of course, a very big thing. Big for Bay St. Lucy."

"I know. Have you told anyone?"

He shook his head.

"Only Peter and Marvin," he said, referring to the two other partners. "And they've kept it to themselves. We'll be having a press conference this afternoon."

"All hell will break loose."

He smiled.

"I'm sure that's true."

"It's strange. I guess fate may be operating here. You know Margot Gavin?"

"From Chicago—runs the shop on Eighth Street?"

"Yes. She and I have kind of bonded in the last few months. Only yesterday morning she was talking about buying the Robinson place."

"She didn't know?"

"No."

"I thought everyone in town did."

"Well, she's not that social. But anyway, it's as though the subject came up in her shop at the precise moment that Mr. Robinson was—"

She found it hard to say the word "dying," but "passing" seemed somehow overly formal, and so what had happened to Arthur Robinson the previous morning simply hung there over the desk, a wordless concept.

"I'm sure that was only a coincidence."

"I hope," she said, "that you're right. And yet, so many bizarre things have happened in connection with that house, that family. I told Margot about it being haunted; but the truth is more strange. It's not that ghosts have been haunting the house; it's that the house has been haunting the town."

"Yes. And for two decades. But now that's over."

"Hard to believe. How much money is involved, do you know?"

He shrugged:

"I really don't. Of course there's the house and the two acres surrounding it, land that no one has been able to claim or build on. But the Robinson's were such— well, entrepreneurs—"

"Gangsters, you mean."

Another smile, this one somewhat broader.

"Some would say that. Attorneys have to be more cautious."

"And attorneys' wives."

"We'll pretend you didn't say it. But there is property all over Bay St. Lucy, property that is now being rented—"

"Like my little house by the ocean."

"Yes. You're paying rent to a kind of holding company, but that company in turn…"

"Is a part of the Robinson estate."

"Precisely."

"We've all been held hostage by that family for decades."

"But that will change now. I've been assured that, with the sister already dead, the youngest heir dying intestate, the property involved will revert to the city, which we can claim in lieu of back taxes. The taxes involved are rather minor; but the loophole will allow the city to take over all the family's holdings."

"So we're talking—"

"Millions of dollars, Nina."

"It's surreal."

"Everything involved with the Robinsons was surreal. Your husband had just hired me, just taken a chance on an ignorant black boy—"

"You weren't ignorant."

"I was desperate though. Anyway, I remember my first days at work. I was sitting in that adjoining office, going through some old files when I heard what had happened the previous evening."

"A horror movie."

He nodded.

"I suppose that every little town—at least every little town in the south—has its Gothic mansion."

"Yes. And now—heavens, the impact that this news is going to have."

"Well, as I say, I have no idea of estimating the windfall that will be coming to Bay St. Lucy; but you and the rest of the City Council will have some tough decisions before it. We'll have the funds to build an entirely new school system, elementary right up through high school."

She smiled.

"Old Dell Mason Dees Hall could be torn down."

"Very possibly."

"And just in time. Before it collapses."

"We can replace the library—"

"—and, if Margot Gavin wishes, she can buy and renovate the house itself."

"What does she want to do with it?"

"Make it into an elegant bed and breakfast. With me to help run it."

"Are you interested?"

"Maybe. I'm pretty happy now just puttering around, but—it would be something new."

"If it happens, you know I'll handle the legal work, deeds, zoning regulations—for free."

"We wouldn't ask you to do that."

"No discussion. It's done"

"So. What happens now?"

"Well, Nina, that's what I wanted to talk to you about."

He leaned across the desk, which groaned with his weight.

"We may need to ask you a favor."

"Of course. How may I help?"

"You're still on the city council I assume."

"Last time I checked."

"You like New Orleans?"

"Love it."

"Want to go?"

"I always want to go to New Orleans and I never can afford it."

"The trip will be paid for by the city."

"What would I be doing there?"

"Since it's almost certain that there is no will, there will be documents to sign following a formal announcement in the offices of Arthur Robinson's attorney. Someone from Bay St. Lucy needs to be there. It is somewhat like the reading of a will. There are legal differences, but you won't need to worry about them. You just need to be there, and sign as a legal representative for the town."

"You don't want to do this yourself?"

"I have to be in court tomorrow. And as for the other council members—"

"They've all got jobs."

He smiled:

"Yes. But somehow, you seem to be the most appropriate person. You've taught everybody in town;

now it's only right that you should represent us in taking back what's rightfully ours."

"Thank you, Jackson. It's very gratifying that you should say that."

"I only wish Frank could be going with you."

"Yes. He'd want to stay at the Monteleone, of course."

Jackson Bennett's smile became a grin:

"And have a beer at Napoleon House."

"Yes. With all their old opera records."

"So. Will you go for us?"

"I'd be happy to."

"The reading will take place in attorney's chambers tomorrow afternoon at two o'clock. We can fly you over tomorrow morning. Will that work for you?"

"Of course."

"If you wanted to stay over a night, enjoy the city—"

She shook her head:

"No. That's all right. I have a cat to feed tomorrow night. But Jackson—"

"Yes?"

"I don't know why but—it just seems that one of us should...I mean, someone from Bay St. Lucy should—"

"Should what, Nina?"

"Should pay last respects. It just seems right."

He was silent for a time. Then:

"Most people here wouldn't want to do that."

"I know. But I do."

"And that's probably why you're the one to go to New Orleans."

"Perhaps."

"Ok. I'll find out where the body can be viewed."

"I would appreciate that."

"Glad to do it."

Silence for a time.

Then Jackson Bennett, getting to his feet, said:

"After all those years, the town is free."

She nodded:

"And that mansion. Standing there, eroding, little by little—"

"With the town powerless to tear it down; powerless to fix it up."

"A cancer, right in our middle."

"That's all over now."

"I hope so, Jackson."

"Like I say, there's nothing to worry about."

She herself stood, and walked in front of him to the office door, leading the way by a step, just as she always did with Frank.

Frank, who seemed to be there with them now, smiling, but holding out two palms in a cautionary way, shaking his head, and saying:

There is *always* something to worry about.

So thinking, she said good bye, descended the stairs, and headed off to her ten o'clock appointment with Macy's Beowulf class.

CHAPTER FOUR: THE HIGH SCHOOL AND
THE JETTY

"Love interest nearly always weakens a mystery because it introduces a type of suspense that is antagonistic to the detective's struggle to solve a problem."

Raymond Chandler

"In literature, as in love, we are astonished at what is chosen by others."

Andres Maurois

She reached the high school at precisely ten o'clock, entering to find the normal scene of bedlam that occurs in any high school at the hourly bell that sends the students storming into the hallways.

"Darn," she muttered to herself, miffed that she, a veteran teacher, had let herself be trapped this way.

The first rule of teaching—at least high school teaching—was:

Never be trapped in the hallway with the students.

Frequently, she'd told herself that Tolstoy, and only in the most violent and dramatic portions of *War and Peace* (perhaps the beginning lines of the Battle of Borodino) could do justice to what actually transpired; the football players hurling themselves against the lockers, bald-shaven coaches grabbing players, placing them in headlocks and, knuckles rubbing on their crew-cuts, shouting over and over again:

"Whaddya think, Suggs? Whaddya think, Suggs?"

—this, whether the player's name actually *was* "Suggs" or not.

She stood as clear from the mélange as possible, secreting herself in a niche she'd discovered years ago between the trophy case and a large paper mache anchor, which told the world that Bay St. Lucy's denizens were "The Mariners."

"Nina!"

Paul Cox, far handsomer and more efficient than any of the principals she'd ever worked for (all of whom either hid in their offices, or prowled the building getting in everyone's way) approached like a vapor through the French and Russian troops dying on The Battlefield of High School Hallway and took her hand, smiling as he said:

"Macy tells me you're talking to one of her classes!"

She shouted something as loud as she could, but couldn't hear herself over the tumult of what seemed to be dozens of identical girls screaming into each other's faces at the same time.

He nodded.

"Good. Good. Thank you so much for doing this!"

"_____," she screamed.

"Yes, I think so too!"

I wonder, she thought, *what I must have said.*

"Come on into my office for a minute. Macy will be down in a second to get you. Besides, there's something I want to show you!"

But I want to stay here, she thought.

"Come on!"

She followed, amazed that the two of them were not trampled.

The office was, as usual, filled with sullen teenagers who'd missed something or forgotten something or done something or not done something and thus were all standing by the counter waiting to be dealt with.

Only after she and Paul were in the office itself, door closed securely behind them, could she feel safe.

How had she done this every day for forty years?

Paul was not a big man, but he exuded confidence. Perhaps that confidence, and not pure muscularity, explained why he'd been one of the best quarterbacks in the high school's history. Did the confidence cause this greatness, she wondered, or result from it?

No matter.

The main thing was he simply represented "PRINCIPALDOM" in its purest form. Starched white shirt, navy blazer, superbly tied club tie—the principal is your pal and such he was to everyone.

"Look at this! We can unveil it now!"

She followed him toward a tripod standing beside one of the paneled walls, a towel hanging over it and covering what seemed to be a painting of some sort.

There was something birdlike about Paul Cox's movements, she found herself thinking. A delicate quality almost. His high cheekbones, aquiline features, bright and inquisitive eyes—this was more an artist than a football player; yet somehow he'd managed to become both, as well as a visionary leader for the school.

"Look!"

He took the cover off.

"Oh my—Paul!" Nina exclaimed.

"Our new physical plant! Elementary, middle, and high school, all conjoined."

The scene painted before her seemed almost something from a science fiction novel. There were the trees, sidewalks, dedicated and happy young people, and blue skies always associated with model developments as depicted by optimistic engineers working with good painters, fanciful planners and—on occasion—ruthless bunko artists.

But here laid out before her was much more. This was not a school but a spaceport, with glass and chrome buildings sprouting high above the city, strange train like vehicles linking porches and archways, windows opening onto the brightest of ocean views, and light, light, everywhere light.

"Paul, this is fantastic!"

"I have," he said, "been keeping it under wraps. It was designed by a firm in New Orleans."

"Is it a moonscape? Or the next Disneyworld?"

"It's our new school."

"How could it be, Paul? This thing would cost a billion dollars."

"Not at all. We can get it at bargain rates: a hundred and forty million. And we're going to have that much, from what I hear."

She was silent for a time, wondering how many seconds after Arthur Robinson's demise it had actually taken for everyone in Bay St. Lucy—from adults to children to senior citizens to pets and porpoises—to know the old man was dead.

"You've heard then."

"First thing this morning."

"Just out of curiosity, who told you?"

"One of the janitors."

"So you knew it to be true."

"Of course. I don't spread rumors. Good luck in New Orleans."

"You know about that, too?"

"Not much. Just the sketchy details I've heard."

"Which are?"

"You leave from here by private car at eleven fifty eight tomorrow morning. The city's private jet flies you from Biloxi to New Orleans. You view the body at McWilliams funeral home sometime around noon. You hear the official dispensation announcement at Raymer Peabody and Fontenot Law firm at two tomorrow afternoon. And after you sign some documents, acting as the city's representative, we're all rich. That's just the basics that are going around town. None of us really know any more details."

"Well, thank you for telling me. I wasn't as yet certain about the proper spelling of "Raymer."

"It's with an 'E.' I checked."

"One can't be too careful with such things."

"No. So how are you and the rest of the city council going to divvy up the dough?"

"We're planning on keeping it all for ourselves."

There was a moment's panic in his eyes, making her wonder if her sense of humor had become too subtle in her old age, or whether it actually was a sense of humor at all.

What if no one else in the world thought funny the same things she thought funny, and, instead of becoming charmingly eccentric, she was simply going insane?

But the panic disappeared from his face an instant after its inception, and his smile broadened.

"You wouldn't be very popular."

"We are now, though, going to be very popular, I suppose."

"You are with me; and with the rest of the school board."

"Where would this school be, Paul?"

"Right here. We have the land. We just tear down what's here now, and start from scratch. It would all be state of the art, from the classrooms right down to the lunchrooms. People would come from all over the country to look at it."

She shook her head.

"It's a marvelous conception, Paul. You should be proud that you had this done."

"We need it, Nina. What we have now is…"

"I know. What we have now is what we had when I started teaching. It wasn't much, even then."

"And now it's about to fall down. It will fall down, some day, and I don't want to be under it when it does. Nor my teachers. Nor my kids."

She liked the way he thought of them as *his* teachers, and *his* kids.

He saw them, she could tell, not as his underlings but as his responsibilities.

There was a difference.

"I wish I could promise you, Paul, that the city will choose to go this way. I can't, you know. Not everyone in town views education as the highest priority."

He nodded.

"I know. But I talked to several people on the school board. We all thought it good to proceed with a drawing, a conception. I assume there will be a meeting when everyone in town makes various proposals."

"More than one meeting. I think we can all be sure of that."

"Then we'll get our chance."

"Of course."

"And when we do, we'll have this to show you."

"Yes. And it's truly impressive, Paul, it really is."

"Can we count on your vote?"

"Of course. You know that."

"Good. Because—"

"Nina! Nina!"

Through a door suddenly flung open, rushed Macy Peterson completely out of breath.

"I'm sorry I'm late! We had a few crises! Are you ready? Sorry to interrupt, Paul! Oh gee! Did you show her? What do you think of it, Nina? Isn't it great? I know already where I'm going to be teaching! Right over there, in that tallest building, the one with a view of the ocean. So when do you think the money will be available? Paul says the construction could start next spring! And we wouldn't have to have it all up front! Just, what was it, Paul, twenty percent? And the rates they're willing to give us are phenomenal. Also, the state may be willing to kick in a certain percentage, given how the elections turn out next month. But Paul is optimistic."

She took two or three more sentences to run completely out of breath, but she had such little control of them that they made no sense at all. They did have the positive aspect of emptying her lungs, and for a few instants, while she was filling them again, there was sufficient time and space for Nina to say:

"Good morning, Macy."

Unable to answer, she nodded, smiling broadly.

Finally she was able to gasp:

"Good Morning!"

But by then, her principal, arms around both of their shoulders, was ushering them out of his office, through the reception area, and into a suddenly vacant hallway, saying all the time:

"BEOWULFBEOWULFBEOWULFBEOWULF!"

With a light shove, he sent them both scampering on their way to class.

"Isn't he a great principal?" said Macy.

"You're lucky."

"Do you think we'll get the new school?"

"I don't know, Macy."

"What are our chances?"

"Well, I—"

She had no idea what to say to that, and was thus greatly relieved at the realization that the classroom lay before them.

They entered, she was introduced, and she made the points she'd made for decades; asked the same questions; received essentially the same answers—

—while the other half of her mind mused, remembered, feared, wondered—in short, fantasized.

This continued for the rest of the day. Through the lunch given gratis to her in the cafeteria as payment for her morning's services. Through the Vespa ride home, through the hour's closet shuffling necessary to plan for a trip—a mourning trip plus a business trip—to New Orleans, plus the tired beginnings and groggy awakenings from an afternoon nap—

—what time was it? five o'clock now?

—plus her daily run/walk on the beach, bare feet deliciously sensitive to the cool, packed, wet and squiggly sand as she attempted to follow a silver sliver of foam that showed the farthest advances of the gentle swell that was now receding—

—through all of these activities it speculated.

What must have happened in that house?

No one had ever known precisely.

Now no one ever would.

The Robinson's. An immensely wealthy family. Roots quite shady. Not a creole name, nor even a well-known Mississippi one. Homer Baron Robinson, the autocrat, standing solitary on the front balcony, looking out over Breakers Boulevard, and over the sea beyond, a sea which must have looked that evening in—what was the precise year? She could never remember—the same way it looked now.

She and Frank, not long married, would take walks on the beach, and she would see him standing there.

He never waved.

That house. Magnificent then in splendor as it still was in decay. The great yard surrounding with its spreading live oak trees, branches two feet in diameter, spread across the ground as though they were spokes of an upturned umbrella. Branches that could be climbed upon and sat upon and hidden within and leapt across by children ecstatic with youth and the ocean breeze—

—but no such happy children had existed in the Robinson house.

In that huge sepulcher of a house, silent ghostlike children had existed.

Hardly appearing.

Privately educated.

And where had all that money come from?

Various people she'd known during her life had claimed to hear the gunfire, which, later accounts verified, must have come at around two A.M.

Some people said two limousines had pulled into the circular driveway.

Gangsters from New Orleans?

Or from Chicago?

But who in Bay St. Lucy would have been awake to see them?

She remembered sitting down to breakfast, and Frank, solemn as a monk, saying: "Something very bad has happened; nobody is sure what."

And, yes, something very bad indeed had happened.

She finished her run, sat on the beach for a time watching lightning trace its golden maze-like slivers through a dark blue thunderhead that billowed far beyond the oil platform.

Then, quite hungry for dinner—the chili dog "au jus" had not been bad at school, but the tater-tots "du jour" were not up to the chef's usual superb performance and the banana pudding was rancid—she made her way toward her shack.

The days were getting shorter. There was a dim gray light in her kitchen as she turned on the small Bose radio, decided against whatever music and banter seemed to be coming out of it, put a disc in the cd player, and listened to the opening strains of Verdi's *I Vespri Sicilliani* as she Furled and Unfurled her cat.

She made and ate dinner, then went out on the deck to watch the ocean.

The tide was coming in. The swells grew, and seemed to be coming closer, closer to the pier posts holding her up. Beyond these swells, lightning became sharper and brighter, the clouds more mammoth, huge cotton balls that had somehow been drenched in ink.

It was eight thirty when, dishes washed, she got into bed and opened the mystery she was reading.

It was nine o'clock when she heard the pounding on the front door.

Was she dreaming?

It continued.

What in heaven's name?

"Yes?" she found herself shouting.

"Ms. Bannister?"

A boy's voice.

A teenager.

What was a teenager doing at her door at nine o'clock in the evening?

What had happened?

"Yes?" she repeated, rather stupidly.

"Ms. Bannister? It's Tommy Boyd."

"Yes, Tommy?"

"Ms. Peterson sent me."

"Macy Peterson?"

"Yes, ma'am."

She got out of bed and opened the door:

"Hello, Tommy. Now what is this about?"

"Ms. Peterson sent me."

"Why?"

"She said to tell you she's sorry to bother you, but she really needs to see you. She's down at the rock pier fishing for crabs—and she says she's got something really important to tell you."

"All right. Hold on, and I'll be right with you."

There was nothing left to do but go back inside, get her windbreaker—because the breezes had freshened now with the approaching storm—and follow Tommy whatever his name was, down the stairs and into his Volkswagen.

"Is Ms. Peterson all right?" she asked.

"I think so. I don't really know. I sometimes run errands for her since she doesn't have a car. She bikes to school you know."

"Yes."

"She just called our place about an hour ago, asked my dad if he would mind me coming to get you and take you to the pier. He didn't mind."

"No, of course not. And you say she's crabbing?"

"Yes, Ma'am."

Curiouser and curiouser.

"Did she seem—all right when you talked to her?"

"Well, actually—"

"Yes?"

"—actually she seemed kind of upset."

Oh damn, Nina did not say.

What was going on now?

She was dropped at the foot of the stone pier, which was just what its appellation described and could not have been described more accurately, no matter how many words were used to do so—except that one could have added its length, over a quarter of a mile, and the fact that it was buttressed on each side by huge red slabs of rock, upon which and through which the great waves roared and sifted.

Bay St. Lucy lacking a wooden fishing pier, this jetty—which is what the townspeople called it—was the only access for fishermen without a boat, to the slightly deeper reaches of the sea.

Nina slipped slightly on the moss-covered cement, feeling spray douse her face and watching somewhat regretfully the receding tail-lights of Tommy's car.

"What in heaven's name is Macy doing out here?"

The great rocks did not answer, nor did the waves crashing against them, nor did the pole-lights marking fifty foot intervals of cement and making the sea glow green beneath them.

"What is going on with her?"

Macy had seemed fine today. More than fine. Bubbly with enthusiasm. What could have happened during the afternoon that—

—well, no need for further speculation.

—for there was Macy herself, huddled in a yellow plastic raincoat, sitting not on the jetty itself but in a niche between two of the great rocks.

"Macy!"

She looked up as Nina approached.

"Oh Nina!" she shouted, trying to make herself heard above the combined roaring of wind and breakers. "I'm so sorry to bother you! Were you ready to go to bed?"

"No," Nina said, not lying, since she had in fact been *in* bed. "But what is happening?"

"I sent Tommy for you!"

"I know."

"He's a wonderful boy; he and his family help me sometimes, when I need things."

Well, wonderful, thought Nina.

And enough of that.

Now what the hell is going on?

"What has happened, Macy?" Nina asked, in lieu of asking, What is going on?

"I come out here, sometimes."

"I can see that."

"It's just—well, sometimes it seems like the only thing to do."

"Well, when you really think about it," replied Nina, crouching near the edge of the jetty, her clothes quite drenched now, whether from the splashing of the waves or the first thin but relatively effective sheets of rain from the squall making its way shoreward and straight along the rock pier, "when you really think about it, most people never do think of anything to do in their lives, in the world whatever, except sit outside at night in a thunderstorm two or three hundred yards from shore on a huge rock pier getting soaked to the skin and catching crabs. I mean, what else *could* one do?"

"Are you mad at me?"

"Too wet."

"I know. I should have thought about the rain."

"It's all right. We'll have plenty of time to think about it now. What is it, Macy?"

"There was no one else to talk to. Except you."

Macy continued to crab. She held, quite gingerly, a string in her hands. At the other end of the string, submerged beneath eddying water and creviced between the cracks of rocks, illuminated green by a torch shining from the jetty, was a chicken breast impaled upon a wire.

From time to time, crabs, hidden in the rock fissures, would make their way to the meat and fasten onto it, claw-forcing it into their horrid-monster like thing that was a mouth, oblivious to the fact that they were being pulled ever so carefully out of the ocean.

Nina found herself watching the meat, looking for the dark approaching shadow that would have been a crab.

Watching for a time as she'd always watched—

—even as a little girl, for she had always loved the jetty.

Though not so much in rain.

"Macy, are you crying?"

"I don't know. It might just be the spray."

"What is it, Macy? You've got to tell me."

"Oh, Nina—"

There was not silence, one would have been dead wrong in saying that; but the complete cacophony of elemental sounds, wave roarings, rain poundings, mournful wailing of some huge tanker a quarter mile at sea—all of these things did lack, at least for a few seconds, a human voice.

Every other manner of audibility was there, and louder than normal.

"Tell me. Tell me now."

"All right," Macy answered, not telling her.

"Tell me, Macy!"

"Oh Nina! Nina, I've given up teaching!"

"What?"

"I signed my letter of resignation late this afternoon!"

"No! No, Macy, I can't believe it!"

"It's true!"

The rain intensified, but neither woman was particularly aware of it, since Nina, having scrambled crablike herself down to where Macy was crouched, the two of them were now embracing.

They did so for a while; when Nina pulled away she could see, in the glow of the electric torch, that the tears behind Macy's glasses had nothing to do with storm or breakers.

"What has happened?"

Macy was almost sobbing.

"It—it all happened this afternoon. I never expected it! It was such a shock!"

"What? You've got to tell me! Why are you resigning?"

"Because—because—"

"Tell me, Macy!"

"Because it's in the rules. The old school rules!"

"What is in the rules?"

"You can't work for a principal—that you're married to!"

"That rule went out decades ago, Macy!"

What had she said?

Oh.

Oh!

"What did you say?"

"We're getting married, Nina! Paul asked me to marry him!"

"Then—then this is a *good* thing!"

"I think so!"

"I thought it was a *bad* thing!"

"No. Good."

"Oh, Macy! How long has this been going on?"

"Since last April. He asked me out to dinner one night, and we went over to Biloxi, so as not to be seen here in town. And then he—"

"I don't want to know."

"Are you sure?"

"Maybe later. No. No, never. But—how did you keep it such a secret?"

"It was hard, Nina!"

"It had to be."

"Oh, it was! But—finally, he told me this afternoon, that it had to end. He's a traditionalist. We shouldn't be a secret anymore; and we should set a date; and—and then he gave me this!"

She held up her non crabbing hand.

"A diamond!"

"Yes! Isn't it beautiful? I'm sorry it's so wet!"

"Diamonds are impervious to wet, silly girl!"

"And Nina—there's something I have to ask you. I don't want to embarrass you, but it's awfully important."

"Ask, Macy!"

"Well—you know that both of my parents have passed, and I'm an only child. But—well, somebody has to—"

"Give you away?"

"That sounds kind of—well—'inexpensive'."

"Sell you?"

"That sounds—"

"I know how that sounds. Listen, don't worry about what to call it."

"Would you?"

"I'd be thrilled."

"It's not like I'm asking you to be my mother—it's just—oh, look!"

Nina did, and saw a shadow passing over the chicken moon that was the breast in the water.

"I think I'm getting a crab!"

"Careful. Let him get his claws into it."

"I know. One second, two seconds—"

"When will the wedding be?"

"Sometime in February, we think. Do you want to help us plan?"

"What would be better? I'd love it, Macy. I'm thrilled about the whole thing. But what you said about teaching—"

Macy nodded, beginning to pull the string up, and with it, the crab, whose shell reflected blue-brown in the watery torchlight.

"I'll have to quit here. But there will be other places. Paul knows I love teaching. Oh! There it is! He's a nice big one!"

"Here, you want me to pull the bucket out?"

"Yes!"

Nina found the silver chain wrapped conveniently around a metal spoke protruding from the cement behind them. She pulled up the crab bucket, yanked open the net wire top, and watched as Macy, with a shake, dropped the crab inside.

"He's your only one!"

"I know, said Macy, smiling. "I hadn't been at it long, before you came. But he's special. I'm going to name him Troy."

"Why Troy?"

"I don't know. But he's very important to me; he's my engagement crab!"

"What are you going to do with him?"

"Eat him."

"Oh! That's so special!"

"I know. But maybe we should go now, Nina."

"That's probably true; the rain seems to be getting harder."

"Can we go back on your Vespa?"

Nina shook her head:

"No. I came with Tommy, remember?"

"Oh, that's right. And he didn't stay, did he?"

"Nope."

"We should have asked him to, I guess."

"Yes, we probably should have, Macy."

The two women clamored off the rocks, the crab bucket, Troy within, between them.

Clouds and pounding wave-spray had obscured the coast, a quarter of a mile inward from them.

"Well. How far is it to your place, Nina?"

"It's nothing. A mile or so."

"I'm so sorry."

"Don't worry. What's a little water? Besides, we have planning to do."

"Yes! There's so much in my mind now. Thank you for being my Best Woman."

"That's a good thing to call it, isn't it?"

"Yes!"

"Come on then. We'll go back to my place and dry off. Then we'll have the last of bottle of wine I opened. Then we'll start planning the wedding."

They hugged, and struck out toward the shore.

The next sodden hour disappeared, immersed in non-stop chatter and cold rain.

It was ten o'clock when they reached Nina's shack.

The wine was broken out.

Some minutes thereafter, various sheets of paper, pictures, and wedding plans covered the kitchen table.

Sometime before midnight, they both went to bed, Nina in her own room, Macy on the couch.

And Nina, snug beneath the covers, realized how excited she was for Macy, and how proud she would be to be in the wedding, and how much she loved her little Bay St. Lucy.

Which was a perfect little seaside town.

And which—Nina had no way of knowing this as she closed her eyes and drifted into pre-sleep reveries—would never be the same again.

CHAPTER FIVE: CORPSES, CASES, AND CAPONS

"Alas poor Yorick! How surprised to see how his counterpart of today is whisked off to a funeral parlor and is in short order sprayed, sliced, pierced, pickled, trussed, trimmed, creamed, waxed, painted, rouged, and neatly dressed— transformed from a common corpse into a Beautiful Memory Picture."

Jessica Mitford

St. Charles Avenue, Nina mused, looking up and down the great palmed and street car-bisected thoroughfare, was the only street in the world where mansions, mortuaries, legal offices, and restaurants all looked precisely the same.

There were other edifices stuck in here or there, of course, and she'd always wondered what drunken pirate crew had thrown together New Orleans' zoning laws.

But that did not matter. The fact that somehow a MacCheezit existed between the Senator Robicheaux Family Estate and what had been the old Pontchartrain Hotel—or that the uptown branch of the New Orleans Public Library sat beneath the same stately live oaks and Mesozoic ferns as Commander's Palace and somebody's two room shack—

—none of this mattered. St. Charles was St. Charles, and as good a reason as she could have wanted for a morning's walk.

The second best thing in the entire world, when one actually thought about it, to walking on the beach.

And so she had flashed the city's credit card to the cab driver, left the vehicle at Audubon Park, given her respects to the backs of buildings at Tulane—or rather, *TU*lane—and the fronts of buildings at Loyola, and sauntered for half an hour, lungs filling with the scent of hot beignets, eyes formulating what one of the painters whose work hung in Margot's shop would have done with the brown bored and completely anachronistic street cars meeting on the median, and yawning to each other as they sauntered on.

She tried to avoid actual thinking, and to engage only in light reveries, but to do so in an organized manner.

A time for every daydream, all of the not-quite-thoughts laid out in precise geographical and urbanized units.

Poydras Street to D'Urberville. Three hundred yards. Memories of the Robinson Mansion, and comparisons with the one over there on the left.

No.

The Robinson Manor was bigger.

Deeper balconies.

Could Margot Gavin actually buy the structure?

After all those years would anything in it be—what was the word? Restorable?

How rich was Margot, anyway?

And would she—Nina Bannister—actually consider going into the hotel business?

No. Of course not.

But the Bed and Breakfast business?

Well, that was something else again.

She imagined a couple not at all like tourists one saw in the Quarter on Big Football Game Days or Mardi Gras week.

What could they do, anyway? A bit of fishing, a little beachcombing, much sitting around the edge of the garden, listening idly to the chatter and gossip of Bay St. Lucy—which went on, of course, in the middle of the garden, presided over by ironically the town's newest true denizen—Margot—

—now how much trouble could it be to look after the two of them?—but more of those reveries later.

For here, canopied, red carpeted, was either a new, beautiful, expensive, and truly sumptuous restaurant—

—Check the small scrunched up note page with the address on it—

What does it say? 228 Toulouse?

Or a Funeral Home.

And it was, indeed, the latter.

McWilliams Funeral Home.

She began to make her way up the steps, and had climbed three of them when the door opened and the corpse emerged. He was certainly just that, was he not? Helping her out with the viewing by coming out to meet her in person.

"Good morning!"

"Good morning," she answered, wondering about the etiquette of greeting the dead.

"It's going to be a lovely day, isn't it?" inquired the cadaver.

"It certainly is," she answered, not adding, 'for those of us who are alive.'

"You must be Ms. Bannister, from Bay St. Lucy?"

"Yes."

"Welcome."

Oh my God he's extending his hand.

She took it.

It was not warm, exactly, but then, the hand being dead, it lacked the strength to lock onto her and carry her to a charnel house.

And then, now that she was closer to the man, she could discern definite non-necromantic tendencies. He was, to begin with, better dressed than most corpses. He was thinner and seemed in worse health.

"I'm Charles McWilliams. Please come in."

She did so, subconsciously wishing for a table beneath the window, and wishing that the soft, monochromatic organ music which seemed to seep from the walls could be played, at least between certain stipulated hours, at Wal-Mart.

"Have there been many people in to—to view?" she asked.

He shook his head.

"You are the first."

He led her through several rooms, making her feel as though she was touring an automobile showroom. Elegant, gray and velvet vehicles reflected quiet lighting and—their lids open and their handles shining——promised the most comfortable ride imaginable.

As well as, she could not help musing, superb mileage.

Stop that, Nina, she told herself.

Arthur Robinson had a small room to himself.

She walked to the casket, having noticed that the funeral director, once beside her, had now dropped off, and now, hands folded appropriately, was standing just inside the door of the room.

There were several large sprays of flowers. Purple flowers, gold flower, and, of course, white lilies.

She leaned over.

The thing that had been 'he' was dressed appropriately for the occasion, charcoal gray suit with red tie. He had not been a small man. She could imagine the gaunt face as having once been young-looking, before being ravaged by whatever had attacked it, as well as the rest of Arthur Robinson.

"Was he ill long?" she found herself asking.

"Yes, Ma'am. For quite some time, I believe."

"Well," she said, looking down at the figure beneath her, "it's over now."

"Yes," came the answer, from behind her (somewhat to her relief) and not below her.

There was nothing else to do.

She could have prayed, but she found herself doing that less frequently now than earlier in her life—she did not know why.

She could have done something appropriate, but there seemed nothing appropriate to do; she was merely reading the day's obituaries, but doing so in 3-D.

And so, having "paid her respects," and wondering how many other phrases the culture stored and used frequently that also had no meaning whatsoever, she turned and left.

There were nods. Quiet condolences. A glance or two at families huddled together in other rooms. The sound of sobbing.

And, finally, she was on the street again.

She took a deep breath.

That was done.

It had needed doing, at least by someone from Bay St Lucy. And she was that person, and she had done the right thing.

Now—a check on time.

Eleven fifteen A.M.

She walked several feet in the direction of Canal Street, thought about the mile or so between her and the law offices she must be in at one o'clock, and decided to take the street car.

There—just in front of her—that was a stop, was it not?

The ponderous clanging of the apparatus behind her told her she was right.

And so she climbed aboard, having, fortunately, the right change, and, giving her coins to Charon she allowed him to pole her over the River Styx, into the

Garden District, and further into the Land of the Dead in the holy-seeming day of Viewings and Wills.

Damn Shakespeare, she thought, the man's infernal writings invading her mind again. He was as bad as Tom Broussard; she could not shake him. "Let's talk of graves," came the words, as automatically as they always came now, as though her brain were a twenty four hour movie theater showing ENGLISH LITERATURE constantly rather than Japanese horror films.

There were times she would have preferred the latter.

> *Let's talk of graves, of worms, and epitaphs;*
> *Make dust our paper, and, with rainy eyes,*
> *Write sorrow on the bosom of the earth.*

The streetcar clattered and sparked along, descending St. Charles.

She tried to think of nothing at all.

It didn't work.

At one o'clock precisely, she entered the offices of Raymer, Peabody, and Fontenot, Attorneys at Law.

Another mansion, of course, rooms here and there, gray men and women making their way about, approximately the same way figures had moved in the mortuary but with less purpose.

She was met courteously and led to the appropriate room, where several men sat around a large burnished table.

She and Frank had always laughed about the measure of a firm's success:

"You can tell how spiffy they are," he insisted, by the length of the secretaries' skirts. The length of their legs, too!"

By that measure, this firm was Fortune 500. A superb woman, absolutely in her prime, was moving around the table, whispering with each of the dark-suited figures who sat sipping cups of coffee.

She was dressed in black, which contrasted starkly and unforgettably with her expensively-tanned skin and radiant golden hair.

This was not, Nina thought, watching her elementally simple but insultingly—to the rest of the human race—graceful movements. *This was not a woman but a constellation.* If the corpse an hour and a half ago had been the obituaries three dimensionalized, this was the Art and Beauty Section animated.

My God, she asked herself, how tall was this woman?

Six feet at least.

Another attorney—for she knew, somehow, that the other men around the table were attorneys—entered the room.

They all nodded to each other, as well as to her.

The vision of beauty that had been serving them, whispering to them, laughing softly with them, and making them simultaneously ashamed of their age and completely oblivious to it—went back to a corner of the room and sat down, as inconspicuous as Helen of Troy in an episode of Perry Mason.

"Thank you all for coming. We're here as you know to discuss the estate of the late Mr. Homer Baron Robinson. There has been some confusion concerning——"

Blah blah blah.

Papers shuffled around.

Legalese.

She had heard so much of it in her life.

It never seemed to change.

Preliminaries.

More preliminaries.

Getting to the heart of it now; briefcase opened, everyone leaning forward just a bit.

"And so. The will reads as follows: I, Homer Baron Robinson, being of sound mind and in possession of my faculties—

What will? she found herself thinking.

There wasn't supposed to be any will.

"Do leave my entire estate to Ms. Eve Ivory."

All eyes turned to the secretary who was sitting in the back of the room.

Except it was no secretary.

Within two minutes proceedings had closed, and Nina found herself sitting alone at the table.

With the woman now bending over her, breath as warm as her smile.

"I can promise you," she said, "that I will try to help Bay St. Lucy in every way I can. I wish only the best for Bay St. Lucy."

And she left.

Nina allowed herself to be stunned for one minute. Perhaps more.

Then she took out her cell phone and dialed a number.

"Jackson Bennett," came the answer.

"Jackson?"

"Yes! Nina! Is it over?"

She shook her head.

"I think, Jackson, it's just beginning."

And she hung up the phone.

By five o'clock that evening she was back in Bay St. Lucy, sitting in the middle of the high school gymnasium, a crowd pouring in, several people seated in a tight circle around her.

Between the reading of the will and this particular moment, several things had happened:

1) She had taken a cab immediately to the New Orleans Airport and boarded the small plane that was to take her home.

2) She had talked frequently by cell phone to Jackson Bennett, learning that he knew nothing, except that all relevant papers would be hand delivered to his office later in the evening.

3) All of Bay St. Lucy had learned that there was in fact a will, and that it left all of the money and property in the Robinson estate to someone named Eve Ivory, and not to them.

4) A press conference/town meeting had been announced for five P.M. in the city gymnasium.

5) She had been whisked directly from her flight to said gymnasium, in the middle of which she now stood, microphone before her, Jackson Bennett, Edie Towler, and four city council members seated around her.

6) Jason Boudreaux, reporter for the Bay St. Lucy newspaper, had raised his hand.

These were the things that had happened between the reading of the will and the posing of Jason Boudreaux's question, which was:

"Nina, what happened in New Orleans today?"

"I don't know."

"Where did this will come from?"

"I don't know."

Someone else in the audience, far in the back, standing on a riser, directly beneath the Visitors basket, shouting:

"Who is Eve Ivory?"

"I don't know."

Front row now:

"Does she own all the Robinson property?"

"I don't know."

Now questions popping like popcorn balls, here, there, wherever:

"What about the money?"

"I don't know."

"What's going to happen to us?"

"I don't know."

"What's going to happen to the town?"

"I don't know."

"Is she going to come and live here?"

"I don't know."

"Could she sell all this property? Does she have a right to do that?"

"I don't know."

"What about the Robinson mansion?"

"I don't know."

Finally the entire crowd, muttering, stunned and disgusted—all left.

Nina turned and said to the small ring of people seated behind her:

"Well. I think I handled that pretty well, don't you?"

None of them said anything.

"Good," she continued. "Now I'm going out to dinner."

CHAPTER SIX: AN EVENING WITH FRIENDS

"Bad news isn't wine. It doesn't improve with age."

Colin Powell

She and Margot Gavin had developed the habit of meeting together for cocktails and dinner at Sergios By the Sea, at seven o'clock precisely, every Thursday evening.

She saw no reason to change the routine now, because things, which so far had gone as badly as they possibly could have, would have hardly been made worse by her sitting around at home.

So she went to Sergios.

The restaurant was slightly ill-named, there being no 'Sergio' connected with it (It was in fact owned by a man named Leonard Katz, who lived in Jackson), and the distance between it and the sea being somewhat more than two miles. Still, she always told herself, it was by the sea, to the degree that all places in the world are by the sea, given a bit of poetic license—and direct ownership of the restaurant by Sergio was not implied by the sign outside it, which contained no apostrophe.

She found Margot standing under the entrance canopy.

"Hello there, traveler! I wasn't sure you'd make it tonight."

"Why wouldn't I make it?"

"No reason. No reason at all. So. You're back from New Orleans!"

"Yes, I am."

"Shall we go in?"

They entered.

The concierge greeted them, took them two steps toward their normal table by the window, noticed the simultaneous turning of all heads in the restaurant, as well as the baleful stares, and asked:

"Would you like a private room?"

And then, not waiting for an answer, he took them to one.

In a matter of seconds they were seated.

"Something to drink for the ladies?"

"Dry martini," said Margot.

"Strychnine," said Nina.

"I'm afraid—"

"She's joking."

"No I'm not."

"Bring her a dry martini. Gin. Olives. More gin."

"Certainly."

They waited until he had disappeared.

"I bet," said Margot, "you had a great trip."

"Absolutely."

"Beignets?"

"Wonderful beignets."

"Preservation Hall?"

"Of course."

"And then, I heard you had a great meeting this afternoon. At the gym."

"Certainly did."

"Also, I heard you had a fantastic time last night with your friend Tom Broussard."

"Once again, you're right on the money."

"How nicely life is turning out for you these days."

"Yep. Oh. Here are the martinis. Right on time."

"Here you are, ladies. For you—"

"Thank you."

"And for you."

"Thank you."

"Now may I bring you something else?"

"Another martini."

"Another martini."

"Ah. Bien."

And he left.

Nina sipped her martini, listening as Margot began:

"So, about this 'Eve Ivory' person: is she—"

"Stop it! I don't want to talk about it!"

Silence for a time.

Only the sipping of the martinis.

"Sorry."

"It's all right."

Silence for another second or so.

Margot began to hum:

"Do you know what it means, to miss New Orleans…"

"I hate you."

"Don't take it so seriously. But, we have to talk about something, Nina. So do you want to talk about Tom walking out on the writers' group last night and all of them hating you for it; or do you want to talk about your meeting Eve Ivory today and finding out the town will maybe cease to exist now; or do you want to talk about talking to all the people this afternoon, so that they all hate you now too, like the ones last night did?"

Nina sipped her martini.

"I think I want to talk about World War II."

The waiter reappeared:

"If I may take your order, Mesdames?"

"Are you," Margot asked him, "French?"

"No," he answered. "I'm from Philadelphia."

"Oh how nice. Well, in that case I'll have the shrimp étouffée."

"Exquisite choice. And for your friend?"

"No strychnine?"

"No, Madame."

"Not in season," said Margot. "And besides, that would be an appetizer."

"Then I'll take the soft shell crab."

"Excellent."

He left again.

"So," Nina said, beginning to feel the effects of the martini, "how was your day in the shop?"

Margot shrugged:

"Okay. I mean, before one o'clock it was ok. Then it changed quite a bit."

"It's all going to come back to that, isn't it?"

"Maybe for a while. A few weeks, months. Forever."

"How did people take the news?"

"Some of them were crying. I personally don't think that's a very good way to deal with grief. I had more sympathy for the ones who were hurling pottery against the wall. Aren't these martinis good?"

"Yes they are."

"I wonder where the second one is."

"Don't know."

"It just seems that—"

They were interrupted by the waiter, who carried no second martinis but rather a question:

Damn, thought Nina. Ready for that martini.

"If I may be so bold—"

"Be so bold," said Margot.

"A lady and a gentleman are here to see you."

"Are they," Margot asked, "from the police?"

"I do not believe so."

"Are they armed?"

"No, Madame."

"Then to hell with them."

"Margot—"

"All right, all right. Show them in."

"Ahhh, oui!"

"It would be fascinating," Margot continued, "to live in Philadelphia some time. Just to be engulfed by language. Perhaps the South of Philadelphia. Arles. Maybe Rocky's neighborhood—"

The door opened.

"Nina, Margot—sorry to bother you."

Jackson Bennett and Edie Towler entered.

"May we join you?"

"Of course," said Nina. "Jackson, have you heard anything since the meeting this afternoon?"

He nodded.

"I've heard a lot. Faxes have been coming in since the meeting this afternoon. And by the way, I'm sorry about that."

"Me too. Why is everybody in Bay St. Lucy mad at me now?"

"You brought them," Edie said, "bad news."

"I'm a schoolteacher; I've been doing that all my life."

"But no one ever listened."

"I suppose that's true."

"I'm beginning to piece it together now pretty well, Nina," said Jackson. " There was a lot we didn't know."

"Apparently."

He leaned forward.

"The shooting happened in December of 1982. No one knows who did it. There are implications that it was organized crime, but further than that, we still don't know."

"All right. Nothing new there."

"Homer Baron Robinson and his wife—I think his wife was Felicia—were gunned down in their own home. The child, Arthur, remained unhurt. He was taken away to New Orleans to be raised by familial connections. It was all very secretive. No one spoke of it. No one talked about exactly where in the city he was, or what these 'connections' might have been."

"So he grew up as a weird kid."

"Is that surprising?" Edie asked.

"No. Not given the circumstances."

Jackson continued:

"You know, he must have seen—well, we don't know what he must have seen."

"True. But go on."

"Well—"

He paused. When the waiter came, Edie ordered a rum and coke. Jackson ordered a scotch on the rocks, before continuing. "Yes. Well, we knew all of the information I've just repeated, about the young Robinson boy. But the girl—"

"The girl?"

"Yes. There was a daughter. Her name was Emily, and she was a couple of years older than Arthur."

"I didn't know a daughter was in the house when it happened."

"She wasn't in the house apparently. She had left home a year or so before. Some say she ran away; others say she was sent. All we do think is that she died quite young, of a drug overdose. She was in New York at the time, or so the story goes."

"The Robinson curse."

"You could call it that. Arthur growing up a recluse in an insane family and then forced to watch two ghastly murders; finally taken away to live—if that's the word for what his life must have been like—taken away to live with God knows who in some New Orleans mansion just as old and musty as the Robinson place is now."

"A Rose for Arthur," Nina whispered.

"What?" asked Jackson.

"Faulkner story. Doesn't matter."

"She does that a lot," interjected Margot.

"At any rate," Jackson continued, "we were all aware of the death of the daughter. What we didn't know was, she herself had a child before dying."

"Uh, oh," said Nina, beginning to understand.

"Right. The circumstances behind this girl's youth are completely shrouded in mystery. She simply disappears from the radar for a time. We don't know who she is, or where she grows up."

"But I think," said Nina, "that I know where she was at one o'clock this afternoon."

"I'm sure you do. Somehow this young girl grew up—not particularly wealthy, but fabulously beautiful."

"And wise in the ways of the world."

"Yes, Nina, I think we can all agree to that. Her grandfather a gangster, her mother a drug addict—we can all agree that she must have known something of the world."

He was interrupted by the arrival of food.

"The étouffée for Madame, the crab for you, my lady. May I bring a menu for the two new guests?"

Edie and Jackson declined.

Nina had always loved soft shell crab, and she tore into this one eagerly, washing it down with gin and stories of human misery.

"So what," she said, crunching a spindly leg in her mouth and feeling like a cannibal, "do we know about her?"

"She married very well."

"I'm sure she did."

"A man named St. Jacques Ivory."

"There are people named St. Jacques Ivory?"

"There was one. From Jamaica. How she met him, God only knows."

"'Was' one? 'Had' money?"

"He died a few years ago. He was elderly when he met her."

"That figures," said Margot. "By the way, this shrimp étouffée is to die for."

"You probably," said Nina, "shouldn't put it that way."

"It's very good," she said.

"Thank you."

"My bad."

"It's all right. So, Jackson, the will—"

"Had originally left everything to Arthur. But Arthur, as we know, had been adjudged insane at age sixteen, when he could have inherited. But the will spoke of Arthur, his sister—"

"—who was dead, God knows how—"

"Yes. Arthur, and Emily—AND THEIR HEIRS."

"Which nobody knew there was one of," said Nina.

"That is the worst sentence," interrupted Margot, "I've ever heard an English teacher make."

"Well, I'm retired."

"So the thinking had always been," Jackson proceeded, seemingly oblivious to dangling prepositions and mangled context, "that young Arthur was mentally incompetent to draw a new will, and that, upon his death, the family's holdings would revert to the city, since they consisted mainly of land."

"But that's not true now."

'No. Somehow word of Arthur's death reached our Ms. Ivory. And she now owns a great deal of land here, plus most of the ocean front property. She owns—"

"Don't say it, "said Nina.

"Don't say what?"

Nina took a deep breathe, not wanting to say for the first time what she knew would be said often in the days and weeks thereafter.

"She now owns The Ivory Coast."

"Well," said Jackson, smiling in spite of everything, "I guess that's one way to put it."

Edie Towler leaned forward:

"Nina, I do want to assure you of one thing."

"What's that?"

"You need to put this afternoon's meeting out of your mind."

"That's a little hard to do."

"No one in Bay St. Lucy blames you for any of this."

"I'm not sure that's true. Those people in the gym–"

"They were just shocked and confused. We all are. But you're still probably the most respected person in this town. Your husband handled the legal affairs for half our citizenry, and you taught grammar and literature to the other half. People love you here, they always have. Nobody would ever hold any of this against you or do a thing to harm you."

"Thank you, Edie. That's very kind of you. I just–"

The door to the private room opened again.

A young, black-haired, slender woman entered.

She was wearing a tan police uniform.

She spoke directly to Nina.

"Are you Ms. Bannister?"

"Yes."

"You need to come with me, ma'am. Your home has been vandalized."

She rode back to her place with the officer, who invited her to sit in the front seat.

"I thought I was supposed to be in back."

"No, Ms. Bannister. You can ride up here with me."

" I thought you were supposed to put your hand on top of my head and press me down. So that I don't hit my head getting in."

"No, ma'am. You're all right the way you are."

"What happened?" she asked, as the car wove its way through traffic.

"It's not very serious. Really. It's not very bad at all."

"But what happened?"

"One of your neighbors heard it."

"Heard what?"

"Some sounds. And he looked out to check."

Nina glanced into the rearview mirror; Jackson, Edie, and Margot were following close behind them in Jackson's town car.

"You're sure it's only minor?"

"Oh yes, ma'am."

"I just really don't understand why—oh!"

They turned the corner. She could see down Beach Lane to her house.

There, in her small parking area, flashing electric blue, was a squad car; young policeman with a flashlight creeping around the side of her house.

"What in heavens' name is happening?"

"I wouldn't worry, Ms. Bannister. It's only—"

"I know. It's only minor."

Her house, she was relieved to see, was still intact.

The car stopped and she got out, looking up, partially blinded by the glare of flashing lights.

How long, she found herself wondering, before the helicopters begin arriving?

She looked at her bungalow.

The stairs seemed all right.

And one of the windows was completely all right.

It was the other one that had been shattered.

Well. Fifty percent—

And then, of course, there on the wall between the good window and the ex-window, was that word, scrawled in black paint, slathered on by what must have been a thick brush, and shining radiantly in the glow of the flashing illumination.

She stood, open mouthed, wondering if someone had gotten the wrong house.

Several people were now beginning to converge on her.

The first was Margot, who, like she herself, was staring at the word, and said:

"Nice job."

"Well," she found herself agreeing, "at least you can read it."

"They used a special kind of paint. Artists use it sometimes. It glows."

"It certainly does."

"And that particular word is—well, it's an old standby. Something one can depend on. Something unchanging."

She could find nothing to say to that.

Margot was shaking her head now.

"It so reminds me of college days in Haight Asbury. If I had a nickel for every time I wrote that word—"

This reverie was interrupted by the convergence of a second person, the town's police chief.

"Nina Bannister!"

She turned and took the outstretched hand of Moon Rivard.

"Moon. How nice to see you!"

"And you, Mz. Nina. Been a long time since we chatted."

"It has, hasn't it?"

"I think it was like two months ago at that thing the Methodist Church put on."

"The pot luck."

"Oooohh, yeah! Did you have some of that gumbo?"

"I don't remember, Moon."

"Well, you didn't then. 'Cause if you had, you'd have remembered. I kept trying to find out who'd made it, so's I could get me the recipe. Never could though. Best shrimp gumbo I believe I ever eat."

Bay St. Lucy was inhabited by a tripartite group of beings, each equally important to the town's welfare and personality, each co-existing with great conviviality, none understanding the slightest thing about the other.

There were the sea people.

There were the artists.

And there were the pure Cajuns, who belonged properly in Lafayette, Eunice, New Iberia, and points west of New Orleans, but who had somehow drifted over here, much as flotsam and jetsam ebb back to the ocean in the wake of a tsunami.

He was no more than five foot eight, and seemed much shorter when standing beside Margot, who was continuing to gawk admiringly at the graffiti—but he had a thick, powerful chest—and his eyes gleamed gleefully when he spoke of the things all Cajuns love.

Food, women, drink, women, food, drink, women, dancing, music, food, drink—

—etc., etc.

A few neighbors had gathered, and were standing just outside the pool of lights thrown by the various vehicles. Two large dogs had banded together under her floor, which was a good twenty feet off the ground. They were standing between the freezer and the charcoal grill, and were baying alternately and terribly, either at the meat stored in the freezer, or at Furl, who was trapped on the deck. Two policemen were now coming out of her house, speaking quietly to each other and writing things on small note pads that each carried.

"So how is retirement treating you, cher?" he said, breaking the silence with that comforting Cajun 'cherie.'

"It's treating me well, Moon. It's not been as difficult adjusting as I thought it would be. I walk on the beach and I work down at Margot's shop. And then, of course, I'm on the City Council—the time goes by pretty fast."

Then, for a few seconds, neither of them spoke.

Then, she said, gesturing at the broken window—

"So—little trouble, I guess?"

He reacted as though he were seeing both the window and the obscenity for the first time, and shrugged.

"Yeh. Dey broke dat window, and dey painted dat word."

"They did. They certainly did."

"You gonna have to get de window fixed."

"And," she added, "I guess I'll probably have to find some way to get the word off of the wall."

"If it's the kind of paint I think it is," added Margot cheerfully, "it can't be removed."

Moon nodded his assent:

"Oh yeh, de kids, dey teenagers you know, dey use dat stuff a lot when dey wan to paint up the water tower. We can't hardly get it off. Usually just have to paint over it."

"It's good to know," said Nina, "that people care enough about you to use good materials."

Everyone looked at her.

No one said anything.

Her sense of humor, her sense of humor—

Of course it was astonishing, she told herself, that she still had a sense of humor.

How long would it last? she found herself wondering.

"Any idea," asked Jackson Bennett, who had now joined the group, "who did this thing?"

Moon nodded:

"Oh yeh. Always de same. Kids. We have a lead on dem. One of the neighbors saw de vehicle drive away. And we had a car not far away."

"You need to catch these kids. This is not funny. Nina might have been inside."

"Why sure. Why sure. Well, we gonna catch dem."

"And," Jackson added, "make them pay for all this."

"Dey won't pay demselves. But de parents will."

Another officer approached him.

Nina found herself surprised at the number of police officers who were employed by the city.

He listened as the officer whispered to him.

"What is the news?" asked Jackson to Moon, who had emerged from his brief meeting.

"You know anything?"

"Yeh we know something. We caught 'em."

"You caught the kids?"

"We caught de ladies."

"The what?"

"The two ladies. Dey housewives. Dey had just come from this meeting at the gymnasium, and dey was mad."

No one said anything.

"Did they have anything to say for themselves after you caught them?" asked Jackson.

"Yeh. Dey say dey sorry."

"Well that's at least good to know. They're sorry for breaking her window, for painting this foul thing on her wall?"

"No," answered Moon. "Dey say dey sorry dey didn't burn de house down."

Again, no one had anything to say.

CHAPTER SEVEN: THE MOST BEAUTIFUL
MANSION ON THE IVORY COAST

"A bad day of fishing is better than a good day of work."

Author Unknown

"A particularly beautiful woman is a source of terror."

Carl Jung

For some time after that, nothing happened, except the town forgave Nina for not having done anything wrong.

The families of the two women who had vandalized her bungalow, being quite well to do, repaired the damage and paid to have the wall re-painted.

And that, for some time, was all that happened.

Then a great deal happened.

It was early November. Nina had succeeded, as had most of the town, in putting the entire matter of *The Robinson Estate* not so much out of her mind entirely as in a small mental attic compartment, much as one used to store sweaters in warm weather.

One has not forgotten about them.

But there is always the possibility that, just this one year, winter will not come at all.

And so, at five thirty A.M., on a crisp pre-dawn in late autumn, she was taking her accustomed once-a-month fishing excursion with Penelope Royale.

Penelope Royale was the most ill-named woman in the world. Her name was perhaps the most feminine and delicate one imaginable. Royale would have connoted British First Family, had not the accent fallen on the last syllable, which made it call to mind exotic casinos and tall women with cigarette cases, as well as kings, queens and ermine robes. The name 'Penelope' was—well, it was simply 'Penelope.' Enough said.

Penelope. Wife of Odysseus. Soul of faithfulness and domesticity.

This woman, though, was not quite what the name implied.

She was a square block of granite, except harder. Everything about her was square. She was five feet tall and five feet wide and five feet deep. Her mouth, the wrinkles on her forehead, the wrinkles on her chin, were all perfectly horizontal, like lines of latitude.

Nowhere on her body were there lines of longitude.

She was a latitudinal human being, with no use for the ups and downs in life.

She had flaming red hair, done in the manner of materials used in packing crates.

"Hold the—tip of the—rod higher in the—air."

Penelope was also the only woman Nina knew who spoke only in obscenities.

It was a remarkable thing, when one thought of it, given the relative scarcity of dirty words in the language, as opposed to the overwhelming abundance of acceptable terms. In the latter group, one had such things to choose from as "chair," "the," "obsequious," "tuna fish," "very," "thunderstorm," "run,"—

—there were really quite a lot of them.

—and for the former group there were only, well, the *a* word, the *b* word, the *c* word, the *d* word—and, when one thought of it—not even so many as all that.

The *e* word for example.

There was no *e* word.

Not even all of the letters in the alphabet had dirty words that could be attached to them.

So how was it possible for Penelope to be a continual cusser, a linguist incapable of admitting the acceptable to her verbal repertoire?

It must have taken, Nina had decided long ago—for she had known Penelope for years, since the woman's expulsion from elementary school, and her expulsion from middle school, and her expulsion from high school—a special kind of dedication. There were pilots who thought only of flying, and who could be seen walking around with their hand held out in space before them, turning and lifting and falling, palm up, palm sideways, palm level, palm falling—imitative of the motions of an aircraft, the mental pilot imagining updrafts and crosswinds and sea squalls and the like.

And in just such a way must Penelope have viewed the possibilities of expression. She saw cursing as pilots saw flying or baseball players saw hitting or loose women saw—well, no matter.

Suffice to say, it was her life.

"You'd—better keep the—rod tip in the—air!"

There were, of course, in almost every one of her sentences, words that, coming from someone else, might have seemed unobjectionable. The one just uttered, for example. But it was Penelope's genius to render, perhaps with the addition of a simple guttural 'cluck,' or the hardening of the line that was her jaw, or the squinting of her anthracitic eyes—to render once normal and rather boring words instantly obscene.

"You," coming from her, had the same effect as the most vicious epithet coming from the most hardened Marine drill sergeant.

"Did you—hear—? B—it! — and — Or G—will h—you!"

"I'm sorry."

"— —!"

"Ok, I'll try."

There were those who found this habit of Penelope's to be rather off-putting—as Penelope herself was said by some to be rather off-putting—but Nina liked her, and had always done so, even when she'd been accused of savagely beating three members of the high school football team's offensive line, only days before a District Championship Game.

She must have had, Nina always told herself, sufficient cause.

And if not, well, no matter. *Somebody* needed to beat up the offensive line, if only because of general principles.

So here they were, in something between a marsh and a bay, the water no more than two feet deep beneath them, trolling for red fish or trout or even the occasional flounder.

Penelope's great passion in life, apart from cursing, was fishing.

How fortuitous, Nina had always thought, that the two could have been so closely connected.

"—! P—, —, o, —! U—!"

"Okay," Nina answered, reeling in a bit, then lowering the tip of the rod.

She could not help thinking, of course, about Eve Ivory. Events from more than a month ago had reminded her of letters received from the IRS. "We are reviewing your returns; we will be in touch shortly with our findings."

Nothing good to come of that.

And now Eve Ivory was the IRS of Bay St. Lucy.

Of course, there was the fact that the woman had seemed gracious in New Orleans, at the law firm.

What had she said?

"I wish only the best for Bay St. Lucy."

Something like that.

But that was a terrible phrase, wasn't it?

It was always the final sentence on letters of rejection.

"We wish you only the best."

It was said to be—thank God, she did not know from personal experience—the final parting line of the middle aged man divorcing his now stranded at age fifty five wife:

"I wish you only the best, dear."

Yeah.

Right.

A much better line—more appropriate for almost any occasion—would have been, "Hey let's go out drinking!"

But, of course, Eve Ivory could hardly have been expected to say that.

"N—! —, —, —, and G—Y—, don't —!"

"Ok, sorry."

She turned a bit in the boat, watching the dot of a line disappear some sixty feet beyond the small wake, and, far beyond it, a ring of palm trees that outlined Broadwater Beach.

For it was within Broadwater Bay that they now found themselves.

"—?"

"Yeah."

"—"

Now, back to thinking.

Jackson Bennett had been busy, of course. Phone calls daily, letters of inquiry, attempts to find out as much as possible.

But his communications with Nina—over coffee, by phone, in chance encounters on the street—all sounded the same.

"We just don't know anything yet. All we can get from her attorney is mumbo jumbo. 'Many matters to look into. Complex legal situations. Finally, 'We will be in touch.'"

Which was pretty much the same as saying:

We wish you only the best.

Right.

If only—

—and she got a bite.

"Hey!"

The rod bent in her hands while the spinner hummed and line disappeared into the ocean.

"Where is he, Nina!"

"There! Out there!"

"Okay, set the drag—are you listening to me?"

"Yes!"

"Set the drag on three! Make him work for it a little bit! I'll come around!"

And there it was, the miracle happening again. For Penelope could not curse while she was actually chasing a fish.

The damnedest thing, thought Nina.

All of time was obscene, save for these few blissful moments ahead of them.

Don't, she told herself, *lose the damned fish.*

Of course now she herself was cursing—

"Don't fight him! Let him go a little!"

The reel in her hand still whirled like a miniature propeller; she found herself pulled forward in the chair on the boat's stern, her hips braced against the seatbelt.

Pull back, she told herself, woozy as the boat turned and slowed.

"Now hit it a little!"

She jerked.

"Just a little, Nina! We don't want to lose him!"

"He's on, I think!"

"Maybe."

"No, he's on good, I can feel him."

"All right! Flip the drag switch to one!"

She did so, the line's screech softening a bit as the pressure on her forearms increased.

Could she do this?

"What do you think it is?"

She turned slightly; Penelope, one hand on the steering wheel, was squinting back against the sun.

"Can't tell yet."

"Could it be a Great White Shark?"

"Maybe. But you don't usually see them in two feet of water."

"But nature always has surprises, Pen."

"Fish."

"Ok."

"Fight a little now; he may be getting tired of this."

"Shall I reel in?"

"No. No."

The fish jumped; a flash of red, a splash of ocean.

"Hey, look!" she shouted. "What is it?"

"Redfish!"

"Are you kidding me?"

She loved redfish..

She began to have visions:

Watching Penelope clean the thing back at the dock; plopping the filets into her portable ice chest, and then depositing them thirty minutes later in the freezer which sat beneath her blue efficiency shack.

"Bring him in a little more; can you still handle him?"

"Think so!"

"Need me to help?"

"No, my arms are ok."

"Keep the rod tip up. Look! There he goes again!"

FLASH! SPLASH!

"How big is he?"

"Eight pounds! Maybe ten!"

"That's a monster!"

"You'll eat for two months."

"You're coming over, of course!"

"Try and stop me!"

They fought the fish for five minutes more, Nina's wrists and arms aching too much to fight a great deal longer, and her heart pounding when they saw two other objects enter the scene.

These were dark brown shapes that seemed to be tearing at the mass of red.

"—!" said Penelope.

"What is it?"

"Sharks."

"I thought you said there weren't any sharks in two feet of water!"

"I said there were no great whites. These are dog sharks. They'll steal that redfish!"

"What can we do?"

"This."

Penelope opened a compartment in the side of her boat. She reached in, and pulled out a handgun, which gleamed oily-metal against the huge orange that was the rising sun.

"What are you going to do?"

"Watch."

"Be careful with that—"

BLAM!

BLAM!

The water exploded in two volcanic atom bomb blasts of sea spray, shark meat, and brown kelp, which rained back down on an otherwise calm bay surface, in which, Nina could see, her redfish was still floating.

"That's better," growled Penelope, putting the still smoking gun away.

"What kind of gun is that?"

"Forty five automatic. Sometimes it's good for sharks."

"So I see. How did you keep from hitting the redfish?"

"Practice. Hey. I think you can pull him in now. He seems to be weakening."

"He's just scared to death, I think."

"Maybe. Anyway, let's try to land him now."

Nina tugged, and, her forearms, like spaghetti, finally succeeded in getting the fish within two feet of the boat.

—where Penelope gaffed the thing and stowed it safely in a compartment half filled with water.

"Whew!"

Nina dropped the rod and reel to her side, unlocked the belt, and threw herself on the bottom of the boat, metal side a nice support for her aching back.

What a wonderful boat this was!

It looked like a child's portable swimming pool; two feet deep, completely square, as was Penelope, and utterly devoid of dash and romance.

But it was perfect for shallow water fishing.

It could chug safely along in water no more than a foot deep, water disdained by tourists out for high adventure on the deep blue sea.

The redfish remained in her mind—along with various possibilities for frying it, broiling it, having it with just a bit of lemon and basil, etc., etc., until Penelope's flat skiff—for what else was it, really?—had chugged its way around Beauforth Beach, skirting the coast and heading toward a sun that had just risen enough to clear the smokestacks of the oil refineries outside of Biloxi and Chicot Island—

—when Bay St. Lucy came into view.

"What in heaven's name is going on?" she asked.

"—," answered, Penelope, the relative mildness in her tone stemming from astonishment and not conciliation.

She did not, in short, understand what she was seeing enough to be properly obscene about it.

For there, a mile before them, was a cross between a circus and the landing at Normandy Beach, with a bit of Turkish bazaar thrown in.

Huge trucks, small trucks, long black automobiles, fifty-foot-tall cranes, moving vans, and people scurrying like ants around rotting fish heads, all surrounding what had been the Robinson mansion, and what was now simply ground zero in the world's largest construction project.

So that was it.

That was the first step.

"Y— —?" asked Penelope.

"I don't know," answered Nina. "But I think our town is meeting Eve Ivory."

"Who the —, and —, —?"

"It's all very complicated. Let's dock. Then we'll go over there in your truck and see what's going on."

The boat harbor of Bay St. Lucy was quite small, with slips for no more than a dozen vessels. Most of them were sleek blue and white outriggers, cabins polished and redolent of mahogany deck work. Penelope's boat did not so much fit in with them as hide among them, and many charter customer's expression could be seen to change from joy to astonished disappointment when, upon passing *The Golden Eagle* and walking just a bit farther down the plank sea walk, he spied the craft that he was actually going to be riding in.

He generally said little, frightened enough by the aspect of Penelope to keep his thoughts to himself—and by the time of his return, the dozen or so game fish he had succeeded in landing outweighed his misgivings about the vessel he'd been in while landing them.

The two of them moored and battened down *Sea Urchin*, which was the craft's name, loaded the Vespa into the back of Penelope's pickup truck, left the catch of the morning under ice for later cleaning and filleting, and drove off down Breakers Boulevard.

"I knew something would happen," said Nina, quietly, as Penelope wove in and out of traffic, cursing each vehicle softly, inaudibly almost, since none of the other drivers were doing anything wrong, except existing on the roadway and moving from one spot to another.

"Clearly, whatever it is, it's going to start with the mansion."

And start it had.

They parked as near to the place as they dared, walked across the Boulevard, and began to make their way through cables, trunks, vans, and electric wires.

The mansion loomed before them, red-clad workers already clamoring out on balconies, up on roofs, and around on porches.

"There must," Nina whispered, "be a hundred men here."

They continued to walk through the carnage that was the result of an effort to combat forty years of decay with a trillion dollar, four-nation, simultaneous destruction-construction-remodeling cataclysm.

They walked over pipes, through tunnels, around mud puddles, and between huge shipping crates. Finally they found themselves in the center of group of workmen, burly beasts, their sweating heads wrapped in pirate bandannas. These men, cigarettes hanging from their lips, would have given them no notice at all, had not Penelope called attention to them by shouting:

"Hey! What—! And why —c—da—!"

They blanched as one, stepping back, horrified.

They looked at each other.

Then they ran.

After two seconds, Nina and Penelope found themselves alone with a shipping crate filled with Carrera marble bathroom fixtures.

"Maybe it would be better," Nina said softly, "if you went back to the landing and started filleting the redfish."

"—?"

"I'll snoop around here for a while; maybe I can get some idea of what's happening."

"OK."

Nina watched the figure turn and walk away from her, surprised to have heard a complete syllable come out profanity-less mixing with her curiosity concerning a hearse-like town car pulling up into one of the mansion's driveways.

The only driveway, actually, that was not now littered with debris of construction.

She watched it come to a halt.

The door opened and Eve Ivory got out.

It was like the sun had come up again, only this time better.

Not that the original sunrise an hour ago had been bad. Clear cool day, no storms approaching, it had done its best with saffron robes and golden cherubs for clouds. "The rosy fingered dawn" it had indeed been.

It simply had too much to compete with.

Eve Ivory had far more radiance. There was more of a life-giving quality about her. She exerted, simply by existing, more claim to being the center of the universe. Things orbited more naturally about her. She tanned things better (not only her own superbly tanned skin, but the skin of those who bathed regularly in her rays).

She was, in short, just too much competition for the stupid regular sun.

The workers who knelt before her as she made her way through them should, Nina found herself thinking, have been wearing not sunglasses but Eve Ivory glasses.

Every instant of this woman's being was a complete and dazzling eclipse.

"Nina!"

And now she had spotted Nina.

"Nina! Over here. Wait! Wait, let me come to you!"

How did one react, Nina found herself asking, to the approach of pure solar energy?

And how surprising was it, that this celestial body-woman would have even remembered her name!

"It's so good to see you again!"

Eve Ivory was dressed in tan, but not as tan as she herself. A purple scarf curled around her neck, and her cheekbones angled down at the world in precisely the same angle as the brim of Fred Astaire's hat.

"I'm so sorry I've not been in contact!"

"It's all right. We did wonder about you."

"I know, I know."

She wrapped her superbly muscled arms around Nina, who now knew what it must have been like to be a sunspot.

Could she now interrupt radio waves?

"There has been so much to do!"

"I can imagine."

"No, no, the legal complications have been perfectly horrid. So many times I wanted to contact you, or at least come over to visit—but every time I was told by this lawyer or that, 'Just wait! Just wait until we have the proper financing in place, or until these attorneys have done their job or we hear from this holding company or that state bureau or'—well, you just can't imagine."

"I'm sure I can't."

"Things are not completely sorted out even now. But we're farther along. And we're able to begin with—well, what you see here! I've been in the house all morning. The rooms are unbelievable. There's even an old tunnel leading from the wine cellar outside to the greenhouse. It's so mysterious and romantic."

"That's incredible."

"Isn't it? Look—can we go somewhere and talk? I did so want to get to know you last month in New Orleans—but there was simply no time. I hope you understand."

"Of course."

"My attorneys have, in the mean time, corresponded with Mr. Bennett—but again, we've not been able to be completely specific."

"No, Jackson has told me as much."

"There is simply so much to say, though—and so many people I want to get to know. Nina, I wonder if––"

"Yes?"

"Well—is there some place we can go now, this morning, so that I can at least introduce myself and begin setting people's minds at ease about what's happening—and what will be happening?"

"There's The Lighthouse. It's just down Breakers."

"The Lighthouse?"

"A coffee shop. It's not much, but—"

"Oh that would be fine! Coffee then! My treat!"

I wonder, thought Nina, watching as forty or fifty men struggled to unload what was either a muddy football field or an obscenely huge black leather sofa, *whether you can afford it.*

"Can we walk to this shop. I have a car here if—"

"No, no, it's just right down the Boulevard. Hundred yards. Look. Right over there!"

"Oh, I see it."

And so they made their way across the immensity that was the Robinson yard, Nina still conjuring memories of lush camellia bushes and gazebos, all forbidden to her and the rest of the town.

Was that, she wondered, *about to change?*

The Lighthouse was so named because of a ten-foot tall replica of a lighthouse that sat squarely on the middle of its roof.

Otherwise there was little lighthouseness about it, and the few pictures scattered about its walls—pictures of fish mostly, with a few beach scenes—did little to make the customer feel that he was in an ocean storm, protecting great ships from dangerous rocks.

No, mostly what the customer felt was that he was in a cheap coffee shop, black and white interior, tables rocking unsteadily on the tile floor, and a few stains on the counter.

The two of them entered.

"Hi there!"

A young Cajun girl, slender and dark haired, smiled shyly at them as they sat on two stools at the counter.

"Can I get y'all something?"

"I'll have," said Eve Ivory breezily, "a mocha infusion cappuccino, with bitter twist and cinnamon extract, light almandine twirl and small brandy insertion."

The girl stared at her for a second, then said:

"What?"

There was silence for a second.

Finally, Nina said

"Two cups of coffee."

The girl brightened:

"Oh. Cream?"

"Yes," said Nina.

And the girl turned away, getting the coffee while Nina apologized:

"We're a little behind the times."

"Oh no matter! No matter at all! But listen, Nina, I—oh, I hardly know where to begin!"

Two men came into the shop, stood in the doorway staring dumbfoundedly either at Nina or at Eve Ivory, Nina being pretty sure which, and then staggered to a table seconds before falling to the floor unconscious and dying.

"There are, I'm sure, a great many things that the people of Bay St. Lucy do not know about me."

We don't know anything about you, Nina found herself thinking. *Who the hell are you?*

That is what she should have said, if she'd had any guts at all.

What she did say was:

"We're not, it's true, as knowledgeable about your background as we should be."

Wimp, she scolded herself.

"Hopefully that will all change soon."

Ok, then, first really big question.

Let's get at it, Nina.

"Do you plan to settle here?"

"Yes, I do. I certainly do."

Well, Nina thought, *that's either very good or very bad.*

"I love this town. I want to come to love all the people in it—I wish only—"

Don't say it don't say it don't say it don't say it—

"I wish only the best for the town of Bay St. Lucy!"

Well, that's it then.

Very bad.

That evening Tom Broussard came to visit her.

She was standing at the grill that she had set up below her shack, two filets of redfish hissing below her as she poured on each of them some drippings of lemon and red wine sauce.

"Hey."

"Well, look who's here; it's Tom Broussard."

"You mad at me?"

"Everybody in the writers' group is mad at you, and has been for a month or so."

"Well. Sorry about that."

"They're mad at me too, of course."

"Why are they mad at you?"

"I don't know. It would have been so easy, Tom. All you had to do was tell them a few anecdotes, a few clichés about writing."

"I know. But Nina, these people use 'workshop' as a verb!"

"So what? They just want feedback from other writers. Didn't you ever get feedback?"

"I got rejection notices. They're different things."

"What about writers' workshops. Don't you ever go to them?"

"When I want to go to a writers' workshop, I go to the library. And, Nina, if these people want a group activity, why don't they just have sex together?"

"Tom—"

"Sex is much more fun than writing, and it's easier."

"I don't want to talk about this anymore. Are you hungry? Want some fish?"

"Wow," he said, coming nearer. "That looks great. Catch it yourself?"

"Yep. Just this morning. Me and Penelope Royale. We were out in her boat."

"Penelope Royale," he said. "That's one strange woman."

She looked at him. He wore a vast white t-shirt, stained by road tar or cooking sauces, with the words "The Seven Dwarfs Suck" carefully stenciled in black across the front, and no pictures.

And you, she thought, *are calling somebody else strange.*

"How did you get here, Tom?"

"Walked."

"That's three or four miles."

"I don't mind. Get a lot of ideas when I'm walking. Hey, listen, I brought you a book."

"Really?"

"Yeah, here."

He handed her a hard-backed novel She took it, then looked at the cover, which depicted several decapitated corpses hanging from meat hooks.

The title, *Remembering Dismemberment,* was splashed in red across the cover.

"It's dedicated to you."

"Thank you, Tom."

"Look inside."

She opened the cover and read:

"To Nina Bannister: The source of all my ideas."

"That's so touching, Tom."

"Well. It's the least I can do. I'm sorry they're mad at you over at the writers' group. I really am."

"Oh, don't worry about it. Friends can be such a bother. So please: will you join me?"

"I don't know. You have anything to drink?"

"I have some wine."

"Too bad. That's all right, though. I'll eat with you anyway."

She told him how much she appreciated his generosity, scooped the fish filets onto a platter that sat upon the freezer—which chugged and sputtered dutifully, a few steps from her charcoal grill—and led him upstairs.

Within a few minutes, they were seated on her deck; she ladling a bowl of Petersilian potatoes out to him, he scornfully sniffing his glass of Chardonnay as though it were urine.

"I would have brought some whiskey if I'd known."

"I know you would have. Believe me it's better this way."

"You don't drink whiskey?"

"I'm sure I have on occasions; I just never seem to be able to remember the occasions."

"Yeah, but that's the point."

"Not sure I follow you there."

"So what's going on at the Robinson place?"

"Lots."

"I can see. Some woman's remodeling it, I hear."

"Yes, and when you say, "some woman," you're quite accurate."

"What's her name again?"

"Eve Ivory."

"That's what I heard. I just couldn't believe anybody would be named "Eve Ivory.""

"Well, she exists. And that's what her name is."

"So what's she aiming to do?"

"She's aiming—or so she told me this morning—to come and live here."

"That's bad."

"Why do you say that?"

He munched his fish, looked at the wine again, decided against it again, and said:

"Her name for one thing. Sounds like she came out of a book: I write novels; I don't want to live in one."

"Well, anyway, that's what she said. She also said she loved the town, and that she wanted everything good for it. She wants to have a series of meetings with the town council, the school board, the library board, the zoning commission, everybody. She's got a ton of money to invest, but before she does it she wants everybody to hear everybody else's proposals. Then we'll all decide how the money gets invested, and how it can help Bay St. Lucy the most."

He nodded.

"Uh huh."

They ate in silence for a time

Finally Nina asked:

"So what are you thinking, Tom?"

He shook his head.

"Something a German writer wrote. I forget his name. He said, "The story is not over until it has taken the worst possible turn of events."

"That's encouraging."

"The only good thing about this, is that we know the next to last chapter."

"What happens in the next to last chapter?"

"You're kidding, aren't you?"

"What do you mean?"

"You really don't know?"

"No. What happens?"

"Eve Ivory gets killed."

He rose.

"Thanks for the dinner. I gotta go."

"So what happens in the last chapter?"

"The worst possible turn of events. That means, we find out who killed her. Bye."

And he left.

CHAPTER EIGHT: WISH LISTS

"When angry, count to four. When very angry, swear."

Mark Twain

Another case of vandalism was to take place on Nina's premises, this one equally disturbing, and differing from the first only in that it was never solved.

The events leading to the crime were these:

She and Margot Gavin were sitting in the living room of her beach house, the seas choppy with a brisk wind out of the south, and pelicans skimming like vultures with dump truck mouths low over the outer breakers. Nina had no idea what she was wearing, but she assumed it to be a colorless sweater of some sort, since that was about all she did wear these days.

Margot wore the Modern Wing of Chicago's Art Institute, and sandals.

It was ten A.M., on a Thursday morning.

They were playing scrabble.

"I think," said Nina, sipping coffee and drawing two tiles, "that we should be in your shop."

"Nonsense. What on earth would be the use of that?"

"You might have a customer."

"All the more reason for staying closed. All that will happen is that Ms. Wilson will descend from her apartment, rattle around in the garden a bit, make herself a cup of coffee—which she now knows quite well how to do—and sit in the garden, reading."

"How long is she going to stay?"

"Two more weeks, she says. She wants to see New Orleans, which she's never visited; then she's going abroad."

"Lots of money, I guess."

"Her husband left her quite well off, apparently. What are you doing?"

"Tripling the 'q.' That's—what? Forty seven points, I think."

"But what's that word you've made?"

"Quires."

"I can see that, darling, but there is no such word."

"Of course there is."

"Do you mean 'choirs'?"

"No. 'Quires.' A 'quire' is a set of twenty-four sheets of paper of the same stock. It's one-twentieth of a ream."

"Well, of course it is. How stupid of me to have forgotten."

"The verb form—I'm making the third person singular—means to fold into quires."

"Which one does all of the time these days, of course."

"I'm not bound to make frequently used words."

"No, nor humanly used ones, either. What is the score at present?"

"I'm up a bit. But you still have a chance."

"What is the score?"

"Now?"

"No, I was inquiring specifically about Tuesday, September 14, in the year 1471. But if you don't have the statistics on that one, I suppose 'now,' the present, might be an acceptable substitute."

"Well, *right* now, I'm two hundred eighty four, and you're ninety seven. But you can turn it around."

"And there are three tiles left?"

"Yes."

"The letters on my rack, Nina, are 'a,' 'u,' 'u,' 'n,' 'r,' 'u,' and 'o'."

"You'll need a break or two."

"When may I smoke?"

"After the game we can go out on the deck and look at the pelicans."

"Good. Let's see then: I don't suppose 'unquires' is a word?"

"Of course not, Margot. Once you had quired, why would you unquire?"

"Simply for want of something to do, I suppose. Pass."

"You can't play?"

"No."

"All right, then. Here. 'Inquires.' Seventeen points. That puts me at—"

"Look."

"Pardon?"

"Look. Out the window. A toy car is coming."

Nina looked over Margot's shoulder. Sure enough, the approaching vehicle did seem to be a toy car. It was green with a tan interior, the color obviously due to the fact that the top was down. It was crawling seaward from the main boulevard, inching its way down toward the beach.

It looked, Nina found herself thinking, *like the car Donald Duck always drove—the duck kids, Huey, Dewey and Louie, all piled into the rumble seat.*

There were no ducks in the car now, though.

Only Eve Ivory.

"What could this be about?" Nina whispered, as much to herself as to Margot Gavin, who, nonetheless, seemed to feel compelled to reply.

"I don't know, Nina, but it's almost certainly something bad."

"How do you know that?"

"Just a good rule of thumb. Why don't you hide?"

"There are two rooms here, Margot. Where can I hide?"

"Nowhere I suppose. Why didn't you think about that when you moved in here?"

"What was I supposed to do, find a beach shack with a panic room?"

"I don't know, they must exist. Oh my heavens—so that apparition getting out of the car is in fact Eve Ivory?"

"That, Margot, is Eve Ivory."

The crevasses in Margot's face deepened, making her expression look all the more dangerous, like the south face of a secondary mountain range after a spring thaw.

"So there really is such a person."

"Yes, Margot, there is."

"I thought she was a myth."

"She is 'Myth' Eve Ivory."

"Please don't do that."

"I'm sorry."

"I can accept 'quires.' I cannot accept puns. What does the creature want here?"

"I don't know. Somehow she trusts me."

"Whatever for?"

"I don't know."

"Have you done anything to make her think she should trust you?"

"No."

"Well then, it's as Shakespeare said: 'Trust unearned is as fragile as suspicion merited.'"

"Shakespeare never said anything like that, Margot."

"No, I suppose not. Look, she's getting out. She's as tall as I am, but prettier."

And she was, in fact, getting out, and she was in fact tall, and she was in fact beautiful. She slammed the door of the sports car—which identified itself with a ring on the trunk upon which the letters 'MG' had been emplated—then looked about her, obviously distrusting everything from the sand in the seashell driveway, to the rickety shacks lining the beach, to the ubiquitous pelicans and gulls, to the gray scudding clouds, to the turquoise ocean which was not bothering to pay her homage of any type—and especially to the stairs leading precariously up to Nina's front porch.

"What could that woman want here?" Nina asked, getting to her feet and turning toward the door.

"Probably fashion advice," answered Margot, following.

By the time Nina had opened the door, Eve Ivory had made her way gingerly to the base of the stairs. She was dressed entirely in leather—black shining beret, black shining jacket with silver buttons, zippers and useless appendages—so that she resembled, as she looked upward and trained her radiation factory of a smile on the two women peering down at her, the various sections of a sealskin tanning factory.

"Nina!"

"Hello, Eve."

"Nina, I do hope I'm not bothering you! I was able to get your address from Jackson Bennett."

"You're not bothering me at all. Please come up!"

"If you're certain—"

"Of course, I'm certain! Just be careful of the stairs—they're a little rickety."

Eve Ivory seemed to think for a second about whether to take her gloves off before grasping the driftwood stair bannister, weighing the relative value of her own skin versus the skin of whatever animal she was wearing, should the wood prove toxic. She chose to risk the animal and launched herself onto the stairs, her voice grinning as broadly and falsely, thought Nina, as her mouth.

"Things are coming wonderfully with the reconstruction of the mansion," she broadcast, waiting a second to gauge the effect of her words on the ecosystem surrounding her.

There was no effect.

She continued climbing, the stairs creaking in unison with various invisible hinges on her pants and boots.

"We should be finished in about a month! I'm planning a gala on December 22!"

"Wonderful. Here, come in!"

"Thank you," said the woman, extending a hand, which Nina clasped while turning to Margot.

"I'd like you to meet my friend! This is Margot Gavin."

"Margot, so wonderful to meet you!"

"Likewise."

"Come, come," said Nina. "Let's go inside. It's breezy out here."

"I'm so sorry to be breaking in on you both unannounced. I know I should have called, but—"

"Nonsense! Can I get you some coffee?"

"That would be nice."

And in a moment, the remnants of the scrabble game were gone, replaced by a third cup of coffee.

A few more meaningless scraps of greeting had been exchanged; Furl had retreated to the farthest corner of the living room, and Nina wondered whether he was simply reacting to a stranger, or sensing evil.

She decided to reserve judgment, since her own feelings were similar.

"So, Margot—may I call you Margot?"

"Of course."

"Are you a long time resident of Bay St. Lucy?"

"No, no. Only a year."

"Ah, I see. And before that?"

"Chicago."

"Chicago! Oh, what an exciting city! I have friends there. Were you there long?"

"Almost twenty years. I worked there."

"I see. Were you a secretary?"

There was an instantaneous pause, which lasted a very long time.

It was a pause which allowed Nina's heart to skip one, two three—now it's going—beats, and her voice to find itself with enough composure to say:

"Margot was—"

That was all she had time to say though, before Margot, smiling archly, answered:

"Yes I was."

"How wonderful! At the same firm?"

"Yes. Same place."

"Do you like secretarial work?"

"I love it. I have excellent typing skills."

"I'll bet you do! You're fingers are very long."

Oh my God, Nina found herself thinking. Or praying. She was never quite sure which was which.

Margot held her hands out and examined them, then raised them with palms toward Eve Ivory.

"I do have very long fingers."

She's wondering, Nina mused, how long it would take her to strangle the woman.

Nina found herself wondering the same thing.

Thirty five seconds, she concluded.

"What do you do here in Bay St. Lucy, if I may ask?"

"Oh, I have a small shop."

"Where you sell curios and such?"

"Yes. Just cheap baubles. Whatever I can lay my hands on."

"It must be difficult, making ends meet."

"A constant struggle. But one does one's best."

"I'm sure. Well, Margot, I don't want to get your hopes up, but—and Nina, this is partially what I've come to share with you—there will almost certainly be major changes coming to Bay St. Lucy."

"So we've all heard," said Margot, taking out a cigarette, smoking it in one long drag, and crushing it out savagely, all invisibly and in her imagination.

"Yes, we're not sure yet which way things will go. But there will be many more opportunities here than exist now, that much I can promise you. And if you're willing to go back into administrative work—"

"Secretarial work, you mean."

"Yes, of course. We're going to be needing people who can—well, do that kind of thing."

"How thrilling."

"It would not involve actually dealing with the public, you understand."

"Of course not."

"But—well, to put it bluntly, we're going to need women who know their way around a keyboard. Are you familiar with Excel, or similar programs?"

"You mean the computer? Oh no, those things are much too complex for me."

"You've never worked with budgets, I suppose?"

"Heavens no. The men in the companies I worked for always took care of such things for me."

"Well, I wouldn't worry about it. We're going to have opportunities for retraining. There may even be some extra in the kitty for wardrobe updates."

"You're joking! Gosh it's been so long since I was able to buy something truly nice!"

"A lot of people around here are going to be buying things that are truly nice, Margot. Like I say, I don't want you to get your hopes up quite yet."

"Of course not. But obviously, anything you might know of that's suitable. For now though—"

She rose and turned to Nina:

"I've got to take my constitutional on the beach. Eve, I come over to Nina's every day and go for a two mile walk down the beach. Sometimes I persuade her to join me, but today I'm running just a bit late. I hope you two ladies don't mind if I excuse myself."

"Of course not," said Eve Ivory, half rising while continuing to maintain the smile which had never left her face.

"Have a good walk," said Nina, simultaneously aware first that Margot had never taken a constitutional in her life, and second that Margo also detested cooking, which made it strange that she was now fumbling through one of the kitchen drawers.

"I'll be back in fifteen minutes or so. You two have a good chat."

"We will," said Eve Ivory, to the disappearing back of Margot, who, Nina reckoned, was now going out somewhere to smoke two or three cigarettes and fume along with the tobacco.

The tone of the conversation, Nina sensed, was now to become more serious.

"Nina—"

A slight lean forward across the table.

"Nina, your friend is perfectly wonderful."

"Yes, she is."

"And I've enjoyed meeting her; I must tell you, though, I'm a bit relieved to have the chance to talk to you alone."

Nina could think of absolutely nothing to reply to this.

'I'm relieved too,' would have been a possibility. Except she was not.

'What's on your mind?' would have been another possibility. Except that it sounded too chatty, and that it was unnecessary, since the woman was clearly going to tell Nina what was on her mind—and that Nina didn't really care anyway.

No, nothing to say.

Not long to wait though.

"I feel—I've always felt—that you are the elder statesperson in the village here. I knew when I saw you at the reading of the will in New Orleans that you represented, almost embodied, Bay St. Lucy."

"I'm flattered. I'm not sure that's true though."

"Oh yes it is. Every moment I spend in the town makes me more certain of the fact."

"Well. I did teach here for a long time."

"And people respect that. They really do. That's why I would like to kind of—well, 'use' you. That's the only appropriate word. I hope you don't mind my imposing on our relationship in such a way."

"No. If you think I can be of use."

"I certainly think that. I think you can be essential."

Almost involuntarily Nina glanced over her shoulder, and saw two things: first she saw Margot walking toward the incoming tide—which was bizarre in itself, since Margot hated the sand—then stop, and, with amazing strength and perfectly professional form, hurl a black object at least one hundred feet into the waves.

Second, she saw Furl peeking out from behind a fern that had somehow found itself shading a magazine stand, in the corner of the room.

Furl's eyes were staring out of a tangle of green foliage and colorless glossy advertising,

Were they glaring with hatred, or did Furl simply need to go out on the deck to use the litter box?

"The main point is, it's been two weeks that I've been here now. I've been in what seem countless meetings."

"So I've heard."

"I have to tell you, I have wished for you."

"I wouldn't have been much help."

"Oh I think you would have been. The voice of reason, that kind of thing."

"It's more likely I would have been in the way."

"No, dear. Not at all. But I do feel I have to share some things with you."

"Good," said Nina.

Uh oh, thought Nina.

"First. Four days ago I sat in on a presentation given by the high school principal. I believe his name is—"

"Paul Cox."

"Yes! Yes, that's it! Several other members of the school board were there, but it was Paul who commanded the most attention."

Why, Nina thought, *are you calling him 'Paul?'*

You don't know him well enough to call him 'Paul.'

Or do you?

"Well, Mr. Cox is a very charismatic principal, and very supportive of his teachers."

"Oh, I can see that! But the vision he laid out for a new school was truly astonishing. Whether that can actually be accomplished or not is—well, you know, everyone has a wish list."

Yes, thought Nina. *And a lot of people are wishing basically the same thing about you.*

"But the thing that stood out in my mind was Paul himself. He's—well, he's a cut above what one usually finds in village life."

"I suppose you could say that."

"I found myself visualizing ways he could be useful to Bay St. Lucy. And to myself."

He could be useful to Bay St. Lucy, Nina mused, by continuing to be the high school principal.

How he could be useful to you, I don't want to even consider.

"He has 'corporate' written all over him. He's a man who walks into a room and commands attention. Don't you agree?"

"Oh yes. Mr. Cox is special. No doubt about it."

"I'm so glad we're on the same page on this."

"I think we definitely are," Nina replied, thinking all the while:

You're going to seduce Paul Cox.

You're going to wait until that damned mansion is fixed up and ready. And you're going to invite him over there.

And you're going to bed with him.

You're not even going to have the decency to shack up with him over in Biloxi or Falls Cove, the way he did with Macy.

"We're definitely on the same page," Nina continued, rather than say I HATE YOU DIE I HATE YOU DIE I HATE YOU DIE.

Because she did.

She hated the woman sitting directly across the table from her more than she had ever hated another human being, except for principals.

And of course, that was a different thing entirely.

It was also a difficult thing to explain.

Why did she realize so clearly that this woman, for all her honeyed tones and sugared words, was utterly evil? Was it jealousy? Was she jealous of the woman's astonishing beauty?

No, everyone was more beautiful than Nina, and she did not hate everyone.

Was it because she was a stranger?

No. No, because she did not seem to be a stranger. She seemed to be someone Nina had known her entire life, hating her every second.

You cannot, Nina found herself thinking, *be prejudiced against a person who has done nothing bad to you; or to anyone else you know, for that matter.*

Then she looked again at Eve Ivory.

Then she said to herself:

Of course you can be prejudiced against her.

It is, in fact, the only concrete thing you can do.

Except sit here and listen.

Which she did, for fifteen or so minutes more. She heard about the various city council meetings, about the zoning meetings, about the plans for allowing people to own property they had up to now been renting, about the new fire station, the new improvements to the admittedly small but still useful marina, the new visitors' bureau—

—and the proposal, made by Allana Delafosse, concerning the cultural center of Bay St. Lucy.

Said center being the actual Robinson mansion itself.

As Eve Ivory paraphrased it, Nina could actually picture Allana herself, standing at the same podium in the library where Tom Broussard had insulted every writer in the village, and holding forth in bizarre and incongruous vowel elongations:

"Here, in these rooms, could be housed a THEEEE ah tah. And here a small nook, where the writers' group might meet. The larger rear salon could be given over to chamber music concerts. With such a maaahvellus range of acoustics—"

Yes, she could hear Allana, saying all of these things.

And thinking they were going to come about.

And not at all visualizing the condescending smile which now spread across the face of Eve Ivory as she said:

"Such a *colorful* woman!"

"Yes. Allana is certainly that."

"And you cannot fault her intentions. Except—when I think of the renovated mansion, with gold inlaid fixtures and oaken bannisters, carrara marble floors—when I think of children running around in there—"

She used the word 'children' as anyone else might have used the word 'squid.'

"Well, like I said. I appreciate Ms. Delafosse's efforts. As I do those of the rest of the village. And I have tried to be a good listener, really I have. But Nina—here is where I may need your help."

"All right."

"Not everyone can be pleased. The wish lists cannot all be fulfilled."

"Of course not."

"I must do what I think is best for the village in the long run."

"Certainly."

"And when the difficult decisions are in fact made, I need you to intercede in some measure between me and any villagers who may be—well—"

"Mad."

"Yes. Although I do hope it won't come to that. Allana Delafosse spoke of you during her presentation. She talked of using teachers—even retired ones such as yourself—to lead the Young Writers' Program. And of course there is no reason why that cannot happen."

"I would hope not."

"No, no reason at all. It's just—"

There was that smile again.

"Just not in rooms with emerald inlaid mirrors."

"No. Of course not."

"So—do you see what I'm asking you?"

"I think I do."

"And may I count on your support?"

"I really don't know what to say. I'll try my best to make the folks realize that not everybody can be satisfied—"

"That's all I'm asking."

"You realize, though, that a lot of these people have lived their entire lives here. They're used to Bay St. Lucy the way it is now."

"That's gone."

The smile disappeared.

Just for a split second.

Then it came back but with a shade more darkness in it, and a few pounds more dead weight.

"Change happens. And it will happen here."

Silence for a time.

"Like I say. I'll be happy to help in any way I can."

"That is all I'm asking, Nina. It really is. Because after all—"

They were interrupted by the entrance of Margot, who, flushed and excited, seemed to have come from making a great discovery.

"Oh, it's lovely out there!"

"Good walk?" asked Nina.

"Absolutely exhilarating. You should both go down to the beach now and walk toward Biloxi at least two miles! The breeze is fabulous and the air is crystal clear!"

Eve Ivory rose.

"It sounds enchanting," she said, "but I'm afraid I have a meeting in several minutes."

"Oh, what a pity! A later time, perhaps?"

"Certainly. There will, I hope, be time for many more walks on the beach and such things. Nina, thank you for your hospitality. Margot, so glad to make your acquaintance."

"Likewise. And I must tell you, for the last half hour I've been thinking about nothing other than what you've said. I know it isn't set in stone, but I'm going home right now and polish my typing skills!"

"Excellent! Well, good bye ladies!"

"Goodbye!"

"Goodbye!"

The sound of steps on the staircase.

Nina looked at Margot.

"Where have you been?"

A shrug:

"Around."

"You hate the beach."

"Not always. Sometimes it's useful. Actually, it's the sea that's so useful."

"A secretary?"

"Well, I've always wanted to be a secretary."

"Really?"

"I suppose it's because I never learned to type."

"Margot—"

"OH FOR—!"

There was a piercing scream from beneath.

"ARE YOU—!"

The two women looked at each other.

"Is Penelope Royale around?" asked Nina, softly.

"No. I think those words came from our friend, Ms. Ivory."

"I've only heard those words—used in that particular syntax, I mean—from Penelope."

"Ms. Ivory and Penelope may have more in common than first meets the eye."

In two seconds, they were on the stair landing looking down at Eve Ivory, who was still kneeling beside her sports car."

She rose, looked up, and, her voice quivering with
rage, screamed:

"Some— slashed my tires!"

There was, for several seconds, only the sounds of
the gulls wheeling and screeching overhead.

Then Nina heard Margot whispering.

"Sonofagun. What do you know about that?

More gulls.

More cursing from Eve Ivory, whose potentially
violent side was beginning to manifest itself for the first
time in Nina's presence.

And the continuous soft strain from Margot, who
was shaking her head, all the while muttering.

"What do you know about that?"

Things were quite busy around Nina's beach shack
for the next half hour. The police were called, of
course. It took no more than five minutes for the first
squad car to arrive, another five for the second.

The third—with Moon Rivard driving it—was
expected shortly thereafter.

Several of Nina's neighbors walked up from their
own beach houses, respecting almost exactly the same
ring of distance they had established a few weeks
earlier, when her own place had been vandalized.
These people were shocked that two crimes had been
committed in Bay St. Lucy within a month, and they
wondered whether the latest outrage might signal an
invasion of 'street gangs'—none of them being quite
certain what a 'street gang' actually was—and the
naturally ensuing onset of urban warfare.

Eve Ivory did nothing for a time except walk back
and forth.

Very fast.

It was strange, Nina thought, *how she seemed to
have established her routine.*

She would kneel beside one of the slashed tires, inspect it for no more than five seconds, then straighten up and walk straight toward the ocean.

She would only walk ten feet.

Then she would stop and, arms folded across her breasts, stare at the Simcon Oil Refinery rig, whose lights had been turned on, despite the strikingly clear weather prevalent on the coast at this time.

Then, seemingly having made a decision, she would whirl and retrace her steps to the car, kneeling in precisely the same pose she had assumed before, and beside the same tire.

It was as though she had expected the tire, this time, to have been made whole again, to have been cured, restored to its former rubbery health.

But finding that it was the same tangle of black strips that it had been a half a minute earlier, she resumed the routine.

Police officers from the first two prowl cars—one of them the young woman who'd come to the restaurant and informed Nina of the earlier vandalism—had no luck communicating with Eve Ivory, who clearly did not deal with underlings.

"Ma'am, if we could just—"

"Where is your boss?"

"He's been called. But if you could just tell us how—
—"

She would say nothing more, but she did, after the first two such encounters, walk two or three steps closer to the ocean.

Under the beach house itself were five figures: the clothes washer, the clothes dryer, the meat freezer, Margot, and Nina.

The only sound or motion that came from any one of them was a slight humming from the meat freezer.

After a couple of days, Nina's reckoning, forty five minutes Mean Greenwich Time, Moon Rivard arrived, parked beside the ventrally mangled MG, got out of his squad car, inspected the four tires, and confronted—or rather was confronted by—Eve Ivory, who said:

"How could you let this happen?"

It was as though a mother had left the house in charge of her teenage son, who, out of pure negligence, had allowed wild wolves to come in and eat all of the drapes and furniture.

"Ma'am, I'm sorry about this."

"Who are you?"

"I'm Officer Rivard."

"You're the head of police here?"

"Yes, ma'am."

"Well, you look like a bum."

There was complete silence after she said this.

Then Moon Rivard—who did, when one thought objectively about the matter, look a little bit like a bum—ran his fingers through his exploded iron-shard hair, and said quietly:

"You don't know who done this?"

Eve Ivory glared at him:

"Of course I don't know who 'done' this, you buffoon!"

Another moment, but there was not quite complete silence.

A kind of gasp escaped from the circle of spectators, who, it could be seen, were weighing the relative disadvantages of having rival Hispanic gangs move into the village, or Eve Ivory.

"Well, it might be kids. It's a new car, and something they ain't seen. So—"

"Kids? Kids? You're saying children did this?"

Another vehicle arrived about then, this one a tow truck, for, clearly, the car owner's seaward incursions and excursions would not cure it, and new tires would have to be installed.

"I'm not sure, ma'am."

"Then when will you be sure?"

"It's just—"

"Just what?"

Moon Rivard shook his head. He had apparently forgotten Eve Ivory's gross insults to him, and, in what Nina took to be a rather stunning display of professionalism, was actually thinking about the crime itself.

"Just that, looking at the tires—"

"Talk, you idiot! What are you trying to tell me!"

"These tires were slashed by somebody, knew what he was doing."

"What?"

"You can't just take a knife to a tire and ruin it. You got to know where to cut. This whole job was done in— like a minute or less. Drunk kids, out to ruin something—don't sound right."

Eve Ivory was silent for a second.

Then, ignoring Moon Rivard, she walked under the beach house, to where Nina and Margot were standing.

Ignoring Margot too, she breathed deeply and said to Nina:

"I'm very sorry this has happened."

"I am too, Eve. I can't imagine—"

"No. Don't worry. It's not your problem. This simply underlines the importance of the subject you and I were discussing."

"Yes. I can see that it does."

"I cannot believe that this—well, I won't use the proper word to describe him. I'll simply say that I doubt his ability to find out who did this thing. I will say this, though. A great deal of money is coming into Bay St. Lucy. And the things bought with that money will be properly looked after. From this moment on, I will have my own security people here. They will not interfere with Officer—whatever his name is. But neither will they allow acts of wanton vandalism to take place."

"I understand."

"I'm sure you do, Nina. In fact, I'm sure you understand a great many things. The problem is, the same can be said for so few of your neighbors. Again, I'm sorry this had to happen. And good bye."

"Good bye."

The MG, whose tires had now been rendered as completely convertible as its top, had been towed to the garage in Bay St. Lucy that had the best chance of getting four antique British tires before New Year—some New Year if not this one—and Eve Ivory had been deposited by The Bay St. Lucy Police Force—in what was to be one of their last official acts, Nina was certain of that—at her mansion.

The circle of spectators had broken up.

Leaving Nina and Margot sitting on the deck, where Margot was actually smoking a real, and not an imaginary, cigarette.

"I cannot tell you," she said, "how exhilarated I feel. But I'm so sorry about your carving knife. If it doesn't wash ashore in a few weeks, I shall certainly replace it."

"Moon had nothing but praise for the job you did. He called it very professional."

"Yes, wasn't that nice of him? But really, it's much like blowing up a building; once you learn, you never really forget."

"That's 'riding a bicycle' that you're talking about."

Margot stared at her.

"What do bicycles have to do with it?"

"You had a very difficult childhood, didn't you, Margot?"

"Nonsense; I had marvelous childhood, both years of it. My only regret is that I didn't destroy the woman herself. In the first place, it takes much less work on an actual human being than on tires. Two nice quick thrusts will do a human, as opposed to sixteen or seventeen on tires. In the second place, the tires, as opposed to human beings, haven't really done anything wrong, have they?"

"No, they haven't. And you probably shouldn't joke about this thing, Margot."

"I'm not joking. I haven't joked about anything in years. I'm simply outrageous. They're different things."

"You're talking about cold blooded murder. That isn't a funny subject."

"It seems to me you're adopting a very provincial attitude."

"Margot—"

"Cold blooded murder is the very centerpiece of Western Civilization. Without it we would have no literature, no visual art, no drama, no government worth mentioning—and certainly, certainly, no sense of fashion at all."

"Margot, I don't know what this woman has planned for Bay St. Lucy. But we just got a look at what she's really like. She can be brutally insulting. And to someone who's done nothing bad to her at all."

"I know. I was appalled."

"Poor Moon: she called him a buffoon."

Margot quashed her cigarette, then lit another:

"I thought you were referring to her calling me a 'secretary.' That's the word she actually used, wasn't it? 'Secretary' or something like that?"

"Yes."

"My heavens, where does one acquire such language? And the damage it does to the soul. Nina, did you ever imagine me as a secretary?"

"Not for an instant, Margot. And certainly not after I first saw you try to make out a receipt."

"Ugghhh. Horrid little things."

"So. What do you think these 'security' people will be like? The ones she's going to bring in?"

Margot rose.

"Oh that's easy. And by the way, thank you for a perfectly wonderful morning. If the ocean were behind us, we could be in California, and I in my youth again."

"So tell. What will they be like?"

"They'll be like what her parents and grandparents were. Thugs and gangsters."

And she left.

CHAPTER NINE: THE GIFTS OF THE MAGI

"The best time for planning a book is when you're doing the dishes."

Agatha Christie

"Handmade presents are scary because they reveal that you have too much free time."

Doug Coupland

Winter reached Bay St. Lucy early on the morning of December 19 at precisely two A.M.

A north wind came roaring in, bringing surges of small rain and winds in excess of twenty miles per hour. The few remaining leaves still hanging, brown now and not golden, to the sycamore and oak trees, were ripped from their spindly stems and sent spinning into yards, alleyways, and parking lots.

Nina awoke to a new world.

Grayer, more windswept.

No cars prowled the streets.

No tourists walked the beach.

The schools, she knew, would remain in session, but Chief Maintenance Engineer Jack McCorkle—who'd once been called a janitor but now was a Chief Maintenance Engineer—would have dreamed his annual dream of purchasing a snow plow, but since one was never needed, he dreamed in vain. Students may have been given some leeway for late arrival.

"Brrrr."

She Furled, watching sympathetically as the shivering animal made its way inside, trying to warm itself on what now seemed rather threadbare carpeting.

She made herself some oatmeal and a cup of tea.

In the closet were two thick blankets. She got them out, unfolded them, shook the dust and spider webs off them, and laid them delicately on her bed.

Next, she ferreted through a box of emergency books: those which, read on a summer day with ice cream wagons passing merrily and balloons floating above the sailboats, were merely wasted.

Here. This would be a Dorothy Sayers day.

Strong Poison.

The Nine Tailors.

Five Red Herrings.

Gaudy Night

The Unpleasantness at The Bellona Club

Have His Carcass

She made two delicate little piles of them, which she placed on the nightstand beside her bed.

She had nothing to do at all, nothing that would force her out of doors, until Macy and Paul's wedding shower, which was to be held at Margot's garden at 7:30 tonight.

"God," she whispered, "How I love retirement."

She went to her closet and found the pink fluffy robe—which resembled an elephant as it would have appeared in a scratch-and-smell children's book—hurled it above her and dived beneath it, so that, after a few seconds of subsummation, she was either wearing it or it was wearing her.

Matching slippers.

The elephant's feet.

Shuffle into them.

Now back into the kitchen.

Another cup of tea, but use the larger cup.

Some lemon. Ah, there, behind the milk, several slices left over from yesterday afternoon.

A few drops in the tea—

Should she go, one last time, out on the deck?

Yes!

Dare to be brave!

Dare to be Beowulf!

Glass door slides open—

"Brrr!"

She spit the syllable into the north wind, which must have been over twenty five miles an hour now.

She went to the rail, peered over and looked to the right, southward, so that the wind did not blow into her face and make her eyes water. House after house seemed deserted, flower boxes shuddering against slate-gray walls, hanging bird feeders swinging like pendulums in precarious four foot half-arcs, and tightly closed window panes rattling against a fine spray of dust and seawater.

The lines came into her mind:

When icicles hang by the wall
And Dick the shepherd blows his nail
And Tom bears logs into the hall,
And milk comes frozen home in pail—

She turned back into the wind, padded back across the deck, and forced herself to look at a digital thermometer that hung on the wall, just beside the door:

Forty four degrees.

"Brrr!" she whispered.

Then she went to bed and stayed there all day.

By early evening, the temperatures were expected to drop into the high thirties, but the bridal shower was not postponed. It was too important. If Nina was perhaps the town's most respected and soon to be dead citizen—she suspected that many citizens had already planned her funeral, elegies, and flower arrangements—Macy Peterson was Teacher of the Future, vibrant, loving, creative, and a maven favorite in a town full of dowagers.

Everyone adored her.

And unexpectedly brutal weather such as this was not about to keep the town from showing its feelings, especially since those feelings extended equally to the perfect fiancé, Paul Cox.

So Nina had slipped out of bed at five thirty, still a bit uncertain why Harriet Vane's lover had been poisoned—even though this was to be her fifth reading of *Strong Poison*—made herself a scrambled egg, gulped down a small glass of milk, imagining it to be mead taken in preparation for her grand Sea Voyage into the Northern Seas of Downtown Bay St. Lucy—

—dressed, and went downstairs.

"I must go down to the sea in ships," she found herself whispering, as she unchained the Vespa, made sure her two sweaters fit tightly beneath her heaviest suede winter jacket—the brown one that had needed dry cleaning since the day Furl had spent sleeping on it, all fault in this matter being of course hers for leaving it spread out on a chair—slipped the thick goggles on, these goggles protecting her from flying gravel shot back by speeding semi-trucks—pulled on the black football-style rider's helmet, fastened it securely—turned on the ignition and sputtered out into the driveway.

Within a minute, she'd reached fifteen miles an hour and might go faster, given the fact that there was no other traffic on the streets.

The weather had turned Bay St. Lucy into a veritable winter wonderland, a marvelous kind of mini-jewel all clothed in white. Cables had been strung across the streets, and innumerable streamers of silver aluminum hung down halfway to the pavement. The streets had been bathed in a film of fake snow. There were snowmen in almost every yard, huge figures consisting of two globes of white fur all shining with Velcro accessories. She counted three Santa sleighs, one in a store window but two on actual yards, with the jolly old elf himself at the helm, completely motionless as though awaiting the big day of his take-off; except at Treasures by the Bay, in whose window he was actually moving, both mouth and arms, the whole effect of which possibly seeming, had it not been so close to Christmas, somewhat ghastly.

Signs saying "Bay St. Lucy Wishes You a Merry Christmas" were everywhere, hanging from power lines, pasted on shop walls, wrapped around telephone poles, and lying on the pavement, having been torn loose by the day's winds.

She was now within half a mile of Margot's shop.

Gradually, during her voyage, she had ceased to be Beowulf and had become William the Conqueror, off to invade England.

There behind her, riding on the small elliptical rack where she had once carried her backpack, were a hundred horses.

She and her men would need those horses.

But it all depended on this wind.

It could not change. Bitter, savage, as it was, it must not change direction. For it was only 1066 and she had not yet learned how to tack, to sail against it.

If it altered, she and her loyal Norse warriors were dead.

But, so far, it had remained constant.

Putt putt putt—

Putt putt putt—

One more turn and—yes! She could see the lights of Margot's shop, just a little in front of the great beaches of Hastings, and a few feet behind The Stink Shak.

It happened.

She made it.

No sea change, no wind change.

And here she was, not Beowulf at all, nor William the Conqueror, but simply Nina Bannister, walking up the steps to Margot's, and opening the door.

"Nina!"

"Nina!"

"Nina!"

"Nina!"

"Nina!"

"Nina!"

"Nina!"

"Hi," she replied.

Then, of course, she was engulfed with people, some of whom she had not seen in—

—how long?

Two weeks?

"Nina you look wonderful!"

"Thank you!"

"I *love* your sweater!"

"Thank you!"

"Is it Alpaca?"

"Rayon and cotton."

A bit more conversation—

—while Nina looked around the shop and the garden beyond—

—and felt awed.

It was a remarkable scene.

It had been dark for some time now, and lights in Margot's were dimmed, most of the illumination coming from either candles, glowing sea shells, or phosphorescent fish. Snow was falling everywhere and covering everything. Not only was the snow ubiquitous but it was variegated. There was felt snow, cotton snow, corn flake snow, candy snow, turtle wrap snow, popcorn snow, hospital bandage snow, gauze snow, clothes remnant snow, fur snow, and discount clothes snow.

Then there were the presents.

The presents!

Of course, Nina admonished herself, the presents should hardly have been a surprise, at least not to anyone at all familiar with the village of Bay St. Lucy.

Most bridal showers centered around a theme.

There were dishware showers.

Lingerie showers.

Cutlery showers.

Cookware showers.

Themes such as those.

But such showers took place in normal villages, towns, and cities, across the nation.

Bay St. Lucy was by its very nature different.

Bay St. Lucy was not a place in which a shower was held.

Bay St. Lucy *was* a shower.

Going into Bay St. Lucy to buy a single shower present was somewhat akin to going into the center of the sun to buy a box of matches.

Approaching the matter differently:

It did happen that, some weeks earlier, elegantly written notices went to all people who might be interested in buying Macy Peterson and Paul Cox a shower gift, might want to be aware that the two were collecting a set of dishware, and that the various pieces might be purchased here or there.

These notices were immediately destroyed.

Why?

Because the people who had received the letters, the potential gift givers, were the proprietors of:

Clay Creatures, Expressions by Claire, Joyce's Shells and Gifts, Maggie May's, The Social Chair, Uptown Interiors, Bay Breeze, The Blue Crab Gifts Gallery, Moore-Haus Antiques, Art Alley in the Pass, Let's Make Up Gifts, Aloha Gallery and Frame Shop, Just Flowers, M&L Gifts, Tuesday Morning, Your Gift Cove, Gratitude, Inside Out, Amano, Stephanie's Stuff, Cool Breeze (an offshoot of Bay Breeze), Bo Jon's Surf and Gifts, Jaynie's Novelties and Gifts, Charlie's Treasures, Mike's Treasures, Shirley's Treasures, Obob's Treasures, Maison El Jardin, Rustic Rail, and Barnes and Ed's Hardware Store.

None of these people were about to be limited to a steak knife or a pair of underwear.

So that Nina saw, as she began to walk about the shop, an array of gifts that was truly astonishing.

Margot had laid them out with the kind of care that might have been expected from The Director of The Chicago Art Museum; so that they almost seemed to be a part of the store itself, their bows and wrappings as natural to them as the oyster to the pearl.

She began to be acclimated into a routine. She would take two steps, and then whisper to herself:

"Oh my God."

Two more steps.

"Oh, my God."

Occasionally:

"I'm doing fine, thank you! No, I've missed you too! Yes, it's beautiful!"

Two more steps:

"Oh, my God."

For Nina was no judge of antiques. But she was no dunce, either, and she knew names.

And she could read cards.

"Handmade clay sculptures by Jennie McCardill. who first opened her business in The French Quarter in 1980. Pieces are sculpted from white clay, hand painted and fired twice in a higher temperature kiln."

And:

"Six assorted white-shell boxes from Joyce's Shells and Gifts, along with Four Cyprian Moneta Center Cut Shells."

And:

From Judy Trice at Tuesday Morning:

"Hummel Keeping Time; Hummel Little Miss Mail Carrier; Hummel Chimney Sweep; Hummel Forty Winks."

And:

From Bay Breeze:

"Hermann Traditional Mohair Bear; Hermann Little Starlight Mohair Bear."

And:

From Denise, at M&L Gifts:

"Limoges: Hinged Chef Hat; Hinged Delft Mini Duck; Swaroski Duck—Fancy Felicia."

And—the names of the shops, the artists, the proprietors begin to fade, but the objects themselves continue:

"Pickle Casters. Meridian Basket. Pin Inverted Thumbprint."

"Ruffled and Quilted Peach Bowl Art Glass Sweetmeat Server."

There, farther along, out toward the garden, a slightly larger group of people.

She would wait until they moved on.

Patches of their conversation:

"…one of the best teachers my child has ever had."

"…just loved her."

"…so glad we had a chance to give her this…"

The group moving on….

What is it?

"Oh, my God."

"Havilland Dinner Service in the Wheat Pattern with Gilt Trim, Eighty Pieces."

So how many are they—

—all of them.

All eighty pieces.

Just a few of them here on display now, of course, but—

—all of them

Twelve each dinner plates, salad plates, cups and saucers.

Bread and Butter holders, four each platters and serving bowls...

All of them.

Eighty pieces.

Havilland Dinner Service in the Wheat Pattern.

"Oh my God."

She went out into the garden.

There she stepped squarely into a pool of Allana Delafosse, who engulfed her, hugged her, not-kissed her first not-on- the right and then not-on- the left cheek, and who finally held her out at arm's length, as though waiting for her to dry before pronouncing:

"You look terrible, dear."

"Thank you."

"Do you feel bad?"

"Now I do."

"You should not have come out in weather like this."

"Well, the shower—"

"You should have called me. I could have arranged transportation. How are you getting home?"

"I have the Vespa."

This caused Allana to attempt an impression of Eduard Munch's "The Scream." Eyes wide, mouth circular and gaping, the complete absurdity and simultaneous horror of The Abyss opening before her—saw Nina's Vespa for what it truly was: The Death of God.

Allana attempted to mouth 'no,' but nothing came out, and there was nothing left to her but to embrace Nina a tightly as she could, and sob.

"It's all right, Allana. It's really not that cold."

She could feel Allana's strong hand patting her back, and this, plus the warm tickle of black ermine in her nose—Allana had come for the evening dressed not as an image from Post War Expressionism but as Cruella De Ville—comforted her and made her not so much resigned to the inevitable wintry death that awaited her during the ride home, as excited by the wake that was to proceed her departure.

Finally, Allana had led her to a vacant chair, gotten two sips of tea into her—not Darjeeling—examined her with the ruthless supernatural gaze of a true Creole medicine woman, and said, hesitantly:

"Your color seems somewhat more natural now. Are you feeling better?"

"Much."

"You simply must allow me to take you home though."

"Someone might steal my Vespa."

"No one will want it, dear."

"There's comfort in that, then, anyway. A person has so little in these final days—"

"Nina!"

Her Last Rites were interrupted by Macy Peterson, who exuded far greater happiness than should have been expected from any woman dressed in a salmon-colored suit offset by octopus ink purple scarf.

"Nina, are you all right?"

"Yes, I—"

"She came here," said Allana, looking first at one woman, then the other, then balefully out a window and into the winter night, "on her moooowwwtacycle."

"Nina, you didn't!"

"It's not that far."

"Why didn't you *call* me? There are so many people I could have gotten in touch with, who would *gladly* have given you a ride! Do you have a way home?"

"I thought I'd just let the ambulance take me to The Emergency Ward."

A complete blank look on both of the faces staring at her.

One second, two seconds—

"That's a joke."

Then both of them knelt forward at the same time and said in one identical voice:

"Don't joke about things like that."

"Well, if you can't joke about death then what—"

The same blank stare.

Change the subject.

"You have some wonderful gifts here, Macy."

A few more seconds for the awesome specter of Nina's demise, the horror of a world without Nina—to be gradually displaced by the visions of glittering little jewel caskets lying around what had become a magic kingdom under drifts and drifts of silvery glittery snow, so wonderfully powdery perhaps because all of it was in fact powder.

"Have you seen the things, Nina?"

"I've seen some of them."

"Aren't they marvelous? Did you see the Hummels?"

"Yes!"

"Paul *loves* Hummels!"

"Does he?" exclaimed Nina, and thinking simultaneously, *then this would make him the first man in the history of the world to do so.*

"Yes, he does! Oh, and by the way, he'll be here soon. He apologizes for being a bit late; he's in a big planning meeting!"

Since Nina had begun a two track conversation, one with herself and one with Macy and Allana, she decided to let the thing go on for a while as it was—four woman chatter, the two Nina's (public and secretive), and the two people sitting before her.

What kind of a meeting? private Nina asked secretively.

"The dishware set was incredible," public Nina said. "Wasn't it?"

I don't suppose Miss You Know Who was at this meeting, was she? asked private Nina.

"The Limoges is also beautiful," stated public Nina.

Allana Delafosse said something to this but Nina was having trouble keeping up with her own two tracks and didn't pay attention.

Something about 'exquisite,' but who cared.

Private Nina leaned forward, put her hands on Macy's knees, looked straight into her beaming face, and said quietly but firmly:

Do you realize that this woman is stealing your fiancé from you, right under your nose? That she's been seen with him all over town for the last days? That she's going to hire him off somehow, give him some fake administrative job for beaucoup money, more maybe than he's ever seen—take him to bed with her, make him a toyboy for a few months, and then throw him out?

These words were fed into the translation center, spliced, processed and reprogrammed, then forwarded into the alternative control center which re-routed them into public Nina talk, so that they came out:

"It's probably the best shower I've ever seen."

"I know, isn't it? People are just so nice."

Florence Thomas came by then and said:

Blah da blah da blah da blah.

To which, Macy replied:

Blah da blah da blah da blah.

Allana seconded that, saying assertively:

Blah da blah da blah da blah.

Leaving an opening which could not be missed by Jaynie, of Jaynie's Antiques, the woman who'd given one of the three pickle casters, and who could always be counted on to say something like:

Blah da blah da blah da blah.

Which she did.

Nine felt compelled to respond, saying:

Blah da blah da blah da blah.

Allana countered:

Blah da blah da blah da blah.

Macy corrected her:

Blah da blah da blah da blah.

Nina supplemented the thought, saying, in a conciliatory way:

Blah da blah da blah da blah.

And then there was a lull in the conversation.

No one knew how long this lull lasted, nor were any records kept, so it will be one of those mysteries of nature. Suffice to say that for a physically indeterminate amount of time the village had become one those black holes that suck in all human suffering, wisdom, and aspiration, condensing them into a tiny ball of immensely heavy matter—which must for unknown reasons remain hidden for a time—and replacing them with utterly useless blather, which was then spread out all over the universe.

Unexplained forces finally blew up this black hole, allowing the return of reason to human speech, so that Allana might say to Nina:

"You know, dear, I did meet with Miss Ivory some days ago."

"I think I heard about that."

"Well. These things do get round, don't they?"

"Yes. Yes, they do."

"I must say, I was impressed with her. And with the way she seemed to listen."

'*Seemed,*' thought Nina, *may be the operative word here.*

"You know she thinks the world of you, don't you?"

"She's been complimentary to me. I'm not really sure why."

"We all know why, Nina. We all know why. She recognized someone who embodies the town's—well how else shall I say it?—the town's soul."

"That's asking a lot, Allana, from someone who's only five feet three."

"I'm not certain what height has to do with it."

"Nina," said Margot Gavin, who, empress of her own domain, had joined the group, "is bringing humor into the conversation."

"Ah. Well, at any rate. She has shown excellent taste in her feelings for you and she was not at all unreceptive to my presentation concerning Auberge des Arts."

"Pardon?"

"'Auberge des Arts' is one proposed name for the mansion itself, renovated in such a way as to become a pure cultural center."

"Oh yes! I'd heard about that—just the basic plans, of course."

"They are quite complex now. I and several others have been working intently on them. I'm sorry I don't have the plans here—"

"That's all right."

"—but we were able to get blueprints of the mansion itself, and it seems perfectly made for such an endeavor. There are two separate areas that might well be transformed into Black Box Theaters. One hall with splendid acoustics, a perfect place for chamber music concerts. There are intimate quarters—one even with a fireplace, if you can imagine that—that remind one of Old English drawing rooms, where Noel Coward, George Bernard Shaw, Dorothy Parker, Oscar Wilde and Edith Wharton, might sit chatting far into the night—"

"—about Paranormal Romance?"

"Nina!"

"Sorry, Margot."

"What was that?"

"Nothing, Allana. Go on."

"Well, that's basically the gist of the proposal. This splendid mansion is now the centerpiece of our town again; as it was always supposed to be. But now we can put art and culture in the center of our community."

"I hope that happens, Allana. I really do."

She was about to something both inspiring and fake.

She was prevented from doing so, though, by the arrival of something even more inspiring and fake.

Eve Ivory.

The woman entered Margot's garden like an appearance of the Northern Lights, radiating fur, jewelry, bangles, and Misrule. She was not so much a human being as a personified boutique, open only for private showings.

"I'm so sorry I'm late! Here, I've at least brought this!"

She held before her a small present. It was wrapped in white paper with a red bow. By its precise measurements, Nina could tell it contained something of no value that was ugly.

"Margot!"

"Eve!"

"This is the first time I've been in your place. It's really quite cute in a kitschy sort of way. I have a dear friend with two kiddoes: some of these little sparklies will be perfect for them!"

"Whatever I can do."

"And—is it—you must be Macy?"

"Yes."

"Well, then congratulations!"

"Thank you!"

"I'm so sorry to have to borrow your fiancé for the evening, but the meeting just will not end. There are some hugely important negotiations going on at city hall and, well, without Paul—"

"I understand. He's excited that he can help. He seems to think something very big is about to happen."

"It is, Macy. It is. Which is why I have brought these!"

Strapped around her neck was an animal of the tundra which she had forced to be motionless so that it could carry her things. She reached into its mouth and withdrew from its pelvic cavity at least twenty letters, all of a hue that would have been called ivory had that not been her name, and which thus would preferably be called 'bone,' since that fit more her nature.

"These are invitations to all of you. A Holiday Gala, December 22, eight o'clock. I think I can promise you to have a truly remarkable announcement to make.

Now I must rush back though: and once again Macy: congratulations to you and Paul!"

So saying, she left.

She'd been gone for perhaps ten seconds before Margot, shaking her head and continuing to peer at the door, asked quizzically:

"Who came in?"

The invitations were opened, analyzed, praised for polish and elegance:

DEAR MR/MS—
MISS EVE IVORY HAS THE PLEASURE OF
REQUESTING YOUR PRESENCE
AT A GALA
TO BE HELD
DECEMBER 22, 8:00 P.M.
AT
THE NEWLY RENOVATED
ROBINSON HOUSE
RSVP

There were envelopes addressed to everyone in the store.

"She did," Nina said, admiringly, "her research. She got all our addresses right."

There was a bit more oohing and aahing about the invitations, and some speculation about what was to go on at this 'gala,' and what announcement was to be made that would be so important to Bay St. Lucy.

But the main thing that Nina could not help noticing was the composure of Macy, who'd lost her fiancé on what might have been the most important evening of her life, up to this point.

All of these presents were to be opened by the two of them, by her and Paul.

And, yet, here she was, left to flit from one table to another, one group to another, one exquisite China display to another, apologizing and gushing, smiling and, Nina knew, wondering.

What exactly did this woman want with him?

Eve Ivory's visit, as welcome here as a camp fire in a dirigible, had cast a pall over the evening.

There was, to be sure, still a kind of cozy glow radiating from the fireplace over by the wall, where three plastic logs turned slowly around an invisible spit, rotating like hot dogs with fake bark.

But people spoke a bit softer, and seemed to be looking at their watches.

This was the way of things for some minutes, half an hour longer.

And then something else happened.

People began to be drawn to the windows.

For what? Nina wondered.

What are they looking at?

She made her own way across the garden, slipping carefully through two crèches and a balloon figure of Frosty the Snowman.

She pressed the tip of her nose against the window glass.

What was that in the street?

"Would you look at that?"

"That is something, isn't it?"

And it was.

For stopped before Margot's shop was a carriage drawn by two white horses—real white horses, which made them the only real things in the village that night—who were driven by a driver with a top hat, and wearing a long coat.

The horses remained perfectly still, and the ringing of their bells was caused by the wind whistling around them, and not by any deviance on their part from pure military protocol.

The door of the coach opened, and Cary Grant got out. He was dressed in a tuxedo, of course, which Cary Grant must always wear, and he had on a black and shining top hat

He straightened, attempted to shake the snow off his shoulders and coat sleeves, could not because there wasn't any, then returned his attention to the carriage itself.

He leaned forward, reached into it, offered his arm, and withdrew Lucille Ball.

No one else could it have been: not simply because Lucy Ricardo had much more in common with the women painters, clay makers, pot throwers, kiln operators, and restaurateurs than did the average medieval nun—but because no film star, with the possible exception of Ingrid Bergman, had this woman's magnificent shoulders.

Not to mention the bonfire burning a brilliant scarlet in curls and yule logs only a foot or so above those shoulders, a face, neck, forehead, nose, ears, throat, etc., naturally intervening, but totally overwhelmed.

Especially since the woman's back was to the shop.

"Who is that?"

"I don't know. Are those actors, or what?"

"Margot, who—"

"Don't ask me."

"Macy, do you know?"

"No idea."

The couple, arm in arm, moved away from the carriage, and disappeared behind a live oak tree that shaded Margot's shop.

So that the entire shower crowd now turned as one toward the shop entrance and waited.

The door eased open, it's bell tinkling gingerly.

"Hello. Sorry we're late. Little trouble with the horse."

A slight gasp.

There in the doorway, inching shyly inside, were Tom Broussard and Penelope Royale.

Arm in arm.

He had been Cary Grant. And was still, if one looked carefully, at least far more than he was disheveled old Tom. His stomach was now held in place by a black, shining cummerbund; his hair had been cut, oiled, slick-backed, and beaten, so that it now cowered servilely upon his scalp, ready to allow children to pet it; his shoes glittered like pieces of anthracite coal; and his slump had been magically cured, adding inches to his height by the simple measure of putting his head directly over his shoes instead of one and a half foot in front of them.

That was remarkable enough.

But as for Penelope—

—that was a bit more.

No one in the shop had ever seen this woman.

They had seen a hard block of granite, tall and unyielding, wrapped with oilskin and topped with carrot fire

But they had no way of suspecting the awesome effect of those rippling muscles revealed by a Bascani Gown, black as night, low-cut, sleeveless, and bejeweled.

They had no way of suspecting that Penelope Royale was an immensely striking woman.

"Oh my—"

"Oh my—"

"Oh my—"

The couple made their way through the shop and into the garden, stopping directly before Macy.

"We're all so proud of you, Macy," said Penelope. "Of you and Paul."

"Oh, Penelope—"

"Your marriage," said Tom, "is the biggest thing that could happen to Bay St. Lucy. Forget all the other stuff you've been hearing about—this is the only important thing. We wanted you to have this."

He gave her a small box, covered in exquisite green wrapping paper.

"Thank you, Tom. Thank you, Penelope."

"We should go now," said Penelope. "I love you Macy. All of us do."

Then the two of them turned and left the store.

Where there was no movement at all until the carriage jangled away.

Finally, the spell was, if not broken, at least eased somewhat, so the inhabitants of the castle could say:

"Open it, Macy."

"Yes, open it."

She did so, fingers trembling.

Then she took an object from the box and held it up to the light, held it up in the room, so everyone could see. An ivory letter opener; the blade carved to a pencil-sharp point, it's hilt carved into an intricate, lace work pattern; a green stone flashing fire at it's end.

"What is that?"

"It's a letter opener!"

"Look at that intricate carving!"

"Look—engraved on the back of the blade, both of your names: Macy and Paul."

"Where is it from?"

"Here in town?"

"Not my shop."

"Not mine."

And then it was for Mrs. Wilson, poor, boring, widowed Mrs. Wilson, she who had spent the last few weeks simply sitting on the edge of Margot's garden and reading, like a statue, hearing silently all of the gossip of Bay St. Lucy while saying nothing—then it was for her to come forward, take the letter opener carefully from Macy Peterson, and say:

"It's from Maurice's Antiques. One of the finest stores in New Orleans. And my favorite. Each of their items is one of a kind."

She gave the letter opener back to Macy and disappeared in the crowd.

"What's the jewel on the handle?"

"What is it?"

The object was laid on a table for all to see, and the few more questions about its identity—which came from those few people in town who did not know jewelry—were answered by the hundred or so craftspeople and artisans who knew very little besides jewelry.

"It's an emerald."

Then:

"How big would you say it was?"

"Oh, I would guess—"

And these people, in turn, were supplanted by the Head of the Chicago Art Museum, who bent over the piece, straightened, and said:

"Twenty five point three carats. Cosquez Mine. Columbia."

The words simply hung in front of her.

Finally, Nina asked, quietly.

"How do you know that, Margot?"

Margot Gavin shrugged.

"We tried to buy one like it once. We couldn't afford it."

Then she turned away, and seemed to go about other business.

After the arrival of an emerald that Tom Broussard and Penelope Royale could buy and the Chicago Museum of Art could not, a great deal more was not to be expected from a bridal shower.

There was only the business of picking up, saying thank you, and just being happy in general.

Nina followed Macy Peterson around the garden and shop, watching the young woman smile, chatter, laugh, gush, and act in a thousand more completely appropriate and utterly joyful ways.

She followed behind, picking up here, discarding there, offering a few thank you's herself on Macy's part.

Finally, after everything was done, she followed Macy outside, hugged her, congratulated her, and watched her get into a van which, driven by friends, was to take her home.

Nina followed the van on her Vespa.

It was a bit of a melancholy drive through the 'Saint' Streets—St. Ambrose St., St. Gerome St., St. Euclid St.—melancholy because it was in one of these small, tree-lined streets, that she and Frank had their first small cottage.

She visualized it for a time, then forced herself to speed up slightly, even though she knew quite well where Macy lived, and would hardly get lost in this part of town.

She parked some fifty yards away while the van disgorged Macy and whatever presents could be carried inside by the three friends surrounding her—the rest having remained at Margot's, while a separate museum could be built to house them.

The four women laughed uproariously on the porch.

The door opened, and they disappeared inside.

After a minute or so the door opened again, and they made their way slowly out to the van, laughing uproariously as they did so.

Then Macy watched the van drive away, waving spiritedly and jumping up and down.

Then she went inside, closing the door behind her.

Nina waited two minutes so that Macy would have time to change into a robe or underwear or whatever, then drove the Vespa into her driveway, parked it, took off her helmet and goggles, went to the door and knocked.

Macy opened the door and threw her arms around Nina, sobbing uncontrollably.

They stood in the door way for a while, and then made their way as a human knot across the small living room floor, like two immensely miserable and stunningly inebriated dancers.

Finally they were seated on the couch, each one's face pressed hard into some kind of fabric on the other one's chest, neither able to talk.

They cried for a time, tried to breathe, could not, gasped, hiccupped, succeeded in breathing, used the air to cry still more, and finally became an inert mass, only capable of panting and squeezing.

Something like words came out of Macy, those being:

"What is he *doing*?"

"I don't know, Macy."

"What can he be *thinking*?"

"He's not thinking."

"What does she *want*?"

"Him."

"She wants *Paul*?"

"Yes, she does."

"Why?"

"Because he's the best we've got. And she wants it all."

"Nina, who is this woman?"

"I don't know, Macy."

"Is she the devil?"

"Yes."

"But the devil is just a story!"

"Ay, think so. 'Til experience prove thee otherwise."

And the other lines came to her, the ones from *Othello*:

There is no such creature; it is impossible.

Unfortunately, it was possible.

"He should have *been* there tonight, Nina!"

"Yes. He should have."

"Can you talk to him?"

"Yes."

"Can you talk to him soon?"

"Yes."

"How soon?"

"Now."

"How?"

"Don't worry about it. I just can."

"Will you tell him for me, please, that I hate him?"

"No."

"I don't, you know."

"I know."

"But what is he *doing*?"

"He's being seduced."

"Oh, God!"

"God doesn't have much to do with it right now."

"What can I do, Nina?"

"Go to sleep."

"How?"

She could have said, 'Sleep, sweet sleep, that knits up the raveled sleeve of care,' but it wouldn't have done much good, and it had never made complete sense to her, anyway.

"Just lie down. Get yourself some warm milk or something."

"And you'll talk to Paul?"

"Yes."

"How?"

"However."

"Will you say bad things to him?"

"Yes."

"Very bad things?"

"Yes."

"Will you tell him he's an idiot?"

"Yes."

"I hate him! I hate him! Oh God, Nina, I love him so!"

"I know. Now try to get some sleep. Good night."

She left, drove to Paul Cox's home, found him just walking up the driveway, pulled up beside him, and said:

"Paul!"

"Nina! What are you—"

"Follow me to my place. Now."

"But what—"

"Now."

She drove to her place, parked, walked up her stairs, and opened the door for him as he arrived.

"Come in," she said.

"Nina, I—"

"Come inside."

She turned on the light, walked to the deck, unFurled, and then went back into the kitchen.

"I know everybody's wondering about—"

"Go in the living room and sit down."

She heard him doing so, and also heard a faint click, as the light came on.

She herself was busy in the kitchen, reaching high on a shelf and finding an almost forgotten bottle of whiskey.

She took two large glasses into the living room with her, set them on the glass-topped table between her and Paul Cox, and filled them.

"I'm not sure I should—"

"Drink."

She drank; he did also.

The whiskey made perfect sense, and was the first thing in quite some time that had done so.

"I should have been there," he said, "tonight."

"Ya think?"

"Does she hate me?"

"She hates you; for that matter, even I hate you."

"But, I'm just trying to—"

"Listen, you idiot: there are two female figures in all of literature. There are a few more of us in real life but we haven't gotten into print yet. We're still trying, and, who knows, with e-books and self-publishing—"

"It's just that—"

"Shut up. These two figures are the 'Eve' figure and the 'Mary' figure. Mary is wholesome, young, blue-eyed, virginal. She represents everything good in the world. Eve is tempting, evil, gorgeous, evil, wily, evil, and destructive. All she wants is to ruin whatever man she happens to be with. Now—drink up! Drink up! Drink up!"

He did so. She poured more for him.

Finally she said:

"Now, it's test time, Paul. Are there two women like that in *your* life?"

"But it's more—"

"Yes, there are, aren't they? There is one who wants to help you and love you and marry you and have your children and do everything, until the day she dies, to make you happy; and there is another who wants to seduce you, and make a fool of you, and throw you off like a piece of garbage."

He was quiet, staring down into his drink.

"And now the really big question on the test. The only question, when you think about it, that really matters at all on the test: which of these women did you choose to spend the evening with tonight, Paul?"

He shrugged again.

Nina took a big drink of whiskey.

"She just seems really encouraging," he said.

She spit the whiskey out.

It came out as part of a huge 'guffaw' and splattered on the table between them, a field of Jim Beam rivulets glittering amber on the glass.

She went into the kitchen, fighting the urge to draw her sleeve across her mouth and chin.

She found paper towels, wiped her face, took them back, cleaned the table, and tried to look at him with a straight face.

This failing, she looked at Furl, who, taking the raining whiskey to be possible food, was now standing beside her chair:

"She seems really encouraging?"

"Yes."

"I bet she does. I just bet she does."

"But—she approached me first."

"Good for her."

"I told her about the school."

"Bet you did."

"She seemed impressed by the plans."

"Bet she did."

"She wanted to talk more."

"Bet she did."

"Will you stop saying that?"

"No."

"Well—she told me I was integral to her plans."

"Bet she did."

"Nina—"

"Go on."

"We might have the school. We might have a new fire department headquarters. We might have Allana's Auberge des Arts. But they would have to be part of a major comprehensive city-wide development. Several bidders were offering visions of this development. But she needed someone from Bay St. Lucy to help her— well, make sense of it all. She needed a right hand man."

"A right hand man."

He took a note pad from the inner pocked of his navy sports jacket, and wrote a figure on it.

"She proposed a salary."

"It's not enough."

"It's more money than I've ever—"

"It's not enough."

"Would you just look at it?"

"Give it to me."

She took the slip of paper.

"With that much money," he continued, "Macy and I could—"

She tore it up, threw the pieces at him, got up, and went to the kitchen.

"Go home," she said, opening one of the cupboard door and then slamming it shut, simply for the pleasure of hearing it go 'bang.'

She listened as he walked out.

For five minutes or so she simply got herself together.

Then she walked downstairs and out toward the beach.

She could hear the cathedral bells of St. Mary's chime the hour.

Eleven P.M.

She listened to the waves for a time, and then walked back to her parking lot.

There did seem to be other bells, from other directions.

It felt like Christmas night.

The world glowed blue in the street light.

But there, outlined against the light—

—was something falling from the sky?

No, it couldn't be—

But, but look up, Nina.

Look up!

There is one, and there—

—fluttering down.

Fluttering down from the sky!

What are—

Then she heard the screech of the low wheeling band of gulls, and she realized what the objects were.

"Damn," she whispered.

She climbed the stairs and went to bed.

CHAPTER TEN: A SURPRISE FOR BAY ST. LUCY

"Everyone needs an editor."

Tom Foote, commenting in *Time*
magazine about the fact that Hitler's original title for *Mein Kampf* was *Four and a Half Years of Struggle Against Lies, Stupidity, and Cowardice*

"A man's face is his autobiography. A woman's face is her work of fiction."

Oscar Wilde

Eve Ivory's security forces arrived on the morning of December 22, a few hours before the gala at which she was to announce her plans for the development of the village.

They came in several vans: black, hearse like vehicles that parked bumper to bumper around the mansion's circular driveway, their lustrous finish gleaming like black, elongated stars, and their grillwork sharpened, smiling, and ready to cut.

They spread first through the gardens, then through the house itself, then through the perimeter of the village, then through the center of the village, then through the very air of the village.

There they stayed.

They hovered like a virus.

They patrolled corners.

They moved in pairs, like twin stars, one the shadow of another.

They were identical. Some were black and some were white, some were male and some were female, some were Asian and some were Indian, some were younger and some were older—but taken all in all they reflected a perfect cross-section of American society, ensuring the awed and gaping community which watched them go about their business that any killing they did would be both diverse and sensitive.

The people of Bay St. Lucy accepted their presence as they would have accepted news of a residual hurricane, one that, if it could not be fled, at least promised not to destroy mobile homes. These newly arrived, black suited, white shirted, red tied people were doing no harm, and, on the plus side, were the only truly well-dressed people the villagers had ever seen who were not Jehovah's Witnesses.

They created, if nothing else, one subject worth talking about.

The other subject worth talking about was the relationship between Paul and Macy.

They were two adult individuals and their privacy was to be respected, of course, so little was talked about after the evening of the shower, beyond the fact that he had not shown up for the shower, and had, in fact, been seen entering Eve Ivory's mansion, with Eve Ivory, at ten o'clock in the evening.

Beyond that, Macy and Paul's affairs remained shrouded in the mists of privacy, as they are generally allowed to do in a small community.

All that was known for certain was that Paul had called Macy at 6:45 the following morning and that she had refused to answer; that he had continued to call, reaching her finally at 7:03. She had, or so the rumor went, expressed her anger, even disgust, at his behavior the previous evening, but the matter of whether she'd actually used the word 'jackass' was conjecture only, and could not be certified one way or another.

It was certain that she had allowed him to come over for coffee, and that he'd stayed for forty five minutes, both of them leaving for school shortly after eight, meaning both of them had arrived somewhat late, but arm in arm, and smiling.

All of the people in the village were careful neither to form, or offer, any personal opinions concerning what might have happened in Marcy's house during the forty five minute period between his arrival and their mutual departure.

"She made him breakfast," said Margot Gavin, standing in the doorway of her shop, glancing at her watch, and observing the darkening streets and blue-glowing lanterns dotting the park opposite.

"Sure she did," said Nina.

"Where is this car?"

"I don't know. Eve Ivory said she'd send a car for us."

"She still likes you."

"Yes."

"And you don't know why."

"No idea. I do have a suggestion, though: when the thing arrives—and I suppose it will be some kind of limousine—I'll get the driver's attention, and you sneak around and slash a couple of the tires. Or—no, maybe not such a good idea."

"Why? I would have been game."

"Two security people. Standing there, just behind the gazebo, at the edge of the park."

"Yes. I see them. Gives one a sense of security, doesn't it?"

"Nobody's going to mess with that gazebo," said Nina.

And then:

"There's the car."

"Where?"

"There. Coming around the corner."

"My God."

"What?"

"It's still coming around the corner. Still coming; still coming—Nina, is this a car or a train?"

"Well. Only the best for us. Everything locked up in the shop?"

"Yes."

"Anything of inordinate value?"

"A few things that are especially nice. But I've placed them well out of view; I don't think we'll have to worry."

"Especially with these new security specialists watching out for things," Nina said. "Look how tall those two are!"

"I know. Why isn't Nazism more appreciated, Nina?"

"People just don't learn history anymore. Oh, there's Allana!"

And, in fact, beaming at them from the front seat of the limousine, which was now parking in front of the shop, Allana Delafosse, identifiable by her Which Color of the Zodiac Am I Going to Wear Today? outfit (orange today), and her full throated "Laaaayyydeeeez" warble, which always came out not so much as a greeting as a theme song.

"How ahhhhhhhhrrrrrryou this maaaahhhhvelous eeeeeeeeeeevening?"

Hearing a simple greeting from Allana Delafosse was like listening to The Star Spangled Banner; one felt the need to stand.

"Fine," said Nina, inadequately as always, approaching the car as the Na—the Security Official—got out and came around opposite, preparing to open the back door for her.

"Good evening, ma'am."

"Good evening," she answered, regretting the fact that she did not know German, while wondering if her shoes were properly shined.

"Well! Are both of you properly excited? It's going to be an historic evening for Bay St. Lucy!"

It's an historic evening anywhere, Nina found herself thinking, *when anybody puts the words 'an' and 'historic' together properly.*

"I have the most wonderful feelings about what is to happen tonight! There are so many ways the projects can go, such an array of possibilities! Ms. Ivory has seemed to take such an interest! And with Mr. Cox working along with her—"

Allana Delafosse continued to describe the varied possibilities, while the limousine wheeled its way through the quiet and somber evening streets of Bay St. Lucy, and Nina watched it all slide by—the shacks, the nicer bungalows, the few children in yards, playing. She watched through windows as the blue patches that were television screens flickered, and through adjacent windows as women bent to wash dishes, raised to shout jokes or gossip or insults or nothings at all to their families inside.

She said the right things to Allana and Margot as the village flowed past her, but all the while she could only see a vision of Frank that would not go away. It was the cynical Frank, the one who, after decades of work, had learned what The Law really was.

It was paper.

It had no more substance than that.

A sheet of paper.

And upon it, everything depended.

That little corner lot, the one with the battered swing set on it.

It had been there forever, a part of the Bay St. Lucy she'd always known.

And there, behind it, the Old Philliber House. Not such a large place, a rickety front porch, some fine trees in the back, the two old ladies, Nancy and Patricia Philliber sitting out on warm evenings, speaking to passers-by.

The school playground.

Roscoe's Gas.

There, down that street, the smaller and more disreputable shacks, where first poorer families lived, and then indigents lived, and then criminals lived, and then nobody lived, and then Tom Broussard lived.

But all a fixed and solid thing. Blocks and blocks and blocks of permanence that tethered Bay St. Lucy together.

And yet there was no permanence and all.

Kafka.

"There was a man from the land who sought access to the law—"

"But the law was protected by a gatekeeper—"

"And there are more gatekeepers, each larger and more ferocious than the last—"

The law.

Papers.

All it would take is one paper. And this entire community could be a vast parking lot.

She had seen it happen. Frank had shown it to her:

Entire farms, hundreds of acres.

But these farms were not owned by human beings; they were owned by papers.

And one day the paper would come, like locusts, but much quieter, and with a power so much more awesome.

And then the farm would be gone, along with the people who had been its soul.

Now there was a housing development.

Or a Wal-Mart.

Such was the law.

"—But the law should be open to everyone, to all the people!"

"—and then the man from the land was dying—"

"—this gate, this access to the law, was meant only for you. I'm going now to close it forever."

The Security Forces are the gatekeepers, she found herself thinking.

And Eve Ivory is The Law.

The limousine pulled onto Breakers Boulevard.

And the Mansion—huge, loud, obscene, gothic, godlike, musical, and glowing golden in the darkening twilight, appeared before them.

"All right," she whispered, "we'll see."

Then she pressed her forehead on the cool glass window and listened to music.

The radio was not playing.

They were deposited at the main entrance to The Robinson Mansion, which, Nina realized even before entering, could not be viewed as a mansion at all, nor a house of any kind, nor even a land-fixed dwelling. The thing she was entering, with its chandelier spinning slowly and sparkling brilliantly like a Cinderella Ball Gown hanging from monstrous metal straps from a ceiling several hundred feet above—this thing could only be compared to the Titanic, dried, refurbished, upended, and wet-barred.

Nothing but the Titanic could have survived from those opulent years.

It had been sealed by millions of gallons of seawater just as the Robinson Mansion had been sealed by impenetrable layers of decadence, criminality, mortgages, hatred, intense sexuality, and The IRS.

The Titanic of course still lay under water.

The Robinson Mansion had been raised.

Nina was not at all certain this was a good thing.

She moved through the various state rooms, talking to Edwena Pelleter, Robert Barnsworth, Allana now and again, Jackson Bennett and wife, the Mayor, and City Councilman—

—but they were not really these people, for these people could not exist in surroundings such as this.

Champagne glass in hand, she entered the Music Room, where an improbable harp leaned against a stained-glass wall, the giant bay windows opposite giving out on a garden redolent with acacias and rhododendrons, which could not of course be growing in December, save for the fact that the garden, she could see now, was no garden at all but a greenhouse. She wondered where the access to the tunnel was in there.

And here before her was a person in a tuxedo, who might have been one of the village's multitudinous insurance salesmen—yes, she was sure he was an insurance salesman, but she had not known that when she'd taught him, or he would have failed—but she would not talk to him as Charles Morgan or Phillip Talbot or whatever his silly name might have been.

For here, in this room, on this marble floor, with this music seeping in from the very walls—here he was Count Rudolf of Buxteholde, a nephew to the Emperor Himself.

"And how is the Emperor?" she found herself asking, in her imagination. The answer she actually received was something about insurance, but the imaginary answer was, "Very well, he sends his greetings!

"Very well! He sends his greeting!"

"Please return them for me."

"Indubitably! Will you and your consort by joining us in Sarajevo for the Grouse?"

"So much," she said, archly, "depends upon the health of the old countess."

"Ah yes. We hold her in our prayers."

"So deeply appreciated."

"Of course. Will you be certain to greet Ferdinand and the Reich's Chancellor, Baroness von Nina?"

"It goes without saying, dear Rudolf!"

This two-pronged—real and imaginary—conversation continued for a short time.

"Great! So you'll come by next Thursday to talk about a policy?"

"I'll try."

What fun, what fun!

Be careful, though, and don't get carried away.

Fine to go down for the grouse; but no insurance policies.

The passageways wound on and on, rooms opening into other rooms, the two hundred or so citizens of Bay St. Lucy strolling from upper deck to lower deck to mizzen deck or captains quarters to the pool area to the dance area to the whatever else area, all asking in quiet tones:

"How much money did it take to build this?"

Or:

"How much money did it take to remodel it?"

Or the biggest statement of all: "Eve Ivory is going to be making the announcement."

And it was true. There was no way to deny it, or to postpone it.

This was like opening the ultimate shower present. Or getting in the mail the official results of the biopsy.

Nina had no idea which.

She could not, though, deny that Eve Ivory The Magnificent had, if nothing else, a touch for the dramatic.

Just to the left of an anteroom was the grand entrance hall. This would have been used for dancing. Above and overlooking the dance floor itself, was an area ten feet deep and fifteen feet long, partitioned by a brass rail, where the orchestra would have sat.

There was only a speaker's platform now.

Nina could not avoid the urge to visualize Mussolini stepping out of the palace doors and onto a balcony, two million Italian fascists cheering beneath him.

There were hardly two million straight chairs on the dance floor, though; there were only about fifty. Reserved for the town's elite,

Of which, she supposed, she was one, since she had been allowed into the room. These chairs were now filling as the clock approached eight.

Nina found a seat. Allana immediately saw her and joined her, sitting on her left.

Then came Macy and Paul, to her right.

"This is so exciting!" gushed Allana.

She looked beyond Macy and whispered to Paul:

"Do you know what she's going to say?"

He shook his head:

"No. Not exactly. Whatever the plan is, I think it's going to have the school we want."

"What about," Allana asked, "The Auberge des Arts?"

He nodded:

"I lobbied hard for it. I think she's going to do it. It's just—"

"Just what, Paul?" asked Nina.

"—there have always been other people involved. People I never got to meet. People with a lot of money."

Uh oh, thought Nina.

"I think she's been trying to pull everything together under some sort of theme But she's never let me in on the whole thing. I don't think anybody in the town knows. She called me only a few hours ago. She said it was a 'done deal' and that we would all be surprised."

Uh oh, thought Nina.

And then Eve Ivory appeared.

She walked out of the wall.

Then she approached the podium, grasped it, and looked down at the people below her, like a leopard looking down at the meat department of a supermarket.

"Hello, Bay St. Lucy!" she said, tapping once on the microphone and beaming as her voice filled the hall.

"Thank you *so* much for coming tonight!"

There was some scattered applause and murmurings.

"I'm so happy to share with you the fact that we have come to the end of a difficult—but immensely productive—three weeks."

Eve Ivory was dressed in ivory but did not look like Eve—who, Nina had always surmised, wore nothing at all earlier in her life and something unfashionable later. Warming herself behind the early evening bonfire that was her smile, she did not, on the other hand, look anything like Benito Mussolini.

She looked rather like The Ice Princess from *The Lion The Witch and the Wardrobe*.

There, in one of those jacket pockets! Nina found herself guessing: Turkish Delight!

"Before continuing, I wish to thank in particular several of the town's citizens who have made this entire project not only possible, but immensely thrilling. First, there is of course the Mayor of Bay St. Lucy, Tom Waterston. Tom, will you please stand."

Tom Waterson did, and waved.

Then he sat down.

"Chief of Aldermen, Lucias Johnson."

Same.

"All of the members of the City Council who are with us tonight."

This of course included Nina, so she rose.

And then sat.

"And so many others, but, finally, my 'right hand man,' as I've been calling him: your school superintendent, Mr. Paul Cox."

Paul rose, to the beaming adoration of Macy, who, through the strength of her grip upon his hand as he smiled and waved to the crowd, gave Nina a good indication of how the two might have spent the phantom forty-five minutes.

Breakfast indeed.

Then he sat down.

A moment for everything to calm down.

Then Eve Ivory, to the business at hand.

"I have now to say a few words concerning—well, some very difficult matters. You all know the stories concerning my family. These are matters that preceded me, that happened here, in Bay St. Lucy, before my birth. I was not responsible for them. I did, on the other hand, fall heir to their consequences. My life, from its earliest moments, was not an easy one. I had many difficulties. I persevered, however, and with luck and fortitude, did well for myself. Much of my good fortune has been lavished on me by my late husband, who, I am deeply sorry to say, cannot be here at this podium to address you."

Pause.

Collective breathing first from Eve Ivory from above, then from Bay St. Lucy from below.

"As a result of all things past, though, a circuitous and highly complex assortment of events has given me the privilege, and rather awesome responsibility, few individuals in our time are called upon to bear. In most towns and villages, the ownership of property divides, subdivides, passes from one generation to another, from one heir to another, so that no one individual or family owns more than an acre, a five acre block, a building, an estate, etc. But I have recently found myself, according to the terms of my grandfather's will, in proprietorship of a great deal of the village of Bay St. Lucy. My first inclination, upon hearing the news, was disbelief. I had no idea how to respond to such a challenge. But after much thought—and, yes, prayer, for that came into it, also—I decided to meet the challenge head on. I decided to come here, meet you, work with your leaders, and prepare a plan that, were my particular land holdings to be scattered through the hands of multitudinous owners, would be impossible to fulfill. I've listened to many proposals, all of them thoughtful, all of them clearly meant to help ensure a prosperous Bay St. Lucy. Some of these plans I have been able to incorporate into the vision you will be sharing within the next minutes. Others, regrettably, have fallen by the wayside—for now. Not, I promise you, forever."

A movement forward toward the rail, the podium rocking somewhat.

"I simply must point out, though, and I wish you to keep this always in your minds. The long term goal, of any master plan, is the welfare not only of you, but of your children. You want beautiful Bay St. Lucy not only to survive today, in the hard economic times that are our environment, but to prosper and grow into tomorrow. You want your children's lot to be better than yours; and their children's lot to better than theirs; and on, and on, into the future."

Applause.

More applause.

Everyone standing now.

Eve Ivory nodding, and finally, palms down, gesturing for everyone to be seated.

Everyone was seated.

Finally she said:

"And so, all of these things said, dear fellow citizens—the time has come. The work has been done. The vision has been completed. And I now give you: the Bay St. Lucy of tomorrow!"

Lights in the hall went down, and they could have been in a darkened theater, except for the filtered light seeping like dust from the green house beyond the great windows.

The faint rasp of static began echoing through the room, and two vast screens fell from the ceiling.

Lights played across the screens, glowing red, yellow, blue, green—

—then blinding white, as the echo turned into a deep sonorous voice, which surrounded them, leaping in and out of rich orchestral music much as Nina's dolphins leapt into and out of the ocean waves.

The dolphins turned into words, which, playing their way down the coastline in rich orchestral chords, were:

"MEGAVENTURES INCORPORATED
PRESENTS: BAYWORLD! A NEW CONCEPT IN
VACATION EXISTENCE!

The music swelled, thundered, rolled, eddied slightly, then mushroomed into a gigantic cloud of melody, lightning, and avalanche, overwhelming the people below and within it as though it were an avalanche of C chords and violin arpeggios.

Meanwhile buildings began to fill the screen.

Massive buildings.

High rise buildings.

Sandstone in color, they appeared, disappeared, dissolved one into another, opened out, zeroed in, and continually invited, invited, invited, revealing themselves as all that could be conceived in a quest for HAPPINESS HAPPINESS HAPPINESS forever, with everything that might be wanted hovering there before one, waiting to be experienced.

THE NEWEST CONCEPT FROM MEGAVENTURES, BAYWORLD EXPLODES UPON THE BEAUTIFUL GULF COAST WITH A MAGIC ALL ITS OWN, ABSOLUTELY UNIQUE IN ITS RICH BLENDS OF CONCEPTS IN VACATION LIVING HERETOFORE UNHEARD OF, HERETOFORE UNIMAGINED!

—while the images went on.
This screen, that screen.
The huge hotels, Nina could now tell, were to be built exactly on the ocean front.
Where her small shack now stood.
They even had names.
Amber Breeze.
Bayview.
Dolphin Rider.

THE FINEST TREASURES OF BOTH SEA AND LAND: CAPTAIN KIDD'S FISHING PIER, TO BE THE LONGEST ON THE AMERICAN COAST, EXTENDING MORE THAN A MILE INTO THE BEAUTIFUL TURQUOISE WATERS OF THE GULF OF MEXICO! LAGUNA SLIPS, THE WORLD'S MOST LAVISH AND WELL EQUIPPED YACHT HARBOR: DUNES '36, THE FIRST GOLF COURSE IN THE UNITED STATES DESIGNED EXCLUSIVELY BY TIGER WOODS HIMSELF,

AND MEANT TO HOST, IN FALL OF 2016, THE
FIRST 'TIGER WOODS BAYSHORE CLASSIC
GOLF TOURNAMENT,' GRAND PRIZE
WINNINGS OF MORE THAN TWO HUNDRED
THOUSAND DOLLARS!

And there it was on the screens in front of them.
The verdant putting greens overlooking deep blue
ocean vistas. There was Tiger Woods himself, his
beaming visage somehow transplanted to the beach,
with yachts and mega-story hotels behind them.

This all continued for some time.

The music was so loud, and the darkness so
complete, that not much could be ascertained
concerning the response of the audience.

That was probably good, thought Nina, who had
busied herself by counting hotels, and was now up to
five of them.

What had the last been called?

Oh yes.

The Waverider.

It had, she was able to note by looking at the screen
on the right, an indoor Olympic-sized pool on the
twenty seventh floor.

How nice, she found herself thinking.

Wake up in one's room on the fifty fourth floor; do a
few weights and calisthenics in the gym on the forty
third floor; a spot of tea in Burmaland, the small
breakfast restaurant on the twenty ninth floor; and then
finally a nice dip on the twenty seventh floor,
swimming in water while looking down at water.

One could work one's way down, the entire day, the
Jacuzzi on the eighteenth floor, the beauty salon on the
fifteenth floor, the small African Market Place
Specialty Grocery Outlet on the ninth floor, the indoor

driving range on the fourth floor, The Cinema Multiplex Sixteen, on the third floor—

–so that by nine or ten P.M., one would, upon staggering out of the hotel, have only just enough energy left to stagger back in again and take the elevator home, ready to begin the entire descent yet again the following day, following, much like Dante, concentric circles ever deeper into the Hell that was now to be Bay St. Lucy.

AND OF COURSE THE CENTER OF IT ALL! THE PIECE DE RESISTANCE! THE PLACE TO BE SEEN, FOR THE DECADE TO COME! LODESTAR OF CINEMA ICONS TO SPORTS HEROES TO POLITICAL LEADERS TO THE FRANK SINATRAS AND DEAN MARTINS OF THE THE TWENTY FIRST CENTURY---**SEA-VEGAS**, THE MOST OPULENT GAMING CENTER, THE MOST RICHLY DECORATED AND FANTASTICALLY ADORNED CASINO—IN THE WORLD!

And there it was.

There it was, all spread out before them.

The very rooms they had just been walking through.

The dining rooms, the galleries, the sun decks, the porches, the studies—

—these rooms were now being shown on the massive screens, but overlaid with crap tables, roulette wheels, and rows after rows of slot machines.

That was to be the center of Bay St. Lucy.

A casino.

Tom Broussard's words came back to her as the "virtual tour" continued.

"The story is not over until it has taken the worst possible turn of events."

The lights were rising now.

The screen was depicting a sunset and three banally idiotic HAPPYPEOPLE, a robot woman and a robot man and a robot child, all hand in hand, watching the sun set into the waves, not caring that such a thing might be more probable on the Pacific coast than here on the Gulf

"The story is not over until it has taken the worst possible turn of events."

A few more bars of music and then, done.

Lights up.

Movie over.

So the presentation is over, Nina found herself thinking.

But the story is not over.

And the worst possible turn of events—

—is still to come.

For a while there was absolute silence.

Then Allana Delafosse rose.

Very slowly, she lifted her arm, and pointed her hand up at the woman who stood above them:

"What—have you done?"

The tone of the words, the expression on Allana's face—they were all ghastly, as though delivered in the Voice of the Dead, in a combination of supplication and damnation.

"What have you done?"

There they hung, not seeming to have reached the demi-heaven from which Eve Ivory was sending down her decrees, but still some few feet above the graveyard where sat the few corpses that were still remnants of what had been Bay St. Lucy.

"What have you done?"

"I am certain, as I have said, that the proposed plan is—well, a bit of a surprise for many of you."

Paul Cox stood, his body trembling, his voice, being a part of his body, also trembling.

"This is not what we talked about!"

"We talked about a great many things, Paul."

"Not this!"

"This school is here, Paul. It wasn't highlighted in the video clip; but it's included in the plan. There is to be a new school."

And now more and more voices began to rise, like rain inverted, the edge of a squall, the first hard showers, and the coming deluge, all spattering on the podium behind which Eve Ivory stood, repeating:

"There is to be a new school!"

First voice:

"For who?"

"For your children!"

"Our children? Our children?"

"We're not going to be here!"

"Where are we in this plan?"

"What have you done to us?"

"You've destroyed the city!"

"These things are detestable!"

"We don't want a casino here!"

"The Hell with you!"

"Go to Hell!"

"Go to Hell!"

'You won't get away with this!"

"You have no right!"

"You have no right to do this!"

"Who do you think you are?"

"You can't come in here and—"

And then a huge black man appeared beside Eve Ivory.

She did not look at him.

He did not look at her.

He simply looked down at the crowd spread out beneath him.

Many were standing now.

He had on a superb black suit.

His eyes glowered.

And his voice rolled down on the people like thunder.

"That will be enough."

—were his words.

And simultaneously, all of Bay St. Lucy was aware of what "Security People" were all about.

They stood, dark-suited, serious of mien, motionless, like church deacons ready to help at communion, at the end of each row.

Each one had fixed in a rigid stare, Nina realized, every townsperson who had spoken.

Once again Baal, the Dark Archangel, spoke to The Children of Israel-Lucy:

"I'm going to need you all to disperse. There are refreshments being served in the dining room."

Tom Waterston, the mayor, stood and said to Eve Ivory:

"Ms. Ivory I just have to ask, as Mayor of Bay St. Lucy—"

She remained motionless as a statue while the man standing beside her said:

"Sir I'm going to have to ask you to disperse."

"But—"

And suddenly there was with the mayor a whole host of angels, praising God and singing:

"That's enough, Sir."

A security guard in front of him; a security guard behind him.

Both saying:

"We're going to need you to leave the room, Sir."

Which he did.

Which they all did.

CHAPTER ELEVEN: THE TROUBLE WITH WINDOWS

"I have an idea that the phrase 'weaker sex' was coined by some woman to disarm some man she was preparing to overwhelm."

Ogden Nash

For the next few hours all hell broke out in Bay St. Lucy. Everybody did everything and nobody did anything.

Everyone called everyone else, sobbing, yelling, screaming.

Until finally all of the telephone lines were jammed, or busy, or overloaded, even the technicians did not know exactly which, but the bottom line was the phone service went dead.

People met on street corners, yelling insults at Eve Ivory, until the small groups that had formed were approached by police cars, ice-blue lights flashing, bull horns intoning:

"Please disperse. Please disperse."

It took only a few minutes to realize that these were not Bay St. Lucy police vehicles.

They were previously unseen vehicles owned by MEGAVENTURES SECURITY SYSTEMS.

The men and women driving them, and using the bullhorns, were no longer dressed as Jehovah's Witnesses.

They now had on uniforms.

The townspeople gravitated to Margot's garden, where, at precisely 10:30 P.M., Allana Delafosse, could be heard holding forth.

"I have always," she said, "decried the use of the word. It is a *detestable* word, made all the more so by the fact that it is so often used to describe persons of my own gender. It is the most vile word, to my knowledge, in the English language. But in reference to this, to this, 'Eve Ivory,' it is the only applicable word."

She paused to let this sink into the ten or so women who encircled her.

Then she continued.

"The woman, let us admit it, is a complete, unadulterated, pure—"

Pause.

Say it.

Say it, Allana Delafosse.

And then she did:

"The woman is a complete parvenu."

Ooooh.

Aaahh.

No one had ever heard Allana Delafosse use that word before.

And these were the kinds of things that happened. Not simply in Margot's now-all-night-shop and planning/complaining center, but all over town. There was an emergency meeting at City Hall.

A great many measures and counter measures were proposed.

An excellent law firm.

The city would hire an outside law firm.

These land developments could certainly be postponed, perhaps locked up in the courts for years.

Couldn't they, Jackson?

To which Jackson Bennett rose and said:

"No."

It was one of the things, remembered Nina, that Frank had always admired about Jackson.

He was not as wordy as most lawyers.

"But couldn't we petition the Joint Zoning and Revenue Office for a Temporary Stay of—"

"No."

"But Jackson, how can she—"

"She owns it."

Then Jackson Bennett left the Emergency City Hall meeting and went home to his family.

The first report of violence came, apparently, around eleven P.M.

Two citizens—their identities kept secret—were brought to The Bay St. Lucy jail and deposited there for Moon Rivard to incarcerate.

They had apparently tried to 'infiltrate' the grounds of the Robinson Estate, and had, of course, been apprehended by representatives of MEGAVENTURES SECURITY SYSTEMS.

Nothing was known of their physical condition, but an ambulance was observed to arrive at the jail some fifteen minutes later.

The ambulance stayed at the jail some time and then left, with no patients riding in it.

One argument, at least, against those who kept avoiding the professional term 'security specialists' and substituting the unfairly premature—given the fact that the people had been in town only slightly more than twenty four hours and were both newcomers and guests—appellation "thugs and goons."

There were more fights, some of which Nina heard about. There were more small meetings; in fact it was almost like bar-hopping.

Meeting hopping.

One antique store to the other.

Contingency plans.

Rumor control.

Still the stories about violence continued.

Once, enroute from Carol's Sea Fantasies, where nothing had been accomplished, to Joyce's Bed and Breakfast, where nothing had been planned, she and Margot and Emily Fontenot encountered a true Bay St. Lucy police car, driven by the young Cajun who'd come to the restaurant weeks before—how long ago that now seemed! To tell her about the damage done to her shack.

This woman and a male partner now pulled beside them, stopped, and rolled down the window:

"Ladies—"

"Yes, officer!'

"You might want to go inside."

"We're going over to the Bed and Breakfast."

"Yes, Ma'am. Whatever you want, but—it would just be good for you to be inside. It's real bad out there."

"Are there more injuries?"

"I don't know. I think so. We keep getting calls. It's just—these other security people—"

There was a crackle of static on the radio.

"I have to take this. But do try to stay inside."

"We will."

And so it went, until midnight, when Nina drove her Vespa home.

She arrived to find two patrol cars parked in her driveway, and the light burning in her living room window.

"What the—"

Someone was in her house.

She parked the Vespa, noting the now familiar logo of MEGAVENTURES SECURITY SYSTEMS painted on the door of the car nearest her.

She climbed the steps, opened the door, and found Eve Ivory standing in the middle of her living room floor, and glaring at her.

"This! This! All of this! All of what is happening in this town! This is what you were supposed to prevent!"

Shocked, she could only ask:

"How did you get in?"

The question had no effect.

Eve Ivory began to pace now, just as Nina had seen her pace on the morning when she'd discovered her slashed tires.

She was smoking.

Nina had not seen her smoke before, but she did it as viciously as Margot Gavin, except that each gesture, each movement of the cigarette to and from her lips, was short and brutal, like punches to the face.

"You were supposed to prevent this kind of thing!"

The presence of Eve Ivory anywhere and in any condition was such a dominant condition that it blotted out other beings; but seeing her this way was so stunning that it even made Nina completely unaware, for a full fifteen minutes, of the two security guards standing on each side of her.

They looked like the offshore riggers she'd seen; faces impassive, one wearing a blonde goatee, the other wearing a light brown goatee.

"Do you know what's been going on in this town?"

Nina shook her head, still speechless.

"Chaos! Stupidity and chaos!"

"People are upset."

"Then let them be upset, dammit! But they will *not* behave like this! I will *not* be treated this way! I will *not*! Can you comprehend that, you, you, you little dolt?"

The word hit her like punch in the stomach.

She forced herself to stammer back:

"I'm not sure what I can do. I think I told you that before."

"You—you *what?*"

"I said, I think I told you that before."

"Are you contradicting me?"

"No. I just—"

"You are! You are! What is the matter with you, are you insane? Have you lost your mind? Are you an imbecile?"

She tried to think of something to say but could not.

The two men standing on either side of Eve Ivory remained motionless, each looking at the other.

Finally Nina was able to say:

"People think you're going to destroy the town."

Eve Ivory glared at her, hurled the cigarette on the carpet and crushed it out viciously with her shoe. Then she took a step toward Nina and shouted:

"*What* town? *What* town? *What* town? There is not a town here—there is a blight. Look at these shacks along the coastline! It's blight, don't you see that? Do you know what actual coast line is worth today? A million dollars per hundred feet. A MILLION DOLLARS PER HUNDRED FEET! Don't you see that? You look at this this 'village' as you choose to call it. One deserted lot after another. You've been isolated by the world for forty years, it's like some, some insane fairy tale. WELL WAKE UP, YOU IDIOTS!"

She lit another cigarette and continued to pace.

"It was coup, a coup, a coup, to bring Megaventures here. These are billion dollar players we're talking about. They could have gone anywhere in the world.

ANYWHERE! But they're coming here, just because they've been able to see what's happened. A veritable jewel of development potential has been trapped in a damn time machine. This is the last package of coastal property of this kind IN THE WESTERN HEMISPHERE, DON'T YOU SEE THAT?"

"But what if we don't want that?"

To which Eve Ivory, in a voice seeping up out of the ice caves over which she presided, hissed:

"Who the hell cares?"

It was at that moment that Tom Broussard arrived.

She knew it was Tom without turning to look, because of the clatter he made on her stairs, which always threatened to collapse with his weight.

She could not take her eyes from the glaring face of Eve Ivory, so she did not see him, but only heard his voice from just behind her, as he entered.

"Penelope," he said quietly, "is out in the harbor. You need to come."

"What?"

"Some big yacht is out in the basin."

"Who is this?"

"Eve, this is my fried Tom Broussard. He's a writer."

"What is he talking about?"

"A yacht," Tom continued, "has anchored out in the basin."

"My God! That's Bill Shipley! He's the president of Megaventures! He's one of the richest men in the world!"

"Tom," said Nina, quietly, "what's Penelope got to do with it?"

"I guess she heard about the meeting tonight. People heard her saying, 'They'll take my boat away. They won't want me here.' And I guess she was drinking some."

"What is she doing, Tom?"

"She's out in her boat."

"Yes?"

"She's about fifty yards abeam the yacht. Shouting at them. Telling them to get out and leave her alone. Leave Bay St. Lucy alone. She's shouting, you know, the way Pen can do."

"Yes."

"And she's got a gun. The people on the yacht say it's a forty five."

"What?" screamed Eve Ivory. "What is this bumpkin saying? Oh my god!"

Nina turned and faced Tom. His hair was black and tangled; he had on black oilskins, which gleamed from the light of the streetlamps beneath.

He was looking not at Nina, though, but straight into the eyes of the security man standing nearest her.

"This man," said Tom, "is white trash."

The room gave a slight gasp.

Then there was no sound, except a slight patter of rain that had begun to fall.

Tom Broussard took another step into the room.

He was no more than a foot from the first man's face.

Into which he whispered.

"Get out. Get out now."

Eve Ivory screamed at him:

"What? What? Who the hell are you, anyway? *You* get out!"

The second security man turned slightly, and said:

"Sir, we're going to have to ask you to moderate your tone."

To which Tom Broussard replied:

"You're white trash, too."

"Sir—"

"You're both white trash. And you're in the home of a lady."

There was more silence.

Furl, who'd been hiding in a closet, saw his chance, and dashed across the room to hide in the clothes hamper, which was in the bathroom.

Eve Ivory spoke more quietly now; she looked at first one of her security men, then the other.

"Throw him out," she said, quietly.

They both moved simultaneously.

The second was a foot behind, though, and thus too slow to help his colleague, who, having attempted an arm bar and failed, fell heavily into the knee of Tom Broussard. This knee, spinning as it was along with the rest of Tom's body, and rising with immense force not often seen in writers of criminal fiction, was sufficient to jettison the man through the window, which exploded with a crash of splintering glass and the shattering of the cheap metal frame in which it had been encased.

In no more than two seconds, the guard was lying sprawled upon the deck, Tom Broussard standing above him, his boot toe squarely against the man's Adam's apple.

He looked at Eve Ivory and said:

"I've been in a lot of places, lady."

She hissed back:

"So have I."

The second security guard had just slipped a hand into his coat pocket when the staircase rattled again, and Nina noticed for the first time a fresh batch of flashing blue lights in her driveway.

Officer Moon Rivard was walking up the stairs, hatless in the increasing rain, both hands gripping and ungripping his impossible mop of iron-gray hair, a smile spreading across his face.

"Good evening Nina, ma cher! Nice night, ain't it?
Maybe a little rain ahead though. That's what
N'Awleens says. Can't never tell though."

No one answered him.

No one moved.

He opened the door and came into the living room.

Then he stepped through the broken window, bent,
and offered a hand to the prostrate security guard,
whose neck was still connected to the pointed toe of
Tom Broussard's boot.

"Tom, you might want to move your foot a little, so
this boy can stand up."

Tom took a step back.

"Officer, you might want to get up off of Mz. Nina's
porch here."

The man got to his feet, glaring at Tom Broussard,
who glared back.

Moon Rivard stood between them for a time, then
moved back into the living room, where he addressed
Eve Ivory.

"Miss Ivory, if I was you I'd go back home now."

"I'll go," she said, squirting syllables out in a short
thick mixture of arsenic and sputum, "wherever I
want."

"Well you have that right."

"You'd better know I have that right! Now will you
put this hoodlum in jail?"

Moon Rivard shook his head:

"Which one? The one that was on the floor or the
one over here ready to pull a gun?"

"That handgun is licensed."

"I'm sure it is, ma'am. Now will you please go
home?"

She was silent for a time, then said:

"By tomorrow afternoon you will be fired; I promise
you."

"That's as it may be, ma'am. But I ain't fired tonight."

"And what is this idiot talking about, concerning the yacht and the marina?"

"There's a situation, but we're taking care of it."

"What kind of a situation?"

"Like I say, it's under control."

"Do you know who owns that yacht?"

"As it happens, I do know."

"One of the richest men in the world."

"Well, he's certainly welcome here in Bay St. Lucy. Just like everybody else is. Now gentlemen—"

He looked at the security officers:

"Now gentlemen, we Cajuns have a saying that we use sometime, not very often, but when we do use it, it's on occasions like this. Wanna hear it?"

No movement, no answer.

"I'm gonna tell it to you anyway. Goes like this. Listen."

He paused for an instant and then said:

"Go home."

Eve Ivory fumed.

Furl continued to hide.

"If that yacht, or anything on it—"

"Go home."

Silence for two seconds more.

Then she stalked out of the room, the two guards following her.

Nina, Tom, and Moon watched them descend, watched as they entered their car, and watched as the car pulled away.

"That window," said Nina, "just keeps getting broken."

"Sorry about that."

"It's all right, Tom. I thought you were great, by the way."

"Could have gotten shot," he said.

"Well, there's that."

"Miz Nina—"

"Yes, Moon. And by the way, you were pretty great too."

"Just doing my job."

"It's a little harder tonight, I guess."

"Yes, ma'am. But Miz Nina, it might be good if you came along with me."

"To the harbor?"

"Yes'm."

"What's going on?"

"There's a war."

"Between who?"

"Well, the Coast Guard is on one side."

"Who's on the other?"

"Penelope Royale."

"So it's kind of even."

"Yahh, for now. I'm afraid if it gets any worse though, some of dose boys gonna get hurt. Dey spend all the time fighting against drug runners and pirates and bomb terrorists and the like; but they ain't never come up against Miss Penelope."

"Why do you want me there?"

"She askin' for you."

"Well, every day has its little surprises."

"Yes, Mz. Nina."

"Can Tom come, too?"

Moon Rivard looked at Tom, and smiled:

"If he promise he won't hurt nobody."

"I'm harmless," Tom replied.

Moon clapped him on the back.

"Sure you are! Just a big 'ole Cajun boy. What did you do to that 'security' man, anyway?"

"He slipped."

"He did? Well how about that?"

"The rain."

"The rain, sure, de rain! Miz Nina, you ought to keep your porch dryer. Somebody gonna get hurt out there!"

"I'll try to remember. Now let's go save the Armed Services from Penelope."

They walked down the stairs.

CHAPTER TWELVE: BACK TO BATAAN!

"I must go down to the sea again...."

John Masefield

"We may not all have come over on the same ship, but we're all in the same boat now."

Martin Luther King Jr.

The trip from Nina's to the harbor was like driving not through a movie but through the "coming attractions."

Avenue E, between Lee and Eustace, was *The Night of the Living Dead.* People were walking like zombies, here or there, sitting on benches, waving flashlights, and, as far as she could see, killing dogs and eating their flesh.   Stonewall Jackson Avenue, where it crossed Lula Lane, was *Mr. Smith Goes to Washington.* There was a great circle of people, and somebody stood in the center of the circle. He was wearing a United States flag like a banner and waving a handgun. Anemone Lane and Worthington Boulevard was *Elmer Gantry.* There was a similar circle of people, with a similar man in the middle. He carried a Bible instead of a flag, but he also carried a gun.

Nina sat in the front seat, noting with surprise Moon's complete indifference to all these groups.

"Should these people all have guns?"

"Dis is America, my sweet."

"Yes, it is. Yes, it is."

"Besides, you want to go out dere and take de guns from those folks?"

"No."

"Me neither."

"How much damage so far, Moon?" asked Tom Broussard from the back seat.

Moon shook his head:

"Not as bad as you might think. We got the liquor stores closed early. Dat helps."

"What about all this woman's 'security forces'?"

"So far, ain't none of them shot nobody. Can't tell if that's gonna last all night. But I think we got most of them out of town and back at the mansion. That's where they belong tonight."

They passed the corner of William Faulkner and Seaview Lane, which was *Seven Brides for Seven Brothers*. Nobody had a gun and nobody had a flag and nobody had a Bible. There was an accordion player, a fiddle player, and a bass guitar.

Everyone was dancing.

"Now that," Moon Rivard said quietly, "is what I like to see."

They moved through the crowd, several people pounding the two step on the roof of the squad car, which whooped its siren intermittently to the beat of "Ma Jolie Blonde."

"Tell me," said Nina, watching the revelers disappear in the distance, "what happened down here at the harbor."

The radio squawked; Moon picked it up, cackled something back into it, replaced it, and said quietly:

"I don't know everything. First reports I got came half hour ago. I was trying to break off something over on the west side, don't even remember it now. Apparently some damn fool from the government tried to serve some papers on Miss Penelope."

"Tonight?"

"Naw, it happened this afternoon."

"What kind of papers?"

"Far as I can made out, dey told her she couldn't put her boat in the harbor no more. Told her it didn't fit 'regulations,' whatever dose are."

It began to make sense. The president of the richest holiday rental resort industry in the world is sailing in tonight on his private yacht. The sale is not yet complete, the papers not yet signed. If you are Eve Ivory, do you want Penelope Royal's washtub creating a blight on the coastal view?

So call your lawyer, dig through the official town zoning laws—or create your own zoning laws for that matter—and evict Penelope.

Threaten to tow her boat off and sell it for junk.

This is the kind of thing, now, she reminded herself, that will be happening every day, until BAYWORLD opens the BAYS of its WORLD.

Something, she continued to tell herself, would have to be done.

This horrible thing could not be allowed to happen.

The only problem: it was happening.

The scene at the harbor was pandemonium, and the brief previews of other movies had been replaced by the main feature: *War of the Worlds.*

Helicopters swung low over the quay itself, and out into the breakers. They whooped and soared, rotors chopping and whapping and roaring, and threatening to suck in entire flocks of pelicans and seagulls, creating tons of GULLMULCH and PELICANIZER which would then be spread over the harbor.

Coast Guard launches plowed the shallow water, floodlights illuminating black-suited commandoes and divers, all of the crafts resembling PT Boats, looking to sink THE YAMMAMOTO.

THE YAMMAMOTO itself had anchored some two hundred yards offshore, disguised as Penelope Royal's floating bathtub.

Another fifty yards beyond it was a magnificent sailing vessel, whose name, The Sea Breeze, was written in gold cursive letters that were clearly illuminated by lanterns filling the two breasts of a wooden lady who'd somehow gotten herself impaled by the ship's prow.

It was this ship that Penelope Royale, standing upright in the middle of her own vessel and waving what Nina genuinely hoped would not turn out to be but of course did turn out to be, a forty-five automatic.

A shouting match between Penelope and a ring of bullhorns encircling her was in full force.

"MA-AM! YOU MUST PUT DOWN YOUR WEAPONS!"

—said the bullhorns.

"_____!!"

—said Penelope.

The match was pretty even.

"Come on, Mz. Nina," said Moon Rivard, helping her out of the car.

The three of them climbed down to the wharf, slipping slightly on the moss-covered concrete as rain intensified.

Nina rebuked herself silently for not bringing rain gear, but, given the fact that one of her best and oldest friends was about to be blown apart by seven fifty-meter howitzers, she felt she could be forgiven.

"Here. Down here. Into the launch."

"Ma'am?"

"Yes?"

"Are you Ms. Bannister?"

"Yes, I am."

"I'm Lieutenant J. G. Brewster, US Coast Guard!"

"Nice to meet you."

"Is that your friend out there?"

I never saw her in my life, thought Nina.

"Yes," said Nina.

"Do you realize she is in grave danger?"

Never would have suspected it, thought Nina. *The torpedo launchers, assault helicopters, fifty-caliber machine guns, grenade launchers, and water cannons, gave me no hint at all.*

"Yes, I do."

"You realize she is armed?"

"Yes."

"Did you know she was in the habit of carrying a handgun with her on her boat?"

Yes. No.

She does carry a little, easily hidden, practically harmless, forty-five caliber automatic, like any lady might carry in her purse.

But she only uses it to blow apart dog sharks.

And anybody from the government.

Those were the precise, correct answers.

But maybe not the ones she needed to give.

What were those answers?

Well, actually there weren't any, so it was good of Moon Rivard to intervene.

"Son," he said. "This lady has come here to try to de-fuse this situation. Don't you think you better stop interrogating her and let her get out there?"

"I don't," said the officer, "know that I'm authorized to do so. That's a very dangerous situation out there. Ma'am—"

"Yes?"

"Are you certain you understand what you're getting into?"

"Yes, I understand."

"And you're willing to do this?"

"Yes."

He breathed deeply, sighed, seemed to weigh the prospect of utilizing Naval ordinance (guns) on a middle-aged woman and a middle-aged something-like-woman, as opposed to sending Nina out into the middle of The Battle of Guadalcanal—and finally decided on the latter.

"All right. You can go."

And so it was that Nina, with Moon Rivard on one side of her and some utterly harmless policewoman on the other, found themselves lurching through ever stronger swells, rain pelting them in the face, and helicopters swooping like eagles made from dysfunctional erector sets above them—

—heading out toward Penelope Royale, who stood just as she'd been for the last half hour—Captain Ahab in the face of THE GREAT WHITE RICHMAN'S BOAT.

Finally they were close enough.

Their own launch cut its engines.

Penelope saw them.

Gun still gripped tightly in one hand, she cupped the other around her mouth and yelled:

"Nina!?"

"Yes!"

"Nina, they —!"

"I know, Pen. I know."

"I —! And if —, then —!"

The driver of the launch, young and inexperienced, blanched. His face had turned ashen, and was horror stricken.

"He hasn't," the policewoman said, "ever been around Penelope."

Moon Rivard said grimly:

"There are some tough things you got to learn on this job."

"Pen, can we pull up alongside? I have to talk to you!"

"—!"

"Yes, I promise."

"Then —!"

"I know."

"—!"

"That won't happen."

"—."

"No, I'm sure."

"—!!"

"I'm coming aboard now, Pen."

And, with Moon helping to steer the craft, they locked onto Penelope's boat.

Boarding was harder than she expected, perhaps because of the increased rocking of the waves, perhaps because of a slight psychological alienation created by the repeated sound of the loudspeaker saying:

WE ARE PREPARED TO OPEN FIRE! WE ARE PREPARED TO OPEN FIRE!

But after a while, there she was, standing now, right beside Penelope, arm around her waist, facing, as Penelope was facing, a complete circle of naval gunboats.

"So," she said to the woman standing beside her, "How've you been, girl?"

Penelope, standing like a statue of George S. Patton, did not answer.

The bullhorns did, however, saying in an intimate kind way:

LOWER YOUR FIREARM OR WE WILL BEGIN FIRING!

"Nina—"

Finally Penelope was at least saying something.

"Yes, Pen?"

I'm sorry I asked for you—I just couldn't think of anybody else."

"It's all right."

"I'm sorry for getting you into this."

"No, don't worry. The truth is, I had run out of something to read. I was going to spend the evening with a Ruth Rendall, but I realized I'd read it already. So I thought, 'Why not go out and stand in the middle of a ring of thirty five-millimeter bazookas?' And just as I was thinking that, the call came that you were here. Isn't it funny how those things work somehow."

"They can't make me go, Nina."

"I know."

"They don't have that right."

"No, they don't."

"Who is this woman?"

"I don't know, Pen. None of us do, really."

"They say she's going to destroy the town."

"Well, she can't do that."

"Who's going to stop her?"

"We will."

"How?"

"I don't know, but we will"

"How can we stop her, Nina?"

"We can stop her, because we'll fight her together."

LAY DOWN YOUR WEAPONS OR WE WILL OPEN FIRE!

"Oh, shut up!" shouted Nina.

Then she said to Penelope:

"They're so intrusive. Just because they have all those torpedoes and machine guns and nuclear rockets and things, they think they're All of That. Can you imagine?"

"I won't let them move me, Nina."

"No. Nobody's going to move you."

"How can you know?"

"I know."

"But look all around us. Look at those guns."

"Yeah, I see them."

"How can we fight them?"

"We'll find a way."

Then she was aware of Penelope, looking at her:
"Will we?"

"Yes, we will, Pen. Because we're the community.
As long as we trust each other, and look out for each
other, and believe in each other—nobody in the world
can touch us. Not even the Big Bad US Navy."

Penelope Royale looked at her for an instant, and
Nina realized that either the rain was truly harder now,
or that Penelope was crying.

She'd never seen Penelope cry before.

Of course a lot of things were happening tonight that
she'd never seen before.

IF YOU DO NOT PUT DOWN YOUR WEAPONS
WE WILL BE FORCED TO—

"ALL RIGHT ALL RIGHT ALL RIGHT!" she
screamed back, simultaneously waving for Moon to
come pick them up and kicking the forty-five
automatic, which Penelope had placed on the bottom of
the boat, over to the side. ALL RIGHT ALREADY.
WILL YOU STOP BEING SO PICKY?"

And within minutes, they were heading back to
shore.

Once there, they were met by several thousand
people, all of them serious and all of them useless.

There were local policemen and federal policemen
and military policemen and doctors and reporters and a
lot of other people, all wondering what to do with
Penelope.

"You can't take her to jail, Moon."

"I have to, Miz Nina."

It's Penelope. She can't spend the night in jail."

"I got no choice."

"Let me stay here with her, at her place on the wharf."

"She pulled a gun on Federal officers."

"No she didn't. Well, technically she did, but it was only a forty-five automatic."

"Miz Nina—"

"And look at what they had! Moon, she was fighting the whole US Navy! Doesn't a woman have the right to defend herself? What's she supposed to use against nuclear torpedoes, a can of pepper spray?"

"Miz Nina—"

"Look, there are five policewomen, all from here in Bay St. Lucy, all surrounding Pen. If you could promise to keep them all here, all keeping guard on her—"

"I don't know if I have the authority, Miss."

"Try! And I promise that I'll stay here too. Five local police officers!"

"Well. I do know that Head Fed. Him and me go coon hunting together."

"And you guys have priority over the military, don't you?"

"Yeah. Far as that goes."

"Please, Moon. Just let us all stay here with Pen tonight. And we'll bring her in tomorrow."

"Well—"

"We've got to stick together now, Moon. All of us in Bay St. Lucy."

"Ok, I'll go and talk to him."

He was gone, and in an instant Nina was in the circle of policewomen and Penelope.

"Nina, don't let them take me."

"They won't."

"I can't go to jail."

"You're going to stay here tonight. We all are."

"Are you sure."

"Yeah. Moon and I have fixed it up."

"Thank you, Nina. You're still my teacher."

"Yes. Well."

"I'm sorry I broke that thing in the fifth grade."

"It's ok. It was just a swing set."

"Miz Nina—"

Moon Rivard.

Let this be good news.

"Miz Nina, we probably all gonna get fired. But he says, long as we keep the five officers here tonight—we gonna let her stay here."

"Moon, I love you!"

"Well, dey's another reason, I gotta be honest wid you."

"What's that?"

"The damn jail is full. No place to put anybody. We got to promise to bring her in first thing tomorrow though."

"You have my word."

"I know I do, ma cher. I know I do. Wait a minute. Getting a call here. Gotta answer this."

He took his call, and Nina turned to give the good news to Penelope.

She took a deep breath, and, watching Moon's face illuminated green by the light from his walkie talkie, kept trying to force from her mind the words Tom Broussard had told her weeks earlier:

The story is not over until it has taken the worst possible turn of events.

The story is not over until it has taken the worse possible turn of events.

Moon Rivard closed his walkie talkie, took two steps toward her, and, in a voice like Hamlet's gravedigger, said:

"We may have to rethink a few things."

"What?"

"We may have to do things—different now."

"Why? Moon, you can't take her in! You promised!"

He shook his head.

"It don't matter no more about her."

"What are you saying?"

"It don't matter no more about Miss Penelope. Stay here or go there; ain't nobody studying up on Miss Penelope no more. Not tonight. Not tonight, anyway."

"Why?"

"Because, Miz Nina, I just got a call: Eve Ivory is dead. Murdered."

CHAPTER THIRTEEN: THE STORY IS NOT
OVER UNTIL—

"I hate small towns because once you've seen the cannon in the park there's nothing else to do."

Lenny Bruce

With the death of the Wicked Witch of the West—or East or South or North or wherever it was that Eve Ivory had come from—the spell that had inebriated Bay St. Lucy, turning it, for at least some rogue hours into a standing yelling cursing dancing bacchanal, was broken.

No one knew precisely why.

News of the murder was kept strictly confidential.

Moon Rivard knew some details, which he steadfastly refused to share with either Nina or Tom during their somber ride back from the wharf, where Penelope Royale had been embedded, under house arrest, for the night, with only two young women officers in charge of her.

No one else seemed to know anything.

And yet the streets had become deserted.

Nina looked at her watch: twelve fifteen AM.

It was as though the midnight chiming of St. Mary's cathedral bells had lifted the curse.

Everyone had come to whatever senses remained, and begun to skulk home.

No more rallies with flags and Bibles. No more shouting and running about. No more dancing.

Just the pale moon overlooking the town and the quiet bay, and just the occasional flash of blue as local patrol cars crawled along the streets.

Nina remained persistent in her attempts to learn something, anything.

"How did this happen, Moon?"

But he, grim faced as she had never seen him, hands gripping the steering wheel, merely shook his head:

"Can't say anything right now, Miss."

"Is she dead?"

"Yes. That's the report."

"How?"

"I can't talk about it. I don't really know."

"Where did it happen?"

"I can't tell you that, Miz Nina."

"Who did it?"

"Can't say."

"Do they know who did it?"

By this time the squad car had traversed most of the three miles between the wharf and Nina's shack. She could see the light glowing in her living room, just behind the now permanently—it seemed—broken window, as Moon growled his rejoinder, or more like his supplication:

"Ms. Nina, we got a tough night in front of us, I think."

She was quiet for a time, watching the streetlights crawl by, and becoming aware of what seemed a curious green glow that had spread over town, as though the deserted streets were now the result of some foreign gas settling on the pavement and not merely the onset of social sanity.

"I know we do, Moon."

"So I gotta give you some orders now."

"All right."

"You and Tom go back and stay inside tonight. Do you both understand that? Whatever happened, has happened. Ain't nothing neither of you can do about it. Tom, you think you might stay here tonight, with Miz Nina? I mean, maybe sleep on the porch or something?"

"Sure."

"It's not that I think anybody's gonna try to come round here. But all kinds of crazy things are happening out there. I ain't seen nothing like this in Bay St. Lucy since—"

He did not have to mention the shootings at the mansion, all those years ago.

"—well, since a long time."

"Moon, you really can't tell us anything?"

"I'm sorry, ma'am. Maybe by tomorrow we'll all know something. So. Here we are. I'm gonna say good night to both of you now."

"Goodnight, Moon."

"Goodnight, Moon."

She found herself thinking, stupidly, of a children's book.

"You both gonna go up there and try to get some sleep, right?"

They watched him drive away.

They waited two minutes, pacing in a tight circle beneath the street light outside Nina's porch. Then they got on her Vespa, with Tom driving, and puttered their way out toward Breaker's Boulevard, heading for the sheriff's office.

She had her arms tightly around him, her chin jutting up against his jacket.

She could still talk though.

"Tom, slow it down! Slow it down!"

"All right! I'm sorry!"

She could feel the pace decelerate.

Finally, she could hear better, and asked:

"How fast were you going?"

"I had gotten it up," he said, "to twenty five."

"Are you crazy?"

"I'm sorry."

"Do you want to get us killed?"

"No."

"I don't want to be a vegetable!"

"I know. It's all right now, though."

"How fast are you going now?"

"It's around fifteen."

"Okay, but keep it there. Do you think she's really dead?"

He shook his head:

"I can't see how. She had fifty armed security police surrounding her."

"Who could have done it?"

"Watch out—turning here!"

"Oh my God! Be careful!"

"It's all right. I got it."

"I'm getting dizzy. You shouldn't take those turns at more than ten miles per hour."

"I know. It's just my old gang days coming back."

"I should have driven."

"I'll try and keep it down."

"Who do you think could have done it?"

"Well, everybody would like to have done it. As for who actually did—your guess is as good as mine."

There was a strange, somber scene at the sheriff's office, which was located in the exact middle of downtown Bay St. Lucy.

It was the World of Late Night Revelry inverted.

Because prisoners, rather than being arrested and booked into the cells, as they might have been after a night's drinking during early morning hours—were being disgorged from the jail, which vomited them forth at regular intervals, into the waiting arms of embarrassed family members, who stuffed them into station wagons and pickup trucks and drove them away.

Tom parked the Vespa at the edge of Magnolia Park, some fifty yards from the entrance to the jail itself.

They sat on a bench, secure behind one of the spreading live oak branches which, huge, ninety years old, and crawling along the ground, served as a reminder of as much permanence as Bay St. Lucy was likely to get this night.

They could, in short, not be seen.

"What's going on?" she asked.

"They're letting prisoners go."

"What prisoners?"

"Probably people they picked up earlier tonight. All those gatherings, shouting matches, you know."

"Yeah. But why are they letting them go?"

Tom shrugged:

"They want the jail empty."

She nodded.

They waited.

It took perhaps ten minutes.

It was a non-descript patrol car, that pulled to the glowing doorway of the jail. Only one car.

"Wouldn't they have needed more people involved in this thing, Tom, if it was a murder?"

"They wouldn't want to call attention to themselves. They don't want a parade."

"No."

The car door opened. Two officers exited either side of the front seat. One opened the rear door, bent down, and emerged leading a hooded figure, so completely wrapped in a bright orange jump suit as to be unrecognizable.

"Who is that, Tom?"

"Can't tell."

Within ten seconds the figure was inside.

The building remained implacable.

"What do we do now?" she asked.

"We could go home, back to your place."

"Yes."

"There's probably not much good we can do here."

"No."

"Moon told us to stay home."

"Yes."

"We probably should have listened to him."

"Yes."

There was silence for a time.

"So what," she asked, "do we do now?"

"I don't know."

"We have to," she said, "find out who they're holding."

"Why?"

"Because," she said, "right now, the way it is, we don't know."

He nodded.

"I guess that's logical. Look! Who's that?"

Another vehicle arrived, this one a large white van.

Jackson Bennett got out and walked into the jail.

"All right," whispered Nina. "Now we're getting somewhere."

"What do you mean?"

"Whoever it is needs a lawyer. And he got Jackson."

More vehicles began to arrive. First came a Megaventures' Security van. Two men got out of it.

"Isn't one of those characters the guy you beat up?"

"I don't know," he said, shaking his head. "They all look pretty much alike."

Yet another car arrived, this one a dark blue limousine.

From this one a woman emerged, tall, bespectacled, beige-suited.

"Edie Towler," whispered Nina. "City Attorney."

"This is all going kind of slow," whispered Tom.

"Probably they're being careful. If this woman was–
–murdered."

"I'm having such trouble saying that word."

"Get over it."

"Yes. Well, if she was in fact the *m* worded, it's a
huge story. Millions of dollars are at stake here."

"Think again."

"Why?"

"You're too low."

"More than millions?"

"Try a billion or so."

"Are you sure about that, Tom?"

He shrugged.

"I have my sources."

"Well. Anyway, they can't let this get to be a water
carnival. Whoever did the killing has got to be booked,
fingerprinted—"

"Arraigned first, then fingerprinted. You're telling
me my business here."

"Yes," she answered. "Well, anyway, they probably
want to get this person out of town as quick as possible,
so they can hold him somewhere safe."

"Him?"

"I always think 'him' when something terrible
happens."

"Well, you may be right."

"Anyway, when word gets out that somebody has
killed Eve Ivory—"

"There's going to be celebrating in the streets."

"Why, Tom?"

"Why? Why? Because the town is saved, that's
why."

"How do you mean?"

"Because the lineage ends with that woman! The situation reverts to what it was when you went to New Orleans!"

"But—but—a town can't profit from a crime!"

"Of course it can! An *individual* can't profit from a crime; but a town? Towns only exist in the first place because of crimes. If there weren't crimes, there wouldn't even be any towns. Our town is just committing its crime a little bit later, and with some poor proxy to act as a defendant, and, maybe, with a little bad luck, go to the gas chamber."

"Tom, don't—"

"Look! Who's that?"

The door opened and a tall, trench coated figure emerged.

"That," Nina whispered, "is Jackson Bennett. Come on."

"You think he'll talk to us?"

"He'll talk to us."

They were halfway across Sans Souci Park before he saw them.

He stood, incredulous, as they approached.

"Nina?"

"Yes, Jackson."

"What are you doing here? And who is this?"

"This is Tom Broussard. He's a writer and a friend of mine."

"All right, but Nina, you shouldn't be here!"

"What's going on, Jackson?"

"I can't tell you that!"

"Sure you can."

"No, I'm an officer of the court! I'll be disbarred if I talk about this!"

"Everybody's going to know in the morning anyway."

"But not from me!"

"Is it true, Jackson? Is Eve Ivory dead?"

"Nina, I just can't—"

"Jackson, you remember that first year, when you didn't think you were going to make it as a lawyer, and Frank kept encouraging you, and encouraging you?"

He was quiet for a time, and then said:

"Of course I remember that year, Nina. But even Frank wouldn't—"

"We could go over to your office right now. Nobody would know."

"But—"

"Frank, I'll be honest with you. A month ago, I wouldn't have cared. A month ago I was just retired old Nina. And you invited me to your office."

"Yes, I know."

"And you persuaded me to go to New Orleans."

"Yes."

"The elder statesperson of the town, you wanted to call me, and didn't, only because you didn't want to say the word 'old'."

A smile played around his lips.

"You aren't that old."

"But I'm in this up to my neck now, Jackson. My house was vandalized; this woman stood in my living room no more than three hours ago, and told me I was responsible for everything that was happening around town."

"That's not true, of course."

"Maybe not. But true or not, I have a right to know what's happened."

He was silent for a time.

In the distance, more sirens could be heard.

"I guess," he said, quietly, "you may be right. The two of you be in my office in five minutes."

Then he got in his car and pulled away.

The rain had begun again shortly before one A.M. Nina could hear it softly pattering on the roof of Jackson's office, and she could imagine in impinging with its little needle droplets on the December garden plots of Bay St. Lucy, readying them for spring plantings.

It was, she found herself thinking, *so strange, to be seated in this same chair, the one where she had received her 'commission' to fly over to New Orleans and perform the 'easy' task of listening to a non will.*

So much had happened since then—

The small office then had been bathed in morning sunlight; now it glowed in what seemed almost like candle light, the green-shaded lamps humming along with a scarcely perceptible buzz of central heating.

They were all seated; Tom beside her, Jackson, large and imposing, behind his desk.

"What happened, Jackson?"

"You must promise me, that you were never here tonight."

"All right."

"This will all come out. But it did not come out from this office."

"Go ahead, Jackson."

He took a deep breath, then launched forth.

"Eve Ivory was murdered tonight, in her bedroom, at the Robinson mansion, at approximately eleven twenty two P.M."

"How?"

"She was stabbed in the neck by a letter opener."

"By whom?"

"Macy Peterson."

"What?"

"Macy Peterson."

"That's insane!"

"No."

"Jackson, Macy Peterson couldn't hurt a fly!"

"Perhaps. But she stabbed Eve Ivory to death."

"This is—this is a mistake!"

He shrugged:

"I wish it was. I wish to heaven it was."

"How do you know this, Jackson?"

"I've just been asked to defend her."

"Did you accept?"

"Of course I did."

"Then you must know she's innocent!"

"I can't say, one way or another."

"What do you mean you can't say? Jackson, Macy Peterson is the gentlest person in the world! What—what makes anybody think she could have done this thing?"

"What makes people think she could have done this thing, Nina, is she was found there."

"Where?"

"The woman's bedroom."

"Okay, for some reason she was in Eve Ivory's bedroom. But that doesn't mean she killed her!"

"Nina, two security men heard screams. They thought Ms. Ivory was screaming. They ran to the door, opened it—and saw Macy Peterson, kneeling beside Eve Ivory's desk. Eve Ivory was dead. Blood was everywhere, still spouting from her neck—out of which Macy Peterson had just pulled a letter opener."

"It had," Tom Broussard said quietly, "Macy's fingerprints on it?"

Jackson glowered at him:

"It had her fingerprints on it," he rumbled, "because she was holding it her hand! There was nobody else in the room! She couldn't stop screaming—and she had just finished stabbing the woman repeatedly in her jugular vein."

There was nothing to say.

The rain intensified, and began rattling on the window beside the desk.

"She did it, Nina. Macy Peterson murdered Eve Ivory."

CHAPTER FOURTEEN: RUMOR

Rumour, compared with whom no other is as swift
She flourishes by speed, and gains strength as she goes.
She flies, screeching, by night through the shadows,
Between earth and sky, never closing her eyelids.

Virgil, *The Aeneid*

A startlingly beautiful multi-millionairess who held the future of Bay St. Lucy in the palm of her hand had just been murdered by the town's most popular young schoolteacher, stabbed repeatedly in the neck as an act of brutal vengeance for the fact that she, the dead woman, had been engaged in a torrid sexual affair with the fiancé of the murderess, the town's most vaunted ex-quarterback and current director of schools.

There was a chance, of course, that this would not be much talked about.

There was a chance that at seven o'clock, at eight o'clock, and nine o'clock, etc., in shops such as Martel's Beauty Supplies, Rosen's By the Sea, Comeuax's Bed and Breakfast, Claire's Shell Designs, Amanda's Pottery Creations, and Just Odds and Ends by Rosette—nothing would be discussed save the nation's affairs at large, the danger of the fiscal cliff, the possible revolution in Syria, the problems involving drilling regulations in Alaska, and the always bothersome issue of global warming.

What actually happened though was that none of these issues, pressing as they were (and continue to be), were talked about at all.

So that, when Nina walked into Margot's shop at 9:15 (She'd been driven back to her shack by Jackson at 2:30, paced until 4, read until 4:05, listened to sirens until 4:30, paced until 6, and blissfully, fallen asleep until 8:30—after which she'd taken a breakfast of sort, gotten dressed of sorts, and wandered like a zombie into town)—when she walked after all of this into Margot's shop, she found herself confronted by a group of people, mostly women—well, actually, all women—who immediately stopped talking about the murder, which was all they had been talking about, looked at her, and asked, as one:

"Did you hear what happened?"

To which she, still somewhat stunned, replied:

"Can I have a cup of coffee?"

She was seated, brought coffee, and asked again:

"Did you hear what happened?"

And, before she could say she did know what happened; that Eve Ivory was murdered and that she knew who murdered Eve Ivory, and where, and what time, and with what instrument—

—she was told all of these things.

But erroneously.

Delia Comeaux, proprietor of Delia's Treasures on the Beach, was the first to be wrong, though not, ultimately, the loudest.

"Macy Peterson shot her."

"She—what?" asked Nina, instantly regretting having said anything at all and wishing for Furl.

"What did she do?"

"Shot her. Right through the heart!"

There was no point in saying anything now. It was like she'd always imagined riding out a hurricane would be, say, from her own deck. There would be no point in speaking, one's voice being both inaudible to the wind and not listened to anyway by the water.

One would only be able to watch.

But it would, at that, be quite interesting.

False statements began to come now from people standing all over the shop, from the calendar area to the pottery area to the dishware area, and even from the "silly shirt" area.

"I heard she shot her in the head!"

"No. The heart. Direct hit. One shot."

"It was out in the garden, wasn't it?"

"I heard it was in the kitchen. And Eve Ivory shot first. It was her gun. Macy took it away from her in the struggle."

"Where is Macy now?"

"In the hospital."

"In New Orleans, I heard."

"Yes. They care-flighted her out last night."

"Where was Paul during all this?"

"Paul was in bed with Eve!"

"Really?"

"Of course! They were doing it when Macy walked in and surprised them!"

"No wonder she murdered the woman!"

"Except I heard she broke a bottle of champagne on the bedstead and cut Eve's throat!"

"That's exactly the way I heard it!"

"But what about the gun? She did shoot Eve, didn't she?"

"Only after Eve shot her first; but Eve was bleeding so bad, she couldn't see."

"What did Paul do?"

"He tried to get the knife away, or so I heard, and that's when *he* got cut!"

"So Paul is the one who's in the hospital?"

"No, Paul is the one who's being care-flighted to New Orleans."

"Poor man."

"Poor man indeed! He's the cause of it all!"

"What about the dog?"

"What?"

"I heard there was a dog involved!"

"Is that what you heard?"

"Yes, it was on the news!"

"What program did you hear it on?"

"Morning Recipes."

"Well, they're usually pretty good."

"I didn't hear any of that about the gun and the knife and the champagne bottle and the naked Paul; I heard they fought in the kitchen and Macy killed her with a paring knife."

"Who told you that?"

'My daughter. She got texted at three in the morning by her ex-boyfriend."

"I thought he was in New Orleans."

"No. Seattle."

"Did you hear about the fire?"

'No, I hadn't heard that!"

"Half of the mansion burned down!"

"How?"

"Macy set the curtains on fire!"

This went on for an interminable amount of time, or at least until Nina had finished one cup of coffee.

Then, having satisfied herself that the people in the shop were no longer attempting to explain anything to her but simply writing their own romance novels and publishing them both orally and in a format that was, thankfully, instantaneously extinguishable and never to come again—she gestured to Margot.

"Come here."

"Where?"

"Come back into the garden."

"But it's more fun here!"

"Come back into the garden."

"But—"

"Come."

She took her friend's arm and led her back into the part of the shop where the two of them were used to sitting in the morning.

In a second they were facing each other across the familiar wrought iron table.

"Macy," she said quietly, "did kill Eve Ivory. She did it with a letter opener. She stabbed her in the neck."

Margot stared at her:

"Nina! That's the most ridiculous thing I've ever heard!"

"But I—"

"Nina, you've got to stop spreading outlandish rumors like that!"

"Margot, Tom and I—"

"You're going to get yourself into a lot of trouble! That's the way crazy stories get started you know!"

She looked at Margot for a time, then nodded and said:

"You're right."

"Now. Promise you won't go wandering around town talking about things you don't understand!"

"I promise."

"Good! Now come back into the shop and listen. Maybe you can learn something."

"No. I want to go home."

She rose, made her way across the garden, and was halfway out of the shop when the door opened before her, the little bell tinkled, and Moon Rivard walked in.

It was certain, the first time he'd ever been in Margot's Treasures by the Sea, and probably the first time he'd ever found himself encircled by thirty women, all of them speaking fluent fiction as fast as they could.

He took two steps into the room, looked around, horrified, gained some sense of composure, and finally said to Nina:

"Miz Nina, you need to come with me, ma cher. Macy's asking for you."

Every eye in the store became riveted on her.

She had immediately become the most admired woman in the village.

From ten feet behind her, she heard a loud 'crash' that was the sound of Margot's mouth falling open and her bottom lip falling on the floor.

"All right," she said, quietly. "I'm coming."

There was massive, intense, continuous, passionate, silent, applause as she made her way out of the store.

Even as she got into the police car, her ears were ringing from the utter silence behind her.

CHAPTER FIFTEEN: MACY'S STORY

*"The best thing about living in small towns is that, when you don't know what
you're doing, someone else does."*

Author Unknown

The confusion concerning Macy Peterson's whereabouts, though prevalent throughout Margot Gavin's store, was not shared by all residents of Bay St. Lucy.

Many of them—and the number was growing—knew exactly where she was.

She was in the city jail.

Around which a crowd of people was growing.

It now numbered more than two hundred souls, who, fluxing and ebbing in an amoeba-like mass, were creating some consternation in the small line of local officers assigned to keep order.

The officers, as it happened, needed not worry.

For this was not an angry crowd.

This was not a lynch mob, but more a PTA crowd; it was not a protest crowd but more a Methodist Church Fifth Sunday crowd.

This was a crowd that had brought casseroles.

For it was, incomprehensibly but undeniably, a fact that in many small villages grief demanded food. The ceremonies marking death, burial, and mourning were invariable accompanied by both soft music and deviled eggs.

If the deceased did not have an appetite, the deeply aggrieved almost certainly did.

So that pre- and post-burial get-togethers were held in small frame homes, the ante rooms, living rooms, kitchens, bedrooms, and screened in porches of which were cluttered with coffee tables, upon which were piled platters of:

Deviled eggs.

Ravioli Florentine.

Buttered squash.

Potato salad.

Chicken salad.

Mashed potatoes.

Brown cream gravy.

Eggplant au gratin.

Fried Chicken.

String Beans and rice casserole.

Green Pea salad.

Cucumber salad.

Sliced turkey.

Lasagna.

Fried butterfly shrimp.

Okra delight.

Gumbo.

Stroganoff.

And various desserts.

Along with iced tea, both sweetened (though not in The North) and unsweetened.

This was the scene surrounding the Bay St. Lucy jail at ten A.M., as Moon Rivard and Nina arrived.

It was a kind of festive atmosphere.

Food was everywhere, and people were eating it.

There were hand-painted placards held high, reading:

WE LOVE YOU, MACY!

And—

WE'RE WITH YOU, MACY PETERSON!
—causing Nina to say:

"What in God's name is going on here?"

Moon, leading her through the crowd, could only shake his head:

"The woman she killed was not too popular."

Nina, turning down a paper cup filled with almond succotash, tried to focus on reality, and said:

"Macy didn't kill anybody. You know that."

"I'm not sure; to tell you the truth, it don't look too good for her."

"Well," she said, entering the building, "at least she won't starve."

"No ma'am. That's the truth."

The receiving area of Bay St. Lucy's jail resembled all government offices anywhere in the world. There was a desk and, behind that desk, several tables with computers on top. The colors in the room were all not-quite gray, not-quite pink, or not-quite brown.

It was, in short, like all other government offices, a horribly horribly horribly depressing place to be and it made Nina feel now, as at all other times in the past, that she would rather have been transported instantly to some gayer place, like the waiting room of an emergency ward.

"Nina!"

Edie Towler emerged from one of the back rooms, approached the counter, and extended a hand:

"Nina, thank you for coming!"

Edie led her into the bowels of the city jail, where Jackson was already waiting. Another officer was sitting at a side table, fiddling with a tape recorder.

In what seemed no more than a minute later, Macy herself, still wearing an orange jump suit that made her look like a member of the County Road Crew, was brought in.

She hurled herself into Nina's arms, and for a time they simply stood in front of Edie's desk, mutually sobbing. She looked terrible, thought Nina.

Of course, what would she be expected to look like?

Her hair was disheveled, her eyes sunken, the remnants of makeup smeared here and there—

—*there was no way,* thought Nina, *she could make any kind of a statement.*

But at least Edie was thoughtful enough to let her sit there, composing herself as best she could.

Finally, with an incredible display of effort, the poor woman managed to smile at Nina.

"Sorry to make you come."

"That's all right."

"I just—I just—"

Then more sobbing.

More patience from Edie, who, after a time, spoke over the gentle weeping sound to say to Nina:

"Macy has been asking for you for some time now."

"I understand."

"Obviously she feels very close to you, Nina."

"I know."

Nina smiled at Macy, who did not see the gesture, since her face, quivering, was buried in her palms, which were also quivering.

"We need to take your statement, Macy," said Edie. "We just want your side of what happened. We're going to read you your rights, and record your statement." Macy glanced at Jackson, who nodded.

The tape recorder was turned on, the rights were read, and Macy began to speak.

"All right. I guess it started after that meeting."

"The one at the mansion," said Edie, gently, probing, but gently—

"Yes. When Eve—when that woman—"

"We know. We know about the meeting. Now go on."

"Well. Paul was furious."

"Paul Cox."

"Yes. Paul felt betrayed. He kept cursing at her—"

"At Eve Ivory?"

"Yes."

"When was he cursing her?"

"In the car, on the way home."

"To your home?"

"Yes. He had to take me home."

"You didn't go to his home?"

"No. He said he had to go to some meetings. Emergency meetings. The school board. I don't know."

"All right. Go on."

"But he did drop me at home, and he told me to stay there. He said the town might be going crazy, after what –that woman—had said. He said, just stay in bed."

"Okay."

"And I was going to do that. I'd drunk a glass of milk and was getting ready to get into my pajamas, when the phone rang."

"The phone?"

"Yes. I wasn't expecting a call, and Paul had just left—so I let it ring several times. I didn't know who it might be. Finally I picked it up, though, and it was—it was her!"

Jackson, Nina noted, bent forward upon hearing this.

Of course there was nothing surprising in that, she realized, because she herself was leaning forward.

"It was who?"

"It was that woman."

"Eve Ivory?"

"Yes."

"Eve Ivory called you?"

"Yes."

"Macy," asked Jackson, 'what time was this?'"

"I'm not sure exactly."

"About what time?"

"Maybe about—well it would have had to be about—eleven o'clock."

"All right, Macy," said Edie Towler, "just go on."

"She said—and I remember it very clearly—she said, 'Is this Macy Peterson?' I told her it was. She said, "This is Eve Ivory." I was—well, kind of shocked—I didn't know exactly what to say. But she went on and said: 'We need to talk about Paul. He and I are lovers. It can't go on this way. We need to talk."

Several molecules of dust came crashing from the ceiling down to the floor.

Nothing else made a sound.

Nina thought she could hear herself breathing.

Then she realized she was holding her breath, and that the clatter from inside her body must have been something else, maybe blood running through veins, arteries, etc.

"She told you that she had made love to Paul Cox?"

"Yes."

"Macy, had Paul ever told you this?"

"No. He said they had met, and that she had offered to hire him. But I asked him straight out, 'Paul, does this woman mean anything to you?' And he said 'no'."

"Macy," asked Nina, "when did you ask him this?"

"On the morning after the shower. You know—you and I talked that night."

"Yes."

"And that morning we—well, we made everything all right."

The phantom forty five minutes, thought Nina.

"She said, I had to come over. I didn't know what to do. I said that probably wasn't a good idea. But she was—crazy sounding, kind of."

Nina found herself remembering the Eve Ivory who had stood, and had paced, in her own living room.

Perhaps an hour or so before this call.

Yes.

She had been crazy.

Psychotic?

Who knew?

"Go on, Macy," said Edie.

"She said I had no choice. She was cursing. Saying awful things. But she said she had pictures of her and Paul. Recordings. Things they had done in bed. She said if I didn't come over right away, right then, she would ruin Paul."

"And so you went."

"I had to."

"Certainly."

"But—she said she didn't want it known that I was coming. She said there were security people everywhere around the mansion. And that I should come up a secret way."

"A secret way?"

"Yes. She said that, about fifty yards from the house, shaded by some oak trees, there was a greenhouse. And that there was a tunnel leading from the greenhouse that you could enter unseen and get into the house. The people who had built the house—well, I guess they were afraid, somehow."

"They were afraid," said Jackson, quietly, "of organized crime. They thought someone might come down out of Chicago and kill them. And that's what happened."

The tunnel, thought Nina. She remembered Eve Ivory telling her about that weeks before.

"So anyway, after that it was like a dream. I called a cab. It was hard to get one. But I did."

"Do you remember the cab company."

"One of the red ones."

"Red Circle. They'll have a record."

"We had to drive around the park some; but I saw the greenhouse. He dropped me there, and I paid."

"Go on."

"Then—well then I was really scared. I didn't know what I would do when I saw her. I couldn't believe it about Paul. I just wanted to tell her it was all lies. But—if it had happened, I couldn't let Paul—"

"I know, honey. Just go on."

"Oh, that tunnel! There were cobwebs everywhere. And I could barely see. And the worst things were— the toys."

"Toys?"

"Old, rusty—children's toys. Dolls. Dump trucks. Lying there on the steps leading up into the mansion. Rusted toys. Raggedy Anns, coming apart, and just staring—"

"All right. So finally you got to the top."

Macy shook her head:

"She had told me over the phone where the tunnel would come out. And how to get to her bedroom. I walked down a hall and knocked on the door to what I thought must have been her bedroom. I knew there were guards in the house, so I didn't want to make much noise. I knocked on the door and said:

"Miss Ivory?"

"There was no answer, so I knocked again. But the door moved. It wasn't locked. It wasn't even shut. So I just—I just pushed it open."

"And was she there, Macy?" asked Nina.

To which Macy Peterson merely stared, a blank stare, a stare through Nina and out into nothing at all:

"She was dead. There was a desk in the middle of the room. A big desk. She was slumped over it. Her eyes were staring straight at me. But they were dead eyes. Blood was everywhere. On the papers covering the desk. On her white gown. It was still dripping down, onto the carpet. And, and—"

"Go on, Macy. You have to get this out."

"I couldn't help it. I just started walking over to her. As though she were, like, sitting there smiling and ready to shake my hand. Finally I was beside the desk and she was there, spread out below me. But—this thing was sticking out from her neck. It's so funny. I couldn't stop thinking of the old monster movie. The Frankenstein one. He had a bolt in his neck. It was like that. She had a bolt in her neck. I think I was screaming then. But I had to pull it out. I was screaming and screaming and—I grabbed the bolt and pulled it out of the monster's neck."

"And I just kept standing there, screaming. With the bolt, that I'd pulled out of the monster's neck."

Macy looked around the room, slowly, and said.

"And that's my statement."

CHAPTER SIXTEEN: SCAPEGOAT

"A community needs a soul if it is to become a home for human beings. You, the community, must get it this soul."

Pope John Paul II

The day, as days are wont to do, worsened.

Having begun with a confession, it progressed to a meeting, and then a conference, and then a little temper tantrum, and then, thankfully, bed.

But as for the meeting—

—it took place on the beach, where, at two P.M., she had persuaded Jackson Bennett to go walking with her.

It was a wintry sea, not cold particularly, but cold looking, with its waves sullen and ill humored, and disguising themselves to resemble the sky, which roiled and darkened and rumbled and harbinged no good.

"So how is she, Jackson?"

He was ill-placed, with his suit on and shiny black shoes.

But they were on the hard-packed sand, and so it mattered little.

"Good as could be expected. They got some lunch in her."

"That's something."

"Yeah. Thanks for coming down this morning."

"Of course. How did her formal statement go?"

"All right. Good that she'd rehearsed it. She keeps asking for you."

"Well. Maybe I can go back down again this afternoon."

He shook his head:

"Too much going on. That girl is going to have herself a busy day."

"Tomorrow morning?"

"Yeah. Much better."

"So how does it look?"

"How does what look?"

"Jackson! The case! You think I'm talking about the Super Bowl?"

He smiled, despite himself.

"No. No, I guess not."

"How does it look?"

"I think it looks pretty good; I've been on the phone with several doctors."

"What kind of doctors?"

"Psychiatrists."

"And they say?"

"It's possible she could have—well, just zoned out."

"What do you mean?"

"Dissociative response, is what they call it. She confronted the woman—and just lost control of herself."

"Without remembering it? Any of it?"

"It has happened."

"So what does this mean regarding the plea?"

"Temporary insanity."

"And that would mean?"

He shook his head:

"Incarceration, certainly. But in a medical facility. And not for too long."

"What is 'too long'?"

"Two years. Maybe three."

"My God."

"Nina, she killed somebody."

"You're sure of that?"

"Do you have another explanation?"

"She says she didn't do it."

"Like I say, do you have another explanation? If so, I'm all eyes and ears."

They walked for a time.

"What," asked Nina, "have you been able to learn about Macy's story?"

"Oh, it checks out. Checks out just fine. Phone records verify that the woman called her, and at almost precisely the time Macy says. Eleven o'clock, precisely. Call lasted forty five seconds, so that would fit. Taxi driver confirms taking Macy over there, and dropping her just about where she said. Security people found that tunnel. Of course, they're kicking themselves that they didn't always know about it; but then Eve Ivory never told anybody about it. So it's not really their fault."

"Now why was this tunnel built again?"

"That's the interesting part. A lot of mansions were built around the middle of the nineteenth century with similar exit tunnels. But most of them were in Ohio, states like that."

"Why Ohio?"

"Part slave, part free. These kinds of tunnels were built mostly by folks who wanted to help runaway slaves. But the Robinsons used it differently."

"They wanted to be able to run from the Mafia."

"Or some similar organization. But like we said this morning: it didn't work."

"Big crime got them anyway."

"Yes," he said, "it did. The pitiable thing was the toys."

"Were they found?"

"Yes. Her security, then our people. Dolls, toy trucks—apparently the Robinson kids used the tunnel as a play area, before—"

He let the rest hang out, and it floated, the unseen description of what must have been machine gun killings, over the ocean, which seemed troubled enough without adding more.

"So this woman," said Nina, "called Macy about eleven thirty."

"Right."

"Macy went over."

"Right."

"Macy entered through this strange tunnel, just as she told us she did."

"Yes."

"And found Eve Ivory in the bedroom, sitting at her desk with her throat punctured."

Jackson Bennett shook his head.

"That's where it gets difficult."

"How?"

"How? Nina, Macy's letter opener killed Eve Ivory. And Macy was clutching that letter opener when security forces opened the bedroom door."

"They're sure it was the letter opener?"

"Absolutely. I just read the autopsy report. As though there were any doubt. It was the same ivory letter opener that, apparently, Macy received, in front of the whole town, at her wedding shower."

"Yes. I know the letter opener. Tom Broussard and Penelope Royale gave it to her. We all saw it. We saw her take it home too."

"Which is where it was, where it must have been, when Eve Ivory called her."

"So she took it over there."

"She *had* to, Nina! There's no other explanation."

"No. Doesn't seem to be."

"In fact, every way you look at it, Macy's story is ninety percent true. She got called, went over, went in—but then that last ten per cent comes in."

"Yes. There is that ten per cent."

"The ten per cent that would have us believe: Eve Ivory called Macy. Someone—apparently having overheard the call—slipped into Eve Ivory's room, through a tunnel that only Eve Ivory knew about, took out the ivory letter opener that only Macy could have been in possession of, and, with no signs of a struggle, stuck the letter opener precisely in Eve Ivory's jugular. Then watched the woman bleed to death and left."

A ragtag patch of gulls had sighted a school of fish some fifty yards out, and were dive bombing a foaming matrix of flash-white and gills, screeching gleefully as they did so.

"That doesn't seem very likely, does it?"

"No. The problem is, Macy keeps sticking to the story."

"And that's a problem?"

"You bet that's a problem."

"Why, Jackson?"

"Because it means neither I nor any other lawyer she can get, can plead her guilty. She would have to plead not guilty, and hope the jury believes a story that on its surface can't be believed."

"And if the jury doesn't believe it?"

He shrugged.

"They'd have no choice. She'd have to be executed."

That was the meeting.

The conference took place in Nina's house.

Margot was the first to arrive, bringing food.

"They say, Nina, that you are the only one who can get in to see Macy."

"Well. I'm as close to a mother as she's got. And sometimes, you need your mother."

"I baked some brownies for her."

"You don't bake."

"I bought some brownies for her, took them out of the box, and put them in an antique container I had in the shop."

"That's good of you. Except the grounds around the jail look like a supermarket now."

"Well. Everybody is pulling for Macy."

"I know. She's the town's most popular killer in quite a long time."

The conversation with Margot idled back and forth for a time, until it was enlivened by the arrival of Allana Delafosse, who'd brought pound cake.

"I thought," she said, "that we might put a saw in it."

"Not too funny, Allana, given the circumstances."

"I'm sorry, darling. But I'm not certain the circumstances are as dire as they might seem."

"How do you mean that?"

"Our little schoolteacher deserves every iota of our support. So she murdered the woman; good for her! I should have done it myself!"

"Allana—"

"Nina, tell me: where is the boat that housed the millionaire who was about to buy our town right out from under us? Where is it, darling Nina? You don't know, do you? Then let me tell you that no one else does either! It's gone! The woman is dead, and, as far as I can learn or anyone else in the village can learn, the old will is now back in force. We own our own destinies."

"As though," Nina found herself whispering, "anybody does that."

"What?"

"Nothing."

"All right, then: so tell me why we should be so glum. One brave young woman did what none of the rest of us had the courage to do!"

"And may," said Nina, quietly, "have to go to prison for it."

"'Stone walls do not a prison make,' I believe the poem goes, 'nor iron bars a cage'."

"No. Not if you're outside writing poems. If you're inside the walls and the bars, they do a pretty good job."

"But Nina—"

She was in turn interrupted by the arrival of Tom Broussard and Penelope Royale, who brought lamb casserole and many apologies for having given Macy the letter opener in the first place.

"We thought it would be—well, appropriate."

No one said anything to that.

"Nina—"

"Yes, Tom?"

"Word around town is—well, that Macy actually killed this woman. But that she was insane when she did it."

"I don't know, Tom."

"We have," Penelope said, "some money available."

"My book royalties are up."

"And," Penelope interjected, "my family left me something years ago. I know it doesn't look like it, the way I live—"

"—but, Nina, you need to know, and you need to tell Macy when you see her. We can help with legal defenses, if we need to."

The room was growing dark. Somehow Margot managed to find a candle, which she put it on the table between the four of them.

Wine appeared also.

They sipped, and listened to the mournful sound of the waves.

"She must have been insane with jealousy," whispered Allana.

Margot said:

"So Paul really did sleep with this woman?"

Voices now helter skelter from around the table:

"Whether he did or not, Macy thought he did."

"It doesn't matter. Macy did what we all wanted to do."

"Everybody in the town."

"That's right; there won't be a problem setting up a legal fund for an insanity defense."

"And we'll all be character witnesses for her."

"Everybody in the town will want to—"

Nina stood up suddenly and said:

"Go home."

They looked at her in shocked silence.

"What did you say, Nina?" asked Margot.

"You heard me. Go home. Go home now. Go home right now."

More silence.

Allana:

"Whatever for?"

"Because I don't want you here anymore. I don't want you sitting here, in my house, having a party."

"Nina—"

"Our friend is in jail. One of us. One of this community, don't you understand that?"

"Of course we understand it, but there's nothing we can—"

"She says she didn't do it."

Silence.

Finally Tom:

"But Nina, from what I can understand, the evidence—"

"She says she didn't do it."

Silence.

Nina again:

"And nobody here believes her. Not one soul."

A mixture now of the waves almost lapping against the poles below them, and gulls wheeling above, the constant gull sound, permanent as the sea.

Somehow, standing there in the middle of her friends, whom she was throwing out, she remembered Sophocles' words:

"—and it brought into their mind the turbid ebb and flow of human misery."

"But we want do everything we can for Macy!"

"Except believe her."

"Nina, it's just that—"

"Don't you understand? Don't you see? Macy went over there in the first place because she didn't trust Paul. She thought there was a tape or something. She took Eve Ivory's word over the word of her fiancé. And now you're all doing the same thing. You think this community is going to be saved because we're all willing to let a beautiful young woman, the best of us, our future, our teacher—go to prison? Oh you can call it a 'mental facility,' but it's still a prison! You think that's the way to save Bay St. Lucy, to make this woman the scapegoat, the tragic heroine, the one to bear all the old sins? Well it won't work. If Macy goes to jail, there will be no more Bay St. Lucy—and not because of some gangster's will—because we didn't trust each other. Because we stopped, right at the most crucial time, being a community."

More silence.

Nina said again:

"So now go home."

And they did.

Leaving her alone.

She poured out the wine and put up the glasses.

"Frank," she said, walking from one room to the next. "Frank?"

But, for the first time since she had lost him, Frank was no longer in the house.

CHAPTER SEVENTEEN: THE FOUL RAG
AND BONE SHOP OF THE HEART

"I have always imagined that paradise will be a kind of library."

Luis de Gongora

Through the combined efforts of many people—Edie Towler paramount among them—Macy Peterson was granted bail, and allowed to go home.

Where Nina visited her at ten o'clock the following morning. The crowds had diminished with the arrival of Christmas Eve. Too many Christmas errands still needed doing. A scattering of die-hard souls still came and went, but were rebuffed by Moon Rivard's officers, who cited the need for Macy to have privacy.

It was one of these officers who ushered Nina though the kitchen, and through the voluminous piles of food that continued, as though by magic, to appear everywhere in the house.

Macy greeted her, coming out of the bedroom.

She was wearing dungarees and a sweatshirt.

It was the first time, Nina remarked, that she'd seen Macy in jeans.

"Hello, Nina."

"Macy."

"Thank you for coming."

"Of course, Macy. I'm always here for you; you know that."

"I do, Nina."

The woman who took her hand, gripped it, and led her to the coffee table beside a bay window, looked as well as she had any right to look, given that she had not slept in forty eight hours, and that she faced the prospect of going to prison, being executed by lethal injection, or both.

"Paul was just here."

"Is he all right?"

"Considering. We both just spent the time crying. Then they made him go. I'm not allowed to have visitors for more than an hour at a time."

"I understand. That's just for now, Macy. It will be better later."

"Yes. I guess so. Do you want coffee?"

"Yes."

"Just wait; I'll get us some."

"Only if it's not too much trouble."

"Of course not. I made a fresh pot when Paul came."

The coffee was poured, sipped, refreshed, sipped again.

"They say," said Macy, quietly, "I went a little crazy."

"I know."

"They have doctors. I'm supposed to be examined."

"When?"

"This afternoon, I think."

"Where?"

"Here. In town somewhere. The doctors are flying in."

"Is Jackson still handling it?"

"Yes. I don't want anybody else. He says he's not a trial lawyer, but—I still want him. I don't know how I'll pay him."

"That won't be a problem, Macy. The whole town will chip in."

"Everyone," she said, "has been so nice."

"That's because they love you. And admire you."

Silence for a time.

Then:

"Do you think I killed that woman, Nina?"

Nina answered immediately, firmly, and without seeming to consider the question at all, even for an instant.

"No."

At which Macy Peterson sprang to her feet, rounded the table, and embraced her, sobbing:

"Thank you! Thank you!"

This went on for perhaps a minute.

Then Macy, eyes watery and bloodshot with tears, returned to her seat.

"They say I went crazy."

"I know."

"They say I just—that I killed a human being. AND THAT I DON'T REMEMBER IT!"

"I know that's what they say."

"Well it isn't true!"

"I know."

"It isn't true, Nina!"

"Of course not."

"Do they think I'm a monster? A lunatic? What have I done in my life that makes everybody think I'm— what? Dr. Jekyll and Ms. Hyde? Do they think this a stupid grade B movie?"

"I don't know what they think, Macy."

"Well I do. They think I went into that room, with my letter opener with me, that I had brought over from this house for just that reason—and that I fought with her, and plunged the thing down into her neck—AND THEN FORGOT ABOUT IT!"

Nina found herself wanting to laugh, given the stupidity of the whole thing.

She fought the urge.

"It's like I told them, Nina. Like I have been telling them. I found her there. At her desk. There was blood everywhere. And she was dead. The letter opener was sticking out of her neck. Somebody else got there before me and killed her."

"Macy—"

"—but Jackson tells me to abandon that story. He tells me I should tell everybody that, after the woman's phone call, it all became blurry. That I don't remember exactly what I did. That I was enraged and hurt and scared all at once. That I may have picked up the letter opener. That I remember going through the tunnel. And that I don't remember anything after that, until they found me beside the desk screaming."

"Well, I think if you say that, then he can—"

"BUT IT'S NOT TRUE! I remember everything! Just like I can remember making coffee this morning! I'M NOT CRAZY, NINA!"

Silence for a time.

Then:

"And I'm not a murderer."

Nina sipped her coffee, put the saucer in front of her, and said, more quietly than she would have expected, so that she halfway sounded in control of some situation, which surprised her, given that there was no situation now which she was at all in control of.

"Okay. Then let's think about this."

"I have been thinking about it, Nina."

"I know. Just talk to me. Or let me talk. Or whatever.'

"All right."

"Everybody in town hated this woman. She was psychotic. I know that. I saw her in action, only a few hours before she was killed."

"How? Where?"

"She came to my shack, with two of her security guards, one of whom Tom Broussard defenestrated."

"De what?"

"Defenestrated. It means to throw through a window."

"There's a word for that?"

"It's needed more often than you might think. Anyway, the woman was hated all over town. Anybody might have killed her. I might have killed her. What happened was, though, that somebody actually did. Somebody heard her call you, then slipped into her bedroom and murdered her."

"With my letter opener."

"Yes. That's the problem. What did you do with the letter opener, after the bridal shower?"

"I brought it back here and put it under my Christmas tree. It stayed there, in its box, like one of the other presents."

"Have you looked in the box since you got back here last night?"

"Yes. The box is empty."

"So it's not like—"

"Like somebody could have bought a duplicate letter opener," said Macy.

"No. It was one of a kind. Tom and Penelope ordered it special from a gift catalogue. It came from Marcel's Antiques in New Orleans."

"Yes. I remember Mrs. Wilson commenting on the shop. She'd been there several times. And they only deal with originals."

Silence for a time.

"It doesn't make sense, Nina."

Nina rose, crossed the room, and hugged Macy again.

"It's like Frank always said, Macy. Start with the truth. Then work back from there."

"But what's the truth?"

"The truth is, Macy, that you didn't kill anybody. And you're not crazy."

"You really believe that, Nina?"

"Of course I do."

"Then I do, too. And—for the first time since this horrible thing happened—I think it's going to be all right."

"Good for you, Macy. Now I have to go and do some thinking."

"Like I say, Nina. I think it's going to be all right!"

"I wish," said Nina, walking out the door, "that I did."

And that time, slightly before eleven A.M., on the day before Christmas in Bay St. Lucy, Mississippi—Nina Bannister felt the need to go to church.

Not to everybody else's church.

Not to The First United Methodist Church, or the Cumberland Presbyterian Church, or the Oakhurst Baptist Church, or the Bayshore Congregational Church.

But to her church.

"We must go down where all the ladders start," she whispered, driving the Vespa at approximately the speed one might perambulate, using a walker, in deep snow.

"We must go down where all the ladders start; in the foul rag and bone shop of the heart."

Who had written that?

It did not matter.

Nothing mattered now.

Except finding out the truth.

And for some strange reason, this job had fallen to her.

She was Oedipus.

"Then we shall begin the search for the truth. Right now! Right here! We shall find the killer, and drive him out. We must—to save our city!"

A plague.

A plague on Bay St. Lucy.

A murderer still loose in the city.

And the citizens, blissfully unaware.

She thought of Tom, of Penelope, of Margot, all sitting around her table, all laughing, all thinking it was over.

The city was safe.

But it wasn't.

It was in more danger than ever.

And somehow, she knew as certainly as she had ever known anything in her life, that she could find out what had happened.

She must only listen to the voices.

The voices that always helped her.

The voices that had gotten her through those months after Frank's death.

Consoling voices.

Voices telling her all the combined wisdom of all those people such as she, and such as Macy, and such as all the rest of them, sitting on a little bay, looking out at a vast untrackless ocean, hurricanes coming toward them, horrible-toothed creatures rising up out of the depths to come and devour them.

Those voices.

That she could always hear in her church.

She pulled into the parking lot of The Bay St. Lucy Public Library, locked the Vespa to a metal bicycle rack, and went inside.

There were few people there, and it made her joyous in a small way even to realize that the place was open on Christmas Eve.

If it had not been—

—well, no need to worry about that.

It was.

Enough said.

The few expectable people were there. A librarian spoke to her; a teenage girl. A mother with two very young children.

She began to prowl the stacks.

No, it was not an imposing library.

But it was enough.

She began to Nina-pray, which was as close as she got to the more conventional kind.

"Who will talk to me today?"

She passed the familiar volumes.

Shakespeare.

Milton.

No voices yet.

There. Pull out that volume, that old Herodotus, which seems almost to be disintegrating.

The Everyman Library.

And there, on the frontispiece:

"Everyman, I will go with thee
And be thy guide
When all else fails
To be by thy side."

She put her forehead against the metal frame of the stack and whispered:

"Be my guide. I need a guide. Where is my guide?"

She walked farther.

A stop more.

McCauley

Wordsworth.

A little farther and then—

—she heard it calling out to her.

She did!

She was not imagining it!

Of course not, because, there it was.

There *she* was.

Nina's sister, closer than any sister could have ever been.

Whom Nina had neglected for too long now.

Calling out to her.

"Nina!"

"All right," she said. "All right, Jane."

She carefully removed a copy of the book that had always been as close to a Bible as any other volume ever written. Then she and Jane Austen's Emma went to have a long talk.

They sat by the window, a portion of Bay St. Lucy's foot traffic passing before them.

They chatted about this and that.

About Harriet Smith and Mr. Knightly and the useless but harmless Bates sisters.

Highbury was of course Bay St. Lucy.

And Emma was Nina.

Jane Austen was talking to her.

Book One.

Good, but not—not what Jane wanted to say. Not quite.

And then it happened.

The book seemed to fall open.

The passage that was meant for her to see, and to see now, right now, and to understand, to really understand, for if not now, then never.

"Emma went to the door for amusement. Much could not be expected from even the busiest part of Highbury. Mr. Perry walking hastily by, Mr. William Cox letting himself in at the office door. Mr. Cole's carriage horses returning from exercise; or a stray letter boy on an obstinate mule. These were the liveliest objects she could presume to expect; and when her eyes fell only on the butcher with his tray, a tidy old woman travelling homewards from shop with her full basket,

two curs quarrelling over a dirty bone, she knew she had no reason to complain, and was amused enough, quite enough, to stand still at the door. A mind lively and at ease can do with seeing nothing, and can see nothing, that does not answer."

A mind lively and at ease can do with seeing nothing, and can see nothing, that does not answer.

A MIND LIVELY AND AT EASE CAN DO WITH SEEING NOTHING, AND CAN SEE NOTHING THAT DOES NOT ANSWER.

"Thank you, Jane," she whispered.

Then she put the book away.

Then she unlocked her Vespa and began to drive back to Margot's shop.

She had halved the distance when she was pulled over by Jackson Bennett, driving a limousine.

He walked back to her, seemingly upset.

"Nina?"

"Yes?"

"I've just come from a talk with Macy Peterson."

"Yes?"

"We've set up a psychiatrist's appointment for her, late this afternoon."

"All right."

"Are you listening to me?"

"Of course."

"Your mind seems—well, it seems like you're somewhere else."

I'm in Highbury, you idiot. I and Emma are trying to do your job for you.

"No. Go ahead."

"She says you were there earlier."

"Yes. You told me yesterday I should go by around ten."

"But I didn't tell you to advise her concerning this case."

"No."

"Nina, she says you advised her to stick to this crazy story about being innocent."

"I advised her to tell the truth."

"The truth is that she killed the woman."

"Oh?"

"What do you mean, 'oh?'"

"I mean I'm not certain that's the truth."

"Nina—"

He bent low over the handlebars and began to speak to her as though she were a child.

"Nina, we all have every bit of respect for you in the world. But you're a retired schoolteacher. This is not your—well, not your area."

"I see."

"Please. Try to keep encouraging Macy. But let the rest of us do our job."

"All right," she lied.

And watched him pull away.

Two minutes later, she was entering Margot's shop, her mind in a state of intense almost feverish activity.

Ringgg went the little bell.

Margot, puttering about.

A customer here and there.

People crossing the street in front of the shop.

Mr. Perry setting up his carriage.

Mr. Fontenot starting up his pickup truck.

Margot, coming out of the garden:

"Well, are you still talking to us?"

No answer.

No answer possible.

Think, Nina.

Something is wrong.

Start with the truth, then work your way back.

Macy did not kill that woman.

There is something you're not seeing, Nina.

Something no one is seeing.

What?

WHAT?

"Are you even talking to me, Nina? What's wrong with you?"

See it all. Remember it all.

See the whole board, the *whole* chessboard.

What doesn't fit? What is wrong?

A mind lively and at ease can do with seeing nothing, and can see nothing that does not answer.

Nina, your mind is lively.

It's always been lively.

BUT IT CANNOT BE AT EASE.

NOT NOW!

MACY'S LIFE IS ON THE LINE!

ALL OF YOUR LIVES ARE ON THE LINE!

THE COMMUNITY IS ON THE LINE!

THINK! LISTEN! LISTEN TO THE BATES SISTERS CHATTERING AWAY!

SOMETHING DOESN'T FIT!

WHAT DOESN'T FIT, NINA?

Margot shrugging.

"All right. I can see you're still mad. Tell me when you want to talk, and I'll make us some tea."

And Margot walked away, humming.

Humming.

Humming.

Follow her.

"What's that?"

"What?"

"What's that, that you were humming?"

"I don't know."

"Hum it again."

"What?"

"Hum it again."

"What is this, Casablanca?"

"Hum it again, Margot!"

"Well it was—oh I remember, I was humming it to you that night after you got back from New Orleans. I was mocking you, actually."

"Hum it, dammit!"

"What's the matter with you?"

"Hum it!"

"All right, it was, let's see—da da da da da daaaa, da da da da da!"

"Do you know what it means," Nina whispered, "to miss New Orleans?"

"Yes, that's it. Old song. Why?"

"She doesn't know."

"What?"

"She doesn't know what it means to miss New Orleans."

Nina threw herself into Margot's arms.

"SHE DOESN'T KNOW WHAT IT MEANS TO MISS NEW ORLEANS!"

After a time, getting ever more excited, she said:

"Where's your calendar?"

"My what?"

"The calendar you always keep; you know, the ins and outs."

"Over there by the cash register. But what does that—"

"Show it to me, Margot."

Margot did.

She read the appropriate entry and said:

"We haven't missed it. Christmas. We haven't missed it!"

"You sound like Ebenezer Scrooge now."

"She doesn't know what it means. She doesn't know what it means, Margot. To miss New Orleans."

"I think you've gone crazy."

"Let me hug you one more time. Then you need to call the police. I need to talk to Moon Rivard.

The two women did hug.

And she stayed there for a while, sobbing against Margot's chest, and thanking Jane Austen.

It took ten minutes for Moon Rivard to arrive at the shop.

He was skeptical.

"Mz. Nina? What is this about an emergency?"

"I can't tell you everything now, Moon. But things are starting to make sense."

"What things, ma cher?"

"Important things. Things about how Eve Ivory really did die."

"Aww, ma'am. That's not your department, you know."

"So I keep hearing."

"I just talked with that lawyer. Bennett. He's awful mad at you. He says you trying to do his job."

"Only because he's not."

"Miss Edie, the town prosecutor, is not too happy, either. They tryin' to get some kind of plea bargain to get Macy Peterson off with a lighter sentence."

"I know that."

"Miss, I don't mean to tell you your business—but if you keep on talking with Macy Peterson, they gonna get some kind of court order."

"Let them."

"You don't want that, Mz. Nina."

"Moon, I need you to help me out."

"I ain't sure I ought to be doing that right now."

"I need you to take me over to Tom Broussard's."

"Can't you ride over there yourself?"

"I need to go fast. We're running out of time."

"Who is?"

"Bay St. Lucy."

"What are you talking about?"

"We might have a few hours. And then, if I'm right. We're done."

"You ain't making no sense."

"No. I am making sense. Just for the first time. Please, Moon—we've got to find Tom. And then we've got to go somewhere else."

"Where else?"

"Down in the ground. And back in time?"

"What?"

"It wasn't big crime, Moon; it was little crime. But all the worse because of it."

"What?"

"The children."

"What children?"

"The children would know. The children saw. And heard. And the children would know. Now come on. Let's go."

He agreed.

And they pulled off toward Tom Broussard's.

They found him where she knew he would be, slumped over the typewriter.

Moon, frightened for his safety, waiting in the patrol car, ready to call for backup.

Nina climbed the steps, knocked on the door, then opened it and went in anyway.

Tom looked up from his manuscript.

"Well. Surprised to see you here."

"Tom, I need you to do something for me."

"I thought you hated me. I thought you hated all of us."

"I'm sorry about that."

"What were we doing last night anyway, that made you so mad?"

"Being happy."

"What's wrong with that?"

"It wasn't the time. There may not be a time, if you can't help me out here."

"What do you want me to do?"

"Fly to New Orleans."

"What?"

"Fly to New Orleans in Bay St. Lucy's jet."

"Why?"

"I'll tell you that in a minute. But didn't you tell me once that you'd spent a year in law school in New Orleans?"

"Well. Kind of."

"What do you mean, kind of?"

"I mean it was a kind of law school. You learn a lot of law there. And you meet a lot of lawyers."

"What was the name of this law school?

"City jail."

"Ok, that makes sense. But Tom, did you make— well, contacts there?"

"Of course I did. Everything I know about crime, I learned in jail."

"If I gave you a name, and asked you to find out everything you could about it—could you do that for me? And for the town?"

"Why are you asking me to do this?"

"Because, Tom, I need somebody who can dig down beneath the surface. And do it quick. And do it right. There's a big, dirty secret Tom. And I need a big dirty man to go find out what it is."

He nodded.

"I'm your man."

The battle to get Tom Broussard on the city's private jet was only won by calling in every favor that every city council member owed Nina.

But it was won, so that, at 4 P.M., the most disreputable—and capable—man she knew was flying off to find out things heretofore unimagined.

While she and Moon Rivard were parking behind the Robinson mansion.

"I can't take you in here. It's a crime scene!"

"I don't want to go into the mansion. I want to go down under it."

"You want to what?"

"I want to see that tunnel. The one that Macy went through."

"Why?"

"Because we have to go down where all the ladders start; in the foul rag and bone shop of the heart."

"But that don't make no sense!"

"Yes it does. It makes all the sense."

"But that's a dirty place down there. I had to go look at it this morning, with all them security policemen. I don't want to go back down there."

"Come on."

"I could order you not to do this, you know. Jackson Bennett and Miss Towler don't—"

"They don't have to go down there, do they?"

"But we don't either!"

"Yes we do. I want to see what she saw."

"Who?"

"I don't know for now. I think I know. But I'm not sure. We have to wait for Tom. I just know, Moon, that somebody was in that tunnel two nights ago. And whoever it was killed Eve Ivory."

"But how, ma'am? That letter opener—"

"She got the letter opener, Moon, because she didn't know what it means to miss New Orleans."

"What?"

"Our minds were lively. But they were at ease."

"You not making any sense."

"We were satisfied with seeing nothing. Even though the whole thing, all the while, was right there under our noses."

"Miz Nina—"

"We could do with seeing nothing; and we could see nothing that didn't seem to our stupid little minds just what we wanted it to seem. It's going to be a very close thing. Now come on, Moon. Take me down into the Robinson tunnel."

"Man. I always hated schoolteachers."

But he got out of the car anyway, led her through the police banner, opened a rusty gate, and pulled up a clapboard trap door.

"Be careful."

"I will."

And the darkness closed upon them.

For a time, the smell of musk, rotting roots and dank soil overwhelmed her.

The first concrete steps led down, and she could hear droplets of water oozing around her.

Moon's broad back swayed before her, and, in front of that, the ray of the flashlight, illuminating cobwebs.

"Be careful where you stop there!"

"I will, Moon."

"Man, it's spooky down here."

"I know."

"Smell that—what is that smell?"

"I don't know. Just—well, just buried things."

"I don't like to smell that. Watch out for them cobwebs!"

"I will."

"Hell, that web there is ten feet across. Like to see the spider spun that thing."

"He's as scared of us as we are of him."

"You sure? That spider, be the size of a rat!"

"Well. Maybe we can eat him."

"What are you looking for down here?"

"I'll know it when I see it."

"Here. Now it levels off. We under the main floor now. In a minute there's a turning place. And then it starts up."

"How long is the tunnel?"

"We measured it. Little more than a hundred feet."

"And you've never been down here before?"

"No, ma'am."

"Moon, you've got to think back. When this-this thing happened at the mansion, you'd just started with the town police."

"Yes, ma'am."

"And what do you remember about it?"

"Well—I and my partner was called over there about four o'clock in the morning. We was told that a shooting had taken place. That two big black cars had been spotted in the driveway. All that happened, they told us, around two P.M. Mr. Homer Baron Robinson and his wife had been shot to death. Shot several times, all shot up. A little boy was safe but had been taken away."

"Why was it all so hush hush?"

"Ma'am, that was big crime, that done that. Maybe out of New Orleans. Maybe out of Chicago. But the word came down, bury the dead. Close up the mansion. And don't ask no questions. So that's what we did."

"I still don't see—wait. Wait. There. Shine the light there!"

He trained the flashlight on a small pile of something rusting not rotting.

Something that did not belong.

And yet did.

Nina knelt beside it.

"Look, Moon."

"Aw, man. Why you have to show me that?"

"Because it's probably a witness. It may be the only witness."

It was a rag doll, with button eyes, and a candy stripe dress.

On one of the white strips, visible in the beam of the flashlight, stenciled in black, were the letters:

E.R.

"Do you want to take that doll with us?"

She shook her head and put the doll back where she had found it.

"No. No, Moon, let's let it stay buried here."

"But what do we do now?"

She straightened up.

"We go back. And hope Margot's calendar is right and that we haven't missed Christmas. And then we wait for Tom Broussard."

She turned, began making her way back toward the entrance to the tunnel, and said softly:

"It's time for the town to meet its past."

CHAPTER EIGHTEEN: DO YOU KNOW
WHAT IT MEANS, TO MISS NEW ORLEANS?

*"If I didn't know the ending of a story I wouldn't begin. I always write my last
line, my last page, my last paragraph, first."*

Katherine Anne Porter

She arrived back at her house at five P.M.

There was nothing to do but wait.

This was easier than she had expected it to be.

It was not like the morning, when the thing had struggled to be born, had fought to come out of her.

It was out now.

She knew precisely what had happened.

She knew what had happened two nights ago.

She knew what had happened thirty years ago.

And here she was, Tiresias.

The blind prophet.

"Mine is a terrifying gift. For what use is knowledge, if it only breeds misery?"

Still, this did not bother her as she made her customary salad, poured the glass of white wine, and turned on The Metropolitan Opera Broadcast.

Turandot.

She checked the clock.

Five forty.

There was no way Tom could be back before ten.

Someone did come, though, around six, or just at the beginning of Act Two.

Two ponderous sedans this time.

So many cars, she found herself musing, all wanting to come see poor little Nina Bannister.

Normally she would have risen, run over to the landing, and opened the door, happy to receive visitors.

That was not the case now.

She did not dread their coming, either.

There was just a kind of numbness about the whole thing.

Edie Towler entered first, Jackson Bennett behind her.

In short order they were all seated around her living room table.

Like the group last night, that she had thrown out.

She could not throw these people out, though.

She did not, on the other hand, have to offer them coffee.

Strictly speaking, Edie ranked higher on the municipal scale than Jackson did.

Jackson, strictly speaking, was not on the municipal scale at all.

So it was only right that Edie spoke first.

"Nina, what in God's name have you been doing?"

Nina actually knew nothing to say to that, and so she simply shrugged, and sipped from what was, she realized, her second glass of wine.

Edie continued.

"I mean this, Nina. We need to know what's is going on."

"Yes," she answered. "We do."

Silence.

Then Jackson:

"Tom Broussard showed up at the airport in Biloxi a few hours ago, with orders, signed by five city councilmen and women, that he was to be taken to New Orleans and escorted, with all due speed, to The Quarter."

"Yes."

"Nina, were you behind this?"

"I was."

"Who is going to pay for that trip?"

"I don't know."

"You don't—"

Edie now:

"Nina, are you all right?"

"No. Yes. I'm not sure."

"Do you need a doctor?"

Again, no answer forthcoming.

They were asking such hard questions!

"You know, Nina—"

Which one of them was talking now?

Or did it really matter?

"—we were attempting to have the psychological examination of Macy Peterson this afternoon at three o'clock."

"So I had heard."

"Macy refused."

"Really."

"She said she wasn't crazy. She said she was quite rational. That she remembered everything that happened that night. And that she would so testify, when the time came."

"Good for her."

"Good for—"

Edie now leaned forward:

"What do you think you're doing? You are in no position to advise this woman!"

"Well. Somebody needs to."

"I take that," Jackson Bennett said quietly, "as an insult."

"Take it, Jackson, any way you want."

Silence for a time. Then Edie:

"You still believe, Nina, that Macy Peterson did not commit this murder?"

"That's what I believe."

"Then who did?"

"Someone else."

"Obviously. But who?"

"I'm not quite ready to say."

"Why not?"

"Because you wouldn't believe me. You already know who committed this murder. It's all snug and tucked away in your minds. And since you can 'see nothing that does not answer,'—well, who am I to waste your time? You're very happy with the truth as you see it. It fits the town's needs. And if it means poor Macy has to be locked away as a homicidal maniac—"

"That's not what anybody's calling her!"

"Oh really? What do we call people who go crazy and commit murder? High strung?"

"You're being unfair to everybody."

"Which is so much harder, isn't it, than being unfair to one little insignificant person."

"No one is saying Macy is insignificant!'

"Really? So are both of you planning to visit her when she's locked away in Bedlam?"

Silence for a moment. Then:

"Macy is going to be well taken care of, Nina. But she has to co-operate."

"She is co-operating. She's telling the truth."

"She's saying that another person killed Eve Ivory!"

"Yes, she is."

"But Nina, that theory simply does not," Jackson thundered, "hold water!"

"It's not supposed to hold water. It's not a dam. It's a cave."

"What does that mean?"

"It starts down under the house, under all the houses, under the town itself. It starts way down deep, where all the ladders go. We were just never willing to go down there."

"I don't understand," said Edie, "what you're talking about."

"No. You don't."

"But, if you wouldn't mind being serious for a minute—"

"I'm being serious. I'm being very serious."

"Then tell us, how did this phantom person come to have Macy's letter opener?"

Upon hearing which, Nina rose, sipped the last of her wine, and said:

"From us. Right in front of us. And under our very noses."

Then she went into the kitchen and started washing dishes.

She listened to the door bang shut as Edie and Jackson left.

The opera ended at nine o'clock.

Rain began at 9:30.

Tom Broussard arrived at ten.

He had on a black slicker.

She could see by his expression as he entered that he had found out what she needed to know.

"Do you want some whiskey?" she asked.

He sat down, shaking his head.

"No. Wouldn't help."

They were both quiet for a time.

The rain drummed harder on the tin roof of the shack.

"You found out, didn't you?"

He nodded.

"Yes. I found out."

"How?"

"Two guys I was in with, were in The Family."

"Which Family?"

"It doesn't matter. Not really. Those kind of guys, if you do time with them, if they get to trusting you. Sometimes they'll help you out."

"Did it take you long to find them?"

"Half hour. The Quarter is small."

"How long would it have taken you in Chicago?"

"Half hour."

"Ok."

There was only the rain, and the sound of Tom, "breathing like dolphins," as Dylan Thomas wrote, and looking at the wall, without seeming to see it.

"It wasn't big crime, was it?"

He shook his head:

"No. It wasn't big crime. It was little crime."

"So it was—"

"Yeah. That's who it was."

"And now she's—"

"Yes. Yes, she is."

More silence, and then:

"Do you have a car, Tom?"

"Yeah. Rented one."

"We have to go to Margot's."

"I know."

"We can call the police from there."

He nodded:

"Well. Let's do it then."

Nina put on her rain gear, turned out the light, and followed Tom Broussard down the stairs.

Margot's shop was aglow, but about to close.

She was huddled in a colorless robe as she opened the door.

"What is going on?" she asked.

"Call the police."

"What?"

"Call the police."

"Why, Nina? Nothing is wrong here!"

"That's not true. Call the police."

"Nina, you've been so strange these last days."

"I am a prophet new inspired. Call the police. Call all the police. Call them now. Call them right now, Margot. And call Jackson Bennett. And call Edie Towler. Call them now."

So saying, Nina walked into the garden and sat down to wait.

The shop filled slowly. First came one of the deputies; then Moon Rivard himself, then another deputy, then Edie Towler, then Jackson Bennett.

Then assorted others.

They were all there in the garden, candles burning in the corner vases, rain drumming ever heavier.

It was, Nina thought, *like a midnight mass.*

There had been rumblings, mutterings.

What does she think she—

She's gone crazy, or at least she—

She won't talk to anybody, and, since this afternoon, she—

But they were all there in the shop.

All the police and all the authority anyone could want.

There simply out of respect for her.

For Nina Bannister.

And now it was time.

She looked at her watch.

Eleven o'clock.

Jackson Bennett approached her, looked down, and asked:

"Nina. What is this? Why are we here?"

She breathed deeply, took from the lining of her pocket a single sheet of paper that Tom had given her upon his arrival from New Orleans, and handed it to Margot Gavin, saying simply:

"Read this."

Margot did.

Then she did again, and she began to understand.

"What is—"

"You have to go get her, Margot."

"But does this mean—"

"Yes."

"Oh my God! All this time?"

"Yes."

"But she was here, and—"

"—and she knew everything. Now go get her, Margot. She has to come home, to Bay St. Lucy. Go up and get her."

Margot disappeared into the staircase that led up to the apartments.

She was gone two minutes, no more.

She came back down, opened the door wide before her—and ushered into the room her boarder, the woman they had all known as Mrs. Wilson—

—but who was really, of course, the elder Robinson daughter.

The daughter known as Emily.

The daughter who had not run away to New York.

And had not died of a drug overdose.

The daughter who had murdered her parents.

And the daughter who had murdered Eve Ivory.

"It's time," said Nina, staring straight into a face with no expression, "to tell us what you've done, Emily."

Emily Robinson had no expression at all as she stared into the flashlight beam that Moon Rivard held trained on her face.

The only expression worth noting at all, for that matter, was Nina's.

She was crying.

CHAPTER NINETEEN: CHRISTMAS

"They can't yank a novelist like they can a pitcher. A novelist has to go the full nine, even if it kills him."

Ernest Hemingway

The following morning, Bay St. Lucy received itself back, as a Christmas present.

The day dawned startlingly clear.

Presents were opened at daybreak, of course, and by ten P.M.—all required relatives having been visited— the children had been let loose on the streets, where the younger ones could show off their Micro-Blasters, Video-Blasters, GI Joe Cannons, Thermo-Nuclear Ray Guns and other gifts associated with the Spirit of Christmas.

The older ones had been given real guns, of course, and could pass them back and forth over the fenders of pickup trucks, while planning hunting trips.

Margot's shop had transported itself magically back in time, and was now Bob Cratchet's living room on Christmas morning.

Everyone was there.

Allana was there, crying; Tom and Penelope were there, crying; Jackson Bennett and his wife were there, crying—

—and precisely at ten o' five, Macy Peterson and Paul Cox arrived, not crying.

Laughing.

For Macy, all charges against her had, one hour previously, been dropped.

As for what had happened, that was all a-tumble in the field of mass confusion.

Emily Robinson had apparently confessed everything, rants of bitterness against the town mixing with cries against the unjustness of life, her parentage, the horrible creature that had grown in her womb and then been taken away from her—and the fact that she would never see the immense amount of money she had spent most of her life expecting.

And Nina was a school teacher again, the entire shop having turned into her classroom.

"But what was this humming thing that put you onto her?" asked Margot.

"Do you know what it means to miss New Orleans?" She didn't. She told you, didn't she, that she planned to go to New Orleans, because she'd never been there before?"

"Yes, she did."

"But," said Nina, "at the shower she talked about Maurice's Antique Shop. As though she went there often."

"Which she did," Margot said, "growing up in New Orleans."

"But what I don't understand," asked Macy, "is what she did as a young girl. And how she could have been kept out of prison."

"Tom explained some of that to me," said Nina. "What happened was this. Emily Robinson and her younger brother Arthur hated their parents, who must have made their life hell. They tolerated it though until Emily became a teenager. She took lovers, I suppose, probably sneaking through that old tunnel to meet them. She became pregnant. Her father must have been outraged, and her mother, too—"

"—and so," added Margot, "a horrible incident happened. She wound up shooting both her parents.

The servants, though, or someone else, made sure that no police were called."

Two black sedans did come," Nina continued. "The one a hearse. The other to whisk the children to New Orleans. Where they continued to grow up as virtual prisoners. In the care of some relative or other, who knows?"

Margot kept up the tale:

"Arthur had seen the killings. And he was never quite right again. His sister continued to live with him, caring for him. Finally she was his nurse, as the other relatives died away."

"A Rose," Nina said softly, "for Emily and Arthur."

"So tell about the legal matters," asked Macy.

"It's pretty clear," said Nina. "Homer Baron Robinson had been a traditionalist, so he made his will out to Arthur and not Emily. He wanted the money and land holdings to go to his male heir. But Arthur could only inherit after his sixteenth birthday. By that time he had been adjudged insane."

"Why didn't Emily simply inherit at that point?"

"There was no "insanity" provision. Emily could not inherit until Arthur died. That was it. So the will remained in probate. Emily waited, and waited. She may have thought about killing her own brother, but she never hated him the way she did her father. He did die of natural causes though, leaving her—finally, she must have thought—an immensely rich woman."

"Except," said Margot, "there was a fly in the ointment."

"Eve Ivory," chimed in Macy.

"Yes," Nina continued. "After learning of Emily's pregnancy, Homer Baron Robinson secretly amended his will. The money was to go first to Arthur, and then to Emily's child. The family attorneys knew this, but had been told to inform no one else."

"Emily," Margot added, "had her child and then had it sent away. She knew nothing of it, save its gender."

"So upon hearing of the will, and learning that Eve Ivory was the beneficiary," Nina continued, "Emily was as shocked as everyone else."

"All that waiting," said Margot, "for nothing."

"But by now, after all those years," Nina continued, "she was desperate. Her daughter had never meant anything to her, except horrible memories of her parents' hatred. She decided to come here, and merely wait."

"In my bed and breakfast," said Margot, with a bit of pride."

"Yes," Macy continued, "because your bed and breakfast is the center of the city."

" She just had to," Nina said, "plant herself in the garden like an ivy vine, and listen."

"She let," Margot went on, "her estranged daughter do all the tough work for her. All the zoning matters, the land matters—it took a month but finally it was all tied up in a neat blue ribbon, ready to be sold to Megaventures."

"All she needed to do was murder her daughter, find a scapegoat to take the blame, and the will would finally revert to her."

"And, as beneficiary, she could sell to Megaventures just as easily as Eve Ivory ever could have."

"And that's what she would have done," said Margot. "She was set to leave town on Christmas day. She would have flown to the Azores or wherever else she wanted to, and sign the contract."

"So the community would have been gone," said Macy. "Nina was right"

"If we had sold you out," said Margot, "we would have been cutting our own throats."

"But what," asked Macy, "about my letter opener?"

"Very simple but very smart," answered Nina. "Emily Robinson observed very closely at the night of the shower. She saw the letter opener, realized that she could use it as a murder weapon, and also realized that the whole community had seen Penelope and Tom give it to you, Macy. She also realized that the shower was chaos, as all showers are. While people were milling around and handling gifts, as always happens, she slipped the letter opener out of its box and put it in her own purse. Then she just closed the box, figuring that you would take it home with you—it being one of the more special gifts—and also figuring that you wouldn't open the box again until after Christmas. Which is the way it actually worked."

But," Macy asked, "how could she know that Eve Ivory was going to call me that night, to threaten me?"

Nina shook her head:

"Macy don't you see? That wasn't Eve Ivory at all who called you. It was Emily Robinson. You, having never actually spoken with Eve Ivory, had no way of telling the difference."

"My God."

"And as for the tunnel, of course Emily Robinson knew about it. She had played in it as a child."

"I can't believe it."

"No one else could, either. But it worked perfectly for Emily. Having sat here for two weeks listening to the town gossip, she knew all about the possible affair between Eve and Paul. And she knew you would have been the logical suspect. So she set you up perfectly."

Then there was silence for a time.

Finally Margot said, quietly:

"Now we've escaped from absolute ruin. From no longer being a community. And, instead of looking for new places to live, we're about to celebrate two weddings. Yours and Paul's, Macy, and Tom's and Penelope's."

Cheering for Tom and Penelope.

Tom said:

"She is, I finally realized after spending time with her these last weeks, the only woman who knows more words than I do."

General laughter.

Silence again, then, from Margot:

"You were the only one who believed, Nina."

And from Macy:

"I wasn't even sure myself. I thought I was going crazy."

"No," said Nina, shaking her head. "You're just in love. It's like the fella says: "Lovers and madmen have such seething brains, such shaping fantasies, that apprehend more than cool reason ever comprehends."

"We were dealing with madmen, all right," said Margot, "but Macy wasn't one of them."

"No. She wasn't," said Nina, quietly.

Margot continued:

"I remember that night at your house, Nina. You threw us out."

"Well. I was too brusque."

"No. I'll never forget what you told us. And it was what we all needed to hear. We had stopped believing in each other."

"You taught us, Nina," said Macy.

"You taught us. Like you always have."

They were silent for a time, and then Paul Cox said:

"We're going to get the school, Nina. It's a certainty now."

"I'm glad, Paul."

"There's just one other thing: I'm going to make a proposal to the school board next week. A proposal concerning the name."

Silence for a time, and then:

"I'm going to propose that Bay St. Lucy's high school be named Nina Bannister High School!"

"Here Here!"

General cheering, and then a general clamor for Nina.

"Speech! Speech, Nina!"

"Speech! Speech!"

She was in the circle of her friends.

The circle of her community.

What could she say?

For they were a community after all.

And she had helped them see that.

What could she say?

She got to her feet.

She looked at Bay St. Lucy smiling around her—and she said the right thing, of course.

A lady always does.

THE END

"Writing every book is like a purge; at the end of it one is empty…like a dry shell on the beach, waiting for the tide to come in again."

Daphne Du Maurier

ABOUT THE AUTHORS

 Pam Britton Reese is a Ph.D. student in Applied Language and Speech Science. She has been a student at the University of Louisiana at Lafayette for two years. Previously, she worked as speech pathologist in various schools and in private practice. She was also a supervisor in communication disorders at **Ohio University**. She likes nothing better, professionally, than helping small, silent two year old boys start talking. She has also **published books** about autism with LinguiSystems for the last 15 years. *The Circle of Autism* was previously published on-line at ken*again e-magazine.

Joe Reese is a novelist, playwright, storyteller, and college teacher. He has published four novels, several plays, and a number of stories and articles. When he is not teaching (English and German), he enjoys visiting elementary schools, where he tells stories from his Katie Dee novels and talks to students about writing. He and his wife Pam live currently in Lafayette, Louisiana. They have three children: Kate, Matthew, and Sam.

CPSIA information can be obtained at www.ICGtesting.com
Printed in the USA
LVOW13s1605180614

390646LV00003B/551/P